Chance Encounters

Rosie Harris was born in Cardiff and grew up there and in the West Country. After her marriage she lived for some years on Merseyside before moving to Buckinghamshire where she still lives. She has three grown-up children and six grandchildren and writes full time.

Also by Rosie Harris

Chance Encounters
Love or Duty
Stolen Moments
Only Love Can Heal

Rosie
HARRIS

Chance
Encounters

CANELO

First published in Great Britain and the USA in 2016 by Severn House
Publishers Ltd

This edition published in the United Kingdom in 2021 by

Canelo
31 Helen Road
Oxford OX2 0DF
United Kingdom

A CIP catalogue record for this book is available from the British Library.

Print ISBN 978 1 80032 303 2
Ebook ISBN 978 1 78863 919 4

Look for more great books at www.canelo.co

Printed and bound in Great Britain by Clays Ltd, Elcograf S.p.A.

For my youngest son… Keith

Chapter One

Megan Lloyd was bored.

A tall, slim girl with long, sleek, dark hair caught back in a bow at the nape of her neck, she was dressed in dark blue slacks and a green cotton top that reached to her hipline. Her expressive face with its high cheekbones, small, square chin and bright, dark eyes under their well-shaped brows normally gave her an alert, intelligent look but at the moment she looked discontented and unhappy.

It was August 1942 and she had just completed a three-year degree course at Aberystwyth University and was undecided about her future.

What she wanted to do immediately was to join up in one of the services and help her country like so many of her fellow students were already doing, but her father refused to give his permission for her to go ahead with her plans.

Her father, Lewis Lloyd, was the owner of a slate quarry in North Wales. A tall, broad man in his early fifties with a shock of thick black hair and piercing dark eyes, he was both wealthy and powerful. His family had lived in the area since the Middle Ages and their imposing grey stone ten-bedroom mansion Yr Glaslyn had been built in the 1600s.

Although the war had been raging between Germany and Britain since 1939 it had made very little difference to his way of life. As the owner of one of the largest slate mines in North Wales, he was held in high regard by his employees and, since many of them had allotments or large gardens, the wartime shortages and food rationing had not made very much difference to him or his way of life.

Items such as eggs, chicken, joints of lamb and pork, and even milk as well as vegetables and fruit in season, which many people were unable to buy because they were in short supply, or rationed, were brought along to him as tokens of their loyalty by the men who worked for him.

He accepted all this as a matter of right and consequently his family never went short of anything. Occasionally his wife Bronwyn, a small, dark-haired woman five years younger than Lewis, weakly protested about them accepting these items, but he would brush her remarks aside.

'Speak sense, woman, if they needed the stuff for themselves they wouldn't be bringing it along here for us now, would they?'

'They only do it because they want to keep in your good books,' she told him.

Lewis gave a derisory laugh. 'If that's the case then believe me, they're wasting their time. They won't be getting a penny more in their pay packets from me just because they bring some trifling thing along and hand it to me.'

'You do pay them, I hope, Lewis, for the produce they bring in, surely,' Bronwyn admonished.

'Half the time I don't know which of them has brought what in,' he said irritably. 'I leave it to the foreman to attend to that side of things and no doubt he takes his pick of what's been brought in before it's handed to me.'

'You should thank them personally, Lewis; it is very, very kind of them to give up items of food and for the wives to give up their clothing coupons just so that we can have more.'

'The women probably can't afford to buy new clothes anyway, and as for the food, most of the fruit and vegetables they bring in is what they've grown themselves.'

'All the more reason for thanking them then,' she insisted.

'Nonsense! They probably have a glut of it and they would have to throw it on the midden or dig it back into the ground if they didn't give it to us.'

'No, Lewis, you know you are speaking nonsense,' Bronwyn told him, her small mouth tightening into an uncompromising line. 'What you're saying might have been true at one time, but these days what with rationing and shortages, every scrap of food is precious.'

'They would far rather be digging in their own gardens than fighting a war over in France,' he told her derisively.

'I'm sure they would, but that doesn't mean we shouldn't say thank you to them for the sacrifice they are making.'

'It's their way of saying thank you to me for giving them the opportunity of working here in safety, in a reserved occupation, rather than being sent over to France or some other place where they'd be risking their necks in the midst of all the mud and bullets.'

Although the Blitz had been raging since 1940, with German bombers attacking London on fifty-seven consecutive nights, the only disruption that Lewis Lloyd was aware of was the occasional difficulties in transporting slate to other parts of the country or other areas of the world. So many of the larger seaports both in Britain and abroad had been bombed either by the Germans or by the Allied air forces. In addition, shipping was constantly under attack from the air as well as at risk from submarines.

Nevertheless, Lewis Lloyd was determined that his life would continue as smoothly as possible. Megan's twenty-first birthday party that April had been the highlight of the year in Beddgelert. It had fallen in the middle of the Easter vacation and all her university friends as well as her many local friends had been invited. For almost a week the Lloyds' mansion Yr Glaslyn had been filled with her friends from Aberystwyth. Lewis Lloyd had gone out of his way to regale them with tales about the history of his ancestors.

He was proud of the fact that his family dated back to the days of Llewellyn the Great and claimed that one of his relations had been present when the famous Prince Llewellyn had returned from a hunting trip and found that Gelert, his faithful dog, which he had left to guard his son, was covered in blood.

Prince Llewellyn had immediately thought that the dog had attacked his small son and killed it. But after the dog had died he found the body of a wolf nearby and realized that his faithful dog had, in fact, saved the life of his son. Prince Llewellyn was so overcome by grief that he began digging a grave for the dog with his own hands and, according to legend, was often to be seen at the graveside where he watered it with his own tears.

Although Megan had returned to university immediately after her birthday, it had been her final term there and in no time at all her course ended. Degree achieved, her future hung in the balance.

Now her student life was over, everything seemed to her to be dull and uneventful. Most of her friends of her own age were already serving in the forces; boys in the army, navy or air force while the girls had joined the ATS or the WAAF or the Wrens. Some had even become Land Army girls working on farms throughout Britain.

All through July and August Megan lazed around playing tennis, partying, swimming, dancing and generally enjoying herself with those who were still awaiting their call-up papers or who were home on their first leave after completing their basic training.

Megan found that it was sheer torment to listen to their exploits and adventures and it made her all the more keen to join them, but no matter how many times she brought the subject up her father adamantly refused to even discuss her joining up.

She would have loved to become a Waaf or a Wren, but her father was strongly against it. To him she was still just a 'little girl', someone to protect from the harsh realities of life. He wouldn't even allow her to work in the offices of his own slate quarry.

'What do you think the men would think if I brought my daughter into work?' he intoned furiously. 'They'd think I was mad, that's what they would think. Anyway, it's quite unthinkable to have a woman working in a slate quarry.'

'I wouldn't be in the slate quarry working alongside the men,' Megan protested. 'I would be working in the office.'

'I don't have any women working in the office. I have young men training to become office managers or accountants. They start as office boys running errands, making the tea and doing the filing. You wouldn't want to be doing work of that nature, would you?'

'Well, there is a war on, Father, and by rights those young men should be in the forces. If you prefer to employ them then perhaps I ought to take their place and join up. A lot of my friends have already joined up,' she added pointedly.

'That will do! I have heard enough from you. I've already told you, you are not coming to work at the quarry, nor are you going to join any of the forces. Help your mother around the house and in the village. She'll find plenty for you to do and think yourself lucky that you are safe and that you don't have to suffer any hardships. Now that is the end of the matter and I don't want to hear another word about it.'

'I have a university degree in economics,' Megan protested. 'What do you think I should do with that?'

'Put the certificate up on your bedroom wall and shut up. I don't want to hear any more. I have enough problems to deal with without some petty domestic quarrel taking over my mind,' he told her angrily.

Megan would have continued the argument but her mother, who was also in the room, motioned to her by placing a finger over her own lips to be quiet. Afterwards Bronwyn Lloyd took her daughter aside and counselled her not to aggravate her father any further.

'He has a lot of problems to deal with down at the quarry,' she told her seriously. 'So many of the ships that he uses to transport slate to other countries have been involved in incidents of one kind or another while at sea; some have even been sunk with all their cargo on board.'

'I'm very sorry to hear that, but it still makes no difference to what I want to do; in fact it makes it all the more urgent. I want to do something constructive; something to help in the war effort. I don't want to sit at home while all my friends are in the services and doing war work of some kind or the other. If he doesn't want me to join the forces then at least he could let me help in his office.'

'No, *cariad*, that wouldn't be at all appropriate. If you are so anxious to help in the war effort then why not write to our boys overseas and help others to send them parcels of food or books and magazines and cigarettes and anything else you can think of. I am sure that your father will be happy to provide funds for you to do that.'

'Mother, I'm twenty-one, not an old dear of seventy. I wonder you haven't suggested that I knit socks or scarves or something for the soldiers.'

'Well, *cariad*, that might be no bad thing either. I'm sure they need those sorts of items now that the winter is coming on. I know that some of the ladies in the village are doing just that and they would certainly welcome a new recruit.'

'I was joking!' She put her arms around her mother and kissed her to try and take the sting out of her words. She could tell how worried her mother was by the fact she had used the endearment in Welsh.

When she had been a child, Megan recalled, they had always spoken in Welsh, but never since she had been at university.

'Well, it would certainly keep your father happy if he knew that was what you were doing. Think carefully about it, Megan. Your father is very concerned about your future. You have a lovely home here and you can invite your friends to come and stay any time you wish. Your father is very good to you and gives you a generous monthly allowance; probably far more than you would be able to earn if you went out to work. Certainly more than you would get in the forces.'

Megan didn't bother to argue. She knew that all this was true but it made no difference to the way she felt about what she wanted to do at the moment. Later, when the war was over, she would comply with her father's wishes for her to become a schoolteacher or anything else he asked her to do. For the moment she wanted to play her part in helping to win the war.

Lewis Lloyd's determination to protect her from the grim realities of the war only made her all the more keen to leave home, even if it meant using devious means to do so.

—

Early in October 1942 she made up her mind to do something positive. She told her parents that she was going to spend a few days with one of her friends from Aberystwyth University who was now a schoolteacher.

She deliberately did not tell them that the friend lived in Liverpool because she knew that her father would forbid her to go there because of all the bombing that had taken place there over the last few months.

Even so, her father was immediately suspicious of her intentions.

'How long are you planning to stay with this friend?' he asked.

'About a week; she has a week off because it's half term,' Megan explained.

Her father looked at her so quizzically she was afraid he had seen through her plan. Her heart was beating so fast and so loud that she thought he must be able to hear it.

Reluctantly he agreed to her going but only on the proviso that she would not take advantage of being away from home to join any of the services. Solemnly she gave her promise that she would not do so.

It was a promise she had no intention of keeping. She intended to discover some way that she could play a useful part in the war. Her conscience wouldn't allow her to sit around doing nothing for the rest of the war. She wanted to play an active part. She knew that joining the forces was impossible because her father would take steps to have her discharged, but she was sure there were other things that she could do apart from those her mother had suggested.

It was difficult to find out what these might be while living in such a remote spot as Beddgelert, but in a large city like Liverpool there would be several places such as a Citizen's Advice Bureau or even the Unemployment Offices where she would be able to obtain the kind of information she needed.

Chapter Two

Megan was shocked when she arrived at Lime Street station; she stared around her wondering if she really was at the right place. Liverpool looked so very different from when she last visited there.

Her friend Audrey Wilson was waiting for her on the platform. Although the same height as Megan, Audrey was much plumper and had dark blonde hair that hung straight to her shoulders. She was smiling broadly as she greeted Megan.

When Megan expressed surprise at her surroundings, Audrey shrugged her plump shoulders and reminded her that Liverpool had suffered very badly from bombing raids during the past year.

As they left Lime Street station Megan was horrified at the sight of the devastation that had been wrought on the city by the German bombing raids. Stores where on her previous visits she and Audrey had spent happy hours browsing; cafes where they had stopped for coffee or a snack as well as offices of all kinds had either vanished or were so badly damaged that they looked like piles of rubble.

Even the people they met or passed seemed to be different from the last time she had been in Liverpool, Megan mused. Most of them looked weary, as though they hadn't had a good night's sleep for weeks. Their clothes seemed drab, wrinkled and uncared for, almost as if they'd been sleeping in them.

They probably had, she thought, and it sent shivers through her and made her all the more determined to become involved in the war effort.

'You seem to have been very fortunate, your house is still all right,' Megan commented when they turned into the street where Audrey lived.

'Yes, we've been very lucky in this part of Liverpool,' Audrey agreed. 'We're far enough away from the docks and not near enough to the industrial area for the bombers to bother about us. Mind you, we did have to spend many nights in our shelter for weeks at a time and we did have damage from bomb blast. Several times we lost our windows and tiles off the roof but that was nothing compared with what some folks had to contend with; sadly a great many of them didn't survive, especially when their homes received a direct hit.'

The two girls spent the next few hours catching up with news of what they had been doing since they had last seen each other. Then Megan explained to Audrey the underlying reason for her visit.

'Why don't you just get a job in one of the companies who are engaged in war work?' Audrey suggested.

'You mean in an office helping to do the accounts and keep the books or something of that sort?'

'Well, someone has to, and those jobs are important to keep the wheels of commerce turning smoothly.'

'I know, but it sounds very tame. I want to be involved in something more dynamic; something that really brings me in contact with what is actually going on.'

'You can always spend your free time as an air-raid warden or work in one of the canteens that serve the troops or something of that sort,' Audrey added helpfully.

Megan pulled a face. 'No, that's not for me. I want to either be in the forces or have some special project of my own. I want to feel that I'm not only pulling my weight but that I am doing something of special value.'

Audrey shook her head. 'I can't advise you. I haven't a clue how you go about solving that one,' she said with a laugh.

'No, but you can direct me to the Citizens Advice Bureau, or whatever it is called, in Liverpool. I am sure if I go to them they'll be able to tell me what is needed or what is of the greatest importance.'

'Let's sleep on it,' Audrey yawned. 'We've talked so much and I'm so tired that I can't think clearly.'

'Agreed! I feel pretty exhausted too. It's been great catching up on all the news, Audrey, and as you say we'll both feel fresher in the morning.'

The next morning Audrey took her to the nearest Citizens Advice Bureau and Megan felt shocked and angry at the same time when she saw more and more of the damage that the bombing had done to the centre of Liverpool.

Several times she stopped and stared, unable to believe what she was seeing. Whole buildings were reduced to a mass of rubble; others looked as if they had been torn apart by a giant hand that had ripped down the centre of them, leaving rooms partially exposed. Others had boarded-up windows and makeshift doors.

She found it a sickening sight and her heart went out to all the people who had suffered as a result of the desolation.

In her mind's eye she compared it with the peaceful countryside around Beddgelert and how relatively unaffected her life and that of her parents had been; the war had barely touched them. She wondered if, had her father witnessed some of this desecration, he might understand her need to do something positive and not simply idle around at home.

Megan joined the queue of people waiting to consult the advisors behind the counter. When it came to her turn the woman tried to be helpful but she obviously didn't understand Megan's predicament.

'You say your home has not been damaged?' She frowned. 'So what is your problem?'

Megan tried hard to explain about not being allowed to go into the forces but that she wanted to do some sort of work that would help the war effort, but the woman still couldn't understand what she meant.

'If you want to join the forces you can apply at any of the recruiting offices,' she told her. 'If it is some other form of war work you want to do then you must find out where their headquarters are and apply there.'

'Thank you.' Megan turned away, realizing that it was hopeless. She would have to find some other way to pursue what was in her mind.

When they met up later in the day Audrey could see that Megan was cross and frustrated. She listened to what had happened but she didn't know what she could do to help. Instead she resolved to take Megan's mind off her immediate problem by suggesting they went dancing that evening.

'You mean they still hold dances when things here are in such a terrible state?' Megan exclaimed in surprise.

'Of course! We need something to take our minds off the stress and strain of being bombed out and all the shortages. Also, it's one of our ways of entertaining the troops. Soldiers, sailors and airmen are allowed in free.'

'Sounds a great idea…' Megan agreed, but her face clouded as she looked down at the black trousers and striped jumper she was wearing under her short coat. 'I haven't anything suitable to wear.'

'Don't worry about that. Simply come as you are. No one dresses up these days like we used to. Wear a dress, or a blouse and skirt, or even come in slacks and you won't be turned away.'

'Well, I have brought a summer dress with me in case we had a warmish day so I suppose I could wear that,' Megan murmured.

'There you are then. So you like the idea that we should go dancing?'

'Indeed I do, I'm looking forward to it.'

'Good. You might even find the answer to your problem there,' Audrey said with a laugh.

'I very much doubt that, but it will be good to let our hair down. I haven't been to a dance since my twenty-first birthday party.'

'Well, I can't guarantee that the surroundings for this dance will be as opulent as they were at your party,' Audrey warned.

'Maybe not, but I am sure I'll enjoy myself,' Megan enthused.

The dance was held in a local hall and it was already packed when Audrey and Megan arrived. The majority of the girls were in their teens or early twenties and most of them were wearing either dresses or a skirt and pretty top. Some of them were bare-legged but they had painted a dark line down the back of their leg to represent a seam so that it looked as if they were wearing very sheer stockings.

Megan was surprised at how many service personnel were there as well. She recognized most of the uniforms but there were some that she was unable to identify. One man in particular stood out from all the others. He was tall, slim but broad-shouldered and he was wearing such a smartly tailored khaki uniform that she asked Audrey what regiment he was from.

'He's one of the GIs,' Audrey told her. 'Judging by his uniform I would say he's an officer.'

'GIs? Whatever are they?' Megan frowned.

'Americans. Yanks! America has joined in the war and men from their army are over here to collaborate with our forces.'

Megan studied him with fresh interest. Even the material of his uniform seemed to be a better quality than that of the British army, she mused.

As if aware that he was being watched he suddenly looked across towards where she and Audrey were standing and caught Megan's eye. She felt her colour rising when he walked over to them and in a very courteous manner asked her to dance.

She hesitated for a moment before accepting. She had never met an American before and she wondered what they would talk about. There were so many prominent notices telling people to be careful what they said because careless talk cost lives so that as a rule it was better not to speak to strangers.

He might be a stranger but he was here in Liverpool because he wanted to help Britain's war effort, she reminded herself.

Even so, as they moved on to the dance floor she found herself asking him questions about why he was in Liverpool and what his company were doing there.

'My name is Hank Jackson. I can't tell you too much of what I do because I am sworn to secrecy. When we join the army we sign a paper to say we will not disclose any information about what we are doing.'

Megan smiled. 'I believe that the members of our forces have to do the same,' she said awkwardly. 'Do you like it here in England?' she rushed on to try and cover up her mistake.

'Sure. It's a fine country and you are a great people and we are eager to help you to fight this war and keep your country and not have it taken from you by the enemy.'

'I'm glad to hear that you enjoy being here,' Megan told him. 'Is there anything you don't like about our country?'

He pursed his lips together and said nothing for a moment. Then he took a deep breath before answering. 'Well, ma'am, since you ask, I am very disconcerted by the number of very young girls who hang around our camp.'

Megan raised a quizzical eyebrow. 'I'm not sure I understand,' she said.

'Soldiers being soldiers, our men are inclined to take advantage of their company, if you know what I mean.'

Megan still looked puzzled. 'No, I don't think I do know what you mean.'

'Well, these young girls hang around outside the camp waiting for our boys to come out. They have been warned not to give the girls nylons and chocolate or cigarettes. Most of them are so kind-hearted though that they cannot see any harm in doing so, and of course the girls come back again and again, for more and more.'

'So what harm is there in that?'

He raised his eyebrows. 'Well, that would be all right, it's what it is that our boys are given in return as a thank you that causes the problem.'

Megan felt herself colouring but said nothing.

Hank went on. 'Far too many of these girls end up pregnant. Many of them have nowhere to go because their parents disown them the moment they discover what has happened as they consider that they have brought disgrace to the family.'

'Oh dear! So what happens to the girls, what do they do? I take it that your men don't intend to marry the girls, not even after they have got them pregnant.'

'That sure is the problem,' Hank agreed. 'Some of the boys already have sweethearts or wives back home in America; some even have young families.'

'So what do these girls do?' Megan repeated.

He shrugged. 'Have an abortion or else go on the game and become prostitutes. A few even take their own lives because disgracing their family distresses them so much.'

Megan looked horrified. 'Are you sure that's what happens to them?' she gasped, her cheeks red with embar-rassment.

He nodded, his handsome face serious. 'It's of consid-erable concern to us because we came over here to help your country, not to bring misery or disgrace on British families.'

'Are you quite sure about all this?' Megan frowned, wondering if it could possibly be true.

'It's what I've been told by my men and I have heard it said by other people who come to our camp to talk to us about our welfare as well as to lecture our men about the girls who flock to entertain us.'

'Is there no way of stopping the girls coming to your camp?'

'We have taken all precautions possible; we've lectured the men and forbidden them to bring girls back to camp. What we've failed to do is prevent our men meeting up with these young girls outside camp or control what goes on when they do.'

'Yet you have come to the dance?'

'Our men are only permitted to do so if there are officers present as well.' He grinned. 'They know we can be trusted to behave ourselves.'

Megan smiled fleetingly; she didn't know what to say in response to his comment. It had however implanted an idea in her mind. The thought of young girls finding themselves pregnant and not knowing how to cope with the situation made her wonder if there wasn't something she could do to help them.

That, she told herself, would be one way of doing her bit to help solve some of the problems brought about by the war. Although she danced twice more with other people what Hank had said stayed in her thoughts and her mind was busy trying to formulate some sort of plan.

When she talked about it afterwards to Audrey, her friend confirmed that what he had said was very true.

'If the girls are Catholics then the nuns will take them into the sanctuary of their infirmary when the time comes for the baby to be born,' Audrey told her.

'And the baby? What happens to that?'

'They keep the baby afterwards and arrange for it to be adopted.'

Megan shuddered. 'I know they are helping the girls, but what an awful fate for both the mother and the baby.

She loses her child and never sees it again or knows what happens to it and the baby is placed with strangers.'

'It's probably better than the poor girl having to bring it up herself, especially if her family have turned her out. She would probably end up becoming a full-time prostitute in order to do so and heaven alone knows what sort of life the child would have.'

'I'm sure you're right,' Megan said, 'but I still find it heartbreaking.'

'I know, but there's not a lot we can do about it,' Audrey stated philosophically.

'What happens if the girl isn't a Catholic?' Megan mused aloud.

'Well, she either goes to a backstreet abortionist or has the baby, I suppose,' Audrey told her.

'And afterwards?'

'I don't know. She either puts it in a home or an orphanage, or else struggles to bring it up herself.'

'Doesn't anyone in authority do anything about it?'

'Well, there's the Salvation Army or Dr Barnardo's, and there are do-gooders who try and talk to the girls and warn them of what will happen if they go out with Yanks, but the girls tend to ignore them. Apart from that, what can anyone do?'

Megan didn't have an answer, but it gave her plenty to think about before she went to sleep that night. She was quite determined to try and help in some way.

Chapter Three

Before Megan left Liverpool she asked Audrey to take her to the Scotland Road area.

'What on earth do you want to go there for?' Audrey asked. 'It's the slums of Liverpool; surely you'd rather go and visit the shops in Lord Street or even visit Bold Street where the really expensive shops are.'

'No, I want to see Scotland Road and the streets around there,' Megan said firmly, her lips clamped together in a tight line.

'Well, all right, if you insist, but there has been a lot of bomb damage in that area because it's so near the docks,' Audrey warned.

The sight that met their eyes when they reached Scotland Road was not merely bomb damage but deprivation. Many of the tenement houses had had windows blown in by the bomb blasts and most of the roads were still littered with broken glass and rubble, as well as old newspapers, boxes, discarded vegetables and general muck. Dogs and cats rummaged amongst the debris and some of the half-starved dogs came sniffing around their heels looking for food.

Megan ignored them; it was the raggedy children, some of them barefoot, dirty and bedraggled, who caught her attention and touched her heart.

Women stood on their doorsteps gossiping to each other. She was aware that they were watching them and whenever she met the gaze of one of the women she was aware of the sharp alertness and suspicion in their eyes.

'Is this the area where most of the girls who visit the Yanks come from?' she asked Audrey.

'Not many of them! In general the girls from around here wouldn't be allowed into the camp because they wouldn't be dressed smartly enough. It's where a lot of the girls who have babies by the Yanks are likely to end up though. Most of the girls who go out with the Yanks come from good homes; often from Wallasey on the other side of the Mersey.'

'So that means that very often the parents of the girls who get into trouble could afford to pay for their daughters to go somewhere and have the baby; and even afford to bring it up afterwards,' Megan mused.

Audrey gave a short bitter laugh. 'You are forgetting the disgrace and the shame that the girl has brought on her family. A few of them do, of course. They send the girl away to a relative in some other part of the country to have the baby, and then have it adopted as soon as it is born. Afterwards the girl comes home again and picks up her life as though nothing has happened. Anyone who asks about her is told simply that she has "been on holiday" or "been away studying".'

'You seem to know an awful lot about it,' Megan murmured.

'Yes, I do, because there have even been girls from our school, girls as young as fourteen, who have been in this predicament.'

On the train on the way home to Beddgelert, Megan tried to think what she could do about the problem in

Liverpool. She wondered whether to keep her ideas to herself or to take her family into her confidence.

Her mother might understand what was involved but she very much doubted if her father would have any sympathy for the girls in question. He would probably tell her that it was up to the local authorities to take care of the girls and to deal with the problem and that it was nothing to do with her.

In a way, Megan knew this was true, but it didn't deter her from construing that something ought to be done about it and contemplating that perhaps it could be her own special war effort.

Ideally what she ought to do, she resolved, was to find a house in Liverpool where the girls would be made welcome and where they could stay until after their baby was born.

What happened after that was up to them. If they could manage to get their families to accept the child then once it was born they could go back to their own home. If not, then she would help them to have the baby adopted; the last resort would be to put it into an orphanage.

She would also try to help the young mother build a new future for herself. She was sure that most of the girls would realize what a mistake they had made and be anxious to make amends and start afresh.

When she told her parents of her idea it was exactly as she had imagined: her mother understood what she wanted to do but her father dismissed it as foolishness.

'We are at war; cities and towns are still being bombed by the Germans night after night. Here you are safe, so let's hear no more about it. Anyway, what the devil do you think you are taking on? Why assume responsibility for the stupid young girls who know no better than to sleep around with soldiers?'

'I simply want to help them; half of them don't know where to turn for help,' Megan explained. 'In many instances their families have disowned them and don't want to know about the baby because they feel it will bring disgrace, or else they can't afford having another mouth to feed.'

Lewis Lloyd grunted but made no reply.

'You really should see the state some of the very poor people in Liverpool live in. There's nothing at all like that here. I was completely shocked when I walked down Scotland Road and saw the terrible places where some of them have to live.'

Megan's voice was high as she tried to make her point and tears were running down her cheeks.

'Yes, and if you go ahead with your silly ideas then that's where you'll end up as well, my girl,' her father told her. 'If they had worked hard and saved and budgeted they wouldn't be in that mess. Most of the women there are sluts who hang around waiting for the pubs to open the same as their menfolk. As for the men, most of them drink their wages away on a Friday night before they even go home.'

Megan knew it was useless to argue with him but it made her all the more resolute to do something to help the girls, so she waited until she was alone with her mother before broaching the subject again.

'Forget about it, my dear,' Bronwyn Lloyd told her daughter. 'What do you think you can do that the local authorities haven't already tried?'

'I'm sure there must be something I can do,' Megan insisted. 'I thought that perhaps I could provide them with some sort of retreat, a house where they knew they would be safe until the baby arrived, something of that sort.'

'That would cost quite a lot of money. Remember, you would have to feed them as well as provide them with a midwife to help deliver the baby. Do you think any of them would be prepared to pay for that?'

'I don't know, and I haven't any way of finding out. I simply thought of providing them with somewhere safe to live until they'd had their baby.'

'It's certainly a very commendable idea, my dear, but I don't think it's very practical. It would take a great deal of organizing as well as a lot of money.'

Megan retreated to her bedroom but she couldn't put the idea from her mind. She was determined to do something to help those girls and she was sure there was some way she could do so.

The answer came to her in the middle of the night; she awoke with a scheme already formed in her mind, one that she felt she would be able to put into practice.

Next morning over breakfast she once more broached the subject.

Angrily her father banged his fist on the table, making the dishes jump as well as Megan and her mother.

'I don't intend to sit here and listen to your babble about fallen girls while I have my breakfast,' her father thundered and again banged on the table with his fist. 'I told you yesterday to forget about it.'

'I simply can't do that, Father,' Megan protested. 'I want to do something to help these girls and I feel that if I did this I would then be playing a vital part in the war effort.'

'And I have said no! As long as you are living under my roof then you will do as I tell you.'

'Father, I am twenty-one now and old enough to make my own decisions, and that is what I intend to do,' she told him rebelliously. 'I want to help these girls and I have an idea of how to go about it, so that is what I am going to do.'

'Not if you want to remain under my roof!'

'In that case I have no option but to move out.'

'Megan! Please don't speak to your father like that,' Bronwyn exclaimed, her face white with dismay.

Megan stared at her mother, willing her to give her support, but Bronwyn had no intention of going against her husband's wishes.

'In that case then I will have to leave,' Megan insisted stubbornly.

'If you defy me, then remember you cannot come back again. If you leave this house now then you leave it for good,' her father told her harshly.

Megan flicked back her long dark hair and tossed her head defiantly. 'I quite understand.'

'So where will you go? How will you live?' her mother asked in a shaky voice.

'I'll manage somehow.'

'You won't get a penny piece more from me,' her father told her. 'Your allowance will be stopped right from this moment, so you will have no money at all. So how do you think you can live?'

'I have money of my own, remember,' Megan said quietly. 'I have the money which my godmother left me when she died two years ago.'

'You have no access to that; it was left under my jurisdiction and as far as I am concerned you can't touch a penny of it.'

'That is where you are wrong, Father,' Megan said smugly. 'I have access to that money when I come of age, and as I have already pointed out to you I am now twenty-one and able to manage my own affairs.'

'You mean you are going to use that money to support girls who have fallen into disgrace!' he exclaimed in a shocked voice.

'Exactly! I am going to use it to provide shelter and help for some of the girls in Liverpool who have fallen victim to the Yanks and who are now expecting their babies.'

'You are completely out of your mind,' her father told her, shaking his head in despair. 'If you do that then you are no longer my daughter; you are no better than the girls themselves. If you join them then that is the end of our relationship; I no longer regard you as my daughter; I disown you! I never want to see you or hear from you ever again.'

Megan felt fresh tears pricking behind her eyes and knew that at any moment they would be running down her face. She bit her lip and held her head high, determined not to give way, and looked at her mother for support.

Her lip trembled when she realized she was not going to get a response from her mother. Bronwyn had moved across the room to the window and was looking out, completely ignoring what was going on in the room behind her. She was making it quite clear that she did not want to be involved in what was happening.

Suppressing a sob, Megan squared her shoulders and walked towards the door. 'So it's goodbye,' she said in a voice that she struggled to keep normal.

Neither of her parents made any response.

With tears streaming down her cheeks Megan went upstairs to her bedroom knowing that she had burned her boats. Now, unless she went back and apologized to them both, she had no option but to pack her belongings and leave the house which had been her home all her life.

She sat down on her bed and tried to think what she must do next. Then, sniffing back her tears, she went over to her wardrobe, took out two suitcases and began to haphazardly pack clothes into them.

The house was eerily silent as she went downstairs and carried her cases along to the garage to put them into the back of her car.

When she opened the garage doors she gaped in amazement. Her mother's Rover was there and so was her father's Rolls Royce, but her Morris was missing.

Frowning, she stared at the empty space, wondering where it was, but in her heart she knew it had been driven somewhere where she would be unable to access it.

It had been a present from her parents for her twenty-first birthday, and this was their way of letting her know that unless she agreed to do as they wanted, then she really had severed all connection with them.

She stood there for a moment contemplating what to do. Pride stopped her from going back to the house and asking where her car was.

If she intended to help the girls in Liverpool then this was her opportunity to stand on her own two feet and do just that, she told herself.

She would go to Liverpool and hope that Audrey Wilson would let her stay at her place for a few days while she sorted herself out. She would find a house she could rent and then put her idea into practice.

Tossing back her long hair, she squared her shoulders and picked up her suitcases, and after taking a long lingering look at Yr Glaslyn, she headed for the railway station.

Chapter Four

Megan felt exhausted when she arrived at Audrey Wilson's front door. The two suitcases had become heavier and heavier as she made her way from Lime Street station to the taxi rank. She knew that really she should take a bus and save what little money she had, but she felt so tired that all she wanted to do was reach her destination as soon as possible.

The taxi driver took her two suitcases from the boot of his car, dumped them on the pavement outside Audrey's house and held out his hand for his fare.

Megan carried the cases to the front door and pressed the bell. Then she waited apprehensively. She hadn't let Audrey know that she was coming and she wondered what sort of a reception she would get.

The door was opened by a tall, fair-haired young man wearing khaki trousers and a khaki shirt that was open at the neck. For a moment Megan wondered whether she had come to the wrong address.

'I... I wanted to speak to Audrey Wilson,' she said hesitantly.

The young man grinned as if he knew her. 'You must be her friend Megan Lloyd. You were staying with Audrey last week at half term?'

'Yes, that's right.' She smiled at him nervously. 'And you are?'

'I'm her cousin Martin Wilson,' he told her. 'I'm here on leave from the army. Actually I'm paying Audrey and her family a quick visit because I'm on embarkation leave. When I return to my regiment in two days' time I'll be off overseas. I can't tell you how much I'm looking forward to seeing some action,' he said with a broad smile.

He ran a hand through his shock of fair hair then turned and called out, 'Audrey, there's a visitor here for you.'

Megan heard the sound of footsteps as Audrey came through from the kitchen into the hallway. Then she heard the gasp of astonishment as Audrey saw her standing there and glanced down at the two suitcases at her feet.

'Good heavens, this is a surprise! I wasn't expecting you! Have you decided to come and live in Liverpool?'

'Yes,' Megan said hesitantly. 'I... I was wondering if I could stay here with you for a couple of days until I can find some sort of lodgings. Do you think your mother would mind?'

For a moment Audrey hesitated, looking from Megan to Martin and back again. Before she could speak, however, Martin had stepped into the breach.

'I can kip down on the settee tonight. I've only one more night left and I have to be up at the crack of dawn so it's much better if I do that, then I won't disturb anyone.'

'No, no, you can't do that,' Megan protested.

'I certainly can,' he assured her. He bent down and picked up her two cases and began walking towards the stairs with them. 'I'll put these in my room and clear my things out and then you can get settled in.'

'Go on through to the kitchen with Audrey,' he ordered when Megan again tried to protest. 'There's fresh tea in the pot; make sure you keep a cuppa for me.'

The moment they were on their own, Megan gave Audrey a brief outline of what had happened before she had left Beddgelert.

Audrey looked shocked. 'Surely they didn't mean it, when they said that they were going to disown you? Surely it's something that your father said in the heat of the moment because he was upset and angry?'

'Don't you believe it! My father meant every word. The only way I can get him to forgive me is for me to grovel and go down on my knees and apologize and then spend the rest of my life doing exactly as he wants me to do.' Megan tossed her head defiantly. 'Well, I am not prepared to do that.'

'So what are you going to do?'

'War work! My kind of war work.'

Audrey frowned looking puzzled. 'What do you mean?'

'When I was staying here, you know we talked about the girls in Liverpool who went out with soldiers, especially the Yanks and ended up having babies? Well, I'm going to do something to help them. I'm thinking of renting a house, somewhere where they can come and be looked after when they have the baby.'

'You can't do that on your own! It'll take an awful lot of money, and you would definitely need to have people to help,' Audrey gasped. 'You'll need a midwife and possibly a doctor, as well as people to help nurse the young mothers and get them back on their feet after their babies are born. And what are you going to do with all the babies if the girls don't want to keep them?'

'I know there's going to be a lot of work and planning and organizing involved. I'm going to spend the inheritance left to me by my godmother to get it started,' Megan explained. 'I can't afford to buy a house, of course, but I'm sure I'll be able to find one to rent. As for the babies, well, that very much depends on what the girls want to do. I realize that some of them will want to get rid of their babies by having them adopted or something but there may be others who'll want to try and bring them up single-handed and I'm hoping I'll be able to help them in some way.'

Audrey shook her head, her grey eyes doubtful. 'You're going to take an awful lot on your shoulders. Are you sure you can manage?'

'That's something I've got to find out, but I'm quite sure I can. I really feel very strongly about these girls and their babies.'

'Well, you're more than welcome to stay here for a few days until you find a house.'

'Are you sure your mum and dad won't mind?'

'Of course they won't. I can help you to find a house, if you like. I know the area a lot better than you do.'

'I know you do, and I'd be more than grateful if you would help me. It needs to be somewhere near Scotland Road.'

Audrey looked startled. 'Why do you want to live there?'

'I think these girls will feel more comfortable because in that sort of area they won't be shunned by so-called respectable people,' Megan explained.

'There's been an awful lot of bomb damage around there so it might not be easy to find a suitable house,' Audrey warned.

'I'm sure we'll find the sort of place I want if we look hard enough,' Megan said confidently.

Audrey looked sceptical but didn't argue with her about it. 'You'll probably have to get some sort of permission from the council or local authority or the health authority, to run that sort of place,' she warned.

They went on talking about it even after Martin had rejoined them. He seemed extremely interested.

'It's not only the Yanks who are responsible for what happens to these girls,' he said as he drank the cup of tea that Audrey had poured out for him. 'Sailors are just as bad. The minute they get into port they pick up a girl and by the time they finally leave she's usually pregnant and she never hears from him ever again.'

'How do you know that?' Audrey asked.

'Your father told me, and he should know because he was a sailor.'

They all laughed at this but they soon became serious again, knowing that what Megan was planning to do was no laughing matter.

The three of them talked for another hour or more; each of them putting forward various ideas that seemed appropriate but none of them too sure of what exactly was involved, or what it would cost to put such ideas into practice.

Realizing that he had to be up at six the next morning to report back to barracks and rejoin his regiment, Martin started to make up a bed for himself on the settee.

'Sorry, we're keeping you up,' Audrey said apologetically. 'I forgot you have to leave early tomorrow morning and that you need to get some sleep.'

'That's fine, you carry on talking as long as you don't mind if I drop off and start to snore.'

'No, it's high time we were both in bed as well,' Audrey said as she stood up and picked up their dirty cups to take into the kitchen.

'Sleep well, Martin,' she said as she came back into the room. 'I don't suppose either of us will be up to say goodbye to you in the morning so we had better do it now. Goodbye and good luck.'

'Thank you; and good luck to you, Megan, with your new enterprise.'

'Thank you, I'm sure all the ideas you've given me will be of great help.'

It was a long time before Megan fell asleep. When she did she dreamed that she was in charge of a large rambling country mansion filled with happy smiling women who were nursing fat bonny babies.

If only that dream could come true, she thought, when she awoke just before eight o'clock the next morning. She lay there thinking back over all the plans and ideas that Audrey and Martin had put forward the night before. Then she hurriedly prepared for the day ahead, vowing that before nightfall she would have set something in motion.

Audrey had already finished her breakfast and was putting on her coat ready to leave for school when Megan came downstairs.

'I'll be home again about four o'clock this afternoon,' she said as she greeted Megan. 'Perhaps then I could take you down to Scotland Road so that you can see it again and have a good look around and find out if there are any empty properties,' she added as she fastened her coat and picked up her handbag and a pile of books.

'In the meantime,' she suggested, 'why don't you make some enquiries to find out if you need to inform the local authorities or anyone else about what you are proposing to do.'

'Yes, I'll do that. I'm not too sure where to start but if I go along to the council offices then I'm sure they'll point me in the right direction.'

'Yes, that sounds the best idea, and when I get home tonight you can tell me what you've discovered. I'm sure there must be some regulations that you'll have to conform to,' she added as she headed for the door.

After Audrey had left Megan helped Mrs Wilson to clear away the breakfast dishes and as they washed up she told her about her plan.

'Yes, I think you're doing the right thing by going to the council offices first,' Mrs Wilson agreed. 'If they can't help you then why not try the police. They always seem to know everything there is to know about those sorts of things. Or you could try the Salvation Army.'

'I'd sooner try the council office and the police,' Megan murmured. 'I feel that they are the right authorities to deal with this.'

The woman in the council office didn't seem to under-stand what Megan wanted. She seemed to think that it was Megan who was in some sort of trouble and told her there were various organizations and charities that helped expectant mothers, but she was rather vague about exactly what was available.

The desk sergeant at the police station wasn't much more helpful.

'You mean that you are in some sort of trouble and need help,' he said.

'No, no not at all,' Megan said quickly.

'So what is your problem then?'

'I want to try and help some of the young girls who are expecting babies… Illegitimate babies.'

'Well, you'll find plenty of them in Liverpool,' he told her, shaking his head sadly. 'It's them Yanks I blame most of all.'

'I know,' Megan agreed. 'That's why I'm trying to do something to help these girls.'

'There are charities all over Liverpool trying to do just that. I'm sure any one of them would be glad of your help. Look in the street directory, you'll find all of them listed there.'

'I want to set up a charity of my own,' Megan explained. 'I want to find a house where they can stay and I will arrange for them to be looked after.'

'Whew!' The sergeant pursed his lips in a whistle. 'That's some undertaking, miss!'

'I know. What I am trying to find out is am I allowed to do it?'

'You mean do you need a licence or something of that sort?' He shook his head from side to side. 'I'm not sure about that. I think you would have to go to the city hall and ask them for advice. You'd probably have to register it with them.'

Megan thanked him for his help and left. She didn't bother to tell him that she had already been there and they had been unable to advise her.

She felt frustrated as she came back out into the street. This was the sort of prevarication she would have received from her father to try and prevent her from doing what she wanted to do.

She had no intention of seeking any more advice. She would wait until Audrey came home and then together they could visit the area around Scotland Road and see if they could find a suitable house to rent.

Once she actually had a place where she could provide accommodation for the girls then perhaps the authorities would take her more seriously.

Chapter Five

Megan had her hat and coat on and was fastening her walking shoes when Audrey arrived home shortly after half past four.

'Are you going somewhere?' Audrey asked with a smile.

'Yes, out with you; you haven't forgotten that we agreed to go and look for a house in the Scotland Road area, have you?'

'Of course I haven't. Give me time to change my shoes because my feet are killing me,' Audrey said. 'I've been standing up most of the day writing on the blackboard and I'm wearing the wrong shoes.'

'If you're so tired do you want to stop and have a cup of tea first before we go out?' Megan asked.

'Would you mind very much? I really am in need of one,' Audrey admitted. 'It's been one of those days.'

Megan tried to be patient while she waited for the kettle to boil and for Audrey to change her shoes and then come downstairs and drink the tea. The moment Audrey replaced her empty cup in its saucer Megan was on her feet ready to go.

They walked to the tram stop nearest to Audrey's home in silence. Once they were on the tram, Megan told her what had happened when she had gone to the council offices and to the police earlier that day.

'So you don't really know what you ought to do or where to go for permission,' Audrey said with a frown.

'No, and I'm not going to waste any more time trying to find out. I'm sure that if I am breaking some law or other then someone will be quick to come and tell me.'

'You are taking rather a risk, you know,' Audrey warned.

'Maybe, but I don't really care. All I want to do now is find a house and get on with what I have in mind.'

They had taken seats on the upper deck of the tram and as it took them down through the heart of Liverpool, Megan was once again shocked by the amount of destruction that had been caused by the bombing.

The streets were busy with people and were reasonably clean and tidy apart from the boarded-up windows of shops that had been bombed and not reopened afterwards. The real truth lay behind the schools and houses the nearer they came to the dock area. At the rear of most houses there were piles of debris, rubble and broken glass.

Where Audrey lived in Grasmere Drive in Everton, there had been some damage, but it was nothing compared to the devastation Megan saw in the heart of Liverpool and which became increasingly severe the closer they came to the docks.

'Do you think there will be any more bombing in Liverpool?' she queried.

'Who knows! I certainly hope not. I'll never forget when night after night the bombers came over dropping their loads and the sound of explosions as factories and warehouses went up in flames.'

'It must have been enough to give you nightmares for life,' Megan said with a shudder.

They got off the tram at Exchange station and Audrey led the way through a maze of streets to Scotland Road. A wide variety of small shops, bookies and barbers stood on either side of the road. There were flats above most of them that appeared to be empty but Audrey told Megan she assumed they were all occupied by the owners of the shops.

'There's nothing here in Scotland Road that is remotely suitable,' Megan said in a disappointed voice.

'No, I didn't think there would be, but I thought you would want to see Scotland Road again to get an idea of what sort of district it is. I think there might be something suitable in one of the roads leading off Scotland Road. Shall we look?'

'Of course; that's what we came here to do,' Megan reminded her.

'Come on then, let's turn down here.'

The road they entered was so shabby and squalid that for a moment Megan was taken aback. She drew in a sharp breath as she saw the grim tenement buildings that lined either side of the road. There were broken stone steps leading down to cellars and, in some cases, stone steps leading up to the front door. Most of them were covered in debris. She had never seen such dirty streets in her life and the thought of living in a house here made her squirm.

They walked the full length of the street then turned the corner and went into the street that stood adjacent. It was hardly any better. Miserable looking half-starved dogs were sniffing through boxes of rubbish that had been left out in front of some of the houses.

There was an air of listlessness; they were so dingy that even the daylight seemed to dim and turn grey as it came into the street.

Megan thought longingly of her mansion home in North Wales and compared it with the sordid scenes around her and for one moment wished she was back there. Perhaps her father had been right and she wasn't cut out for living in this sort of place.

She squared her shoulders and took a deep breath, knowing that if she didn't go ahead with her plan then she would have to go back home and let him know that he had been right after all, and she couldn't bring herself to do that.

They spent a long time walking up and down the streets that led from Scotland Road and criss-crossed to other streets and all the roads leading off until their feet were aching, and still they hadn't found anything that they thought remotely suitable.

By mutual consent they headed back towards Exchange train station to pick up a tram to take them back to Everton. They were both feeling tired and disillusioned. As they were walking down one of the streets they met a youngish woman coming towards them.

She was tall, with short fair hair, and she was heavily pregnant. They noticed that she was swaying from side to side. Suddenly she stumbled and would have fallen had Megan not rushed forward and grabbed her arm, steadying her and holding her upright until Audrey came and did the same on the other side.

'Thank you,' the woman gasped. She tried to smile at them but she was still breathless and trembling too much to do so.

'Have you got very far to go?' Audrey asked.

'No, not very far,' the woman said breathing heavily. 'Only around the corner into the next street.'

'We'll walk along with you then,' Megan said, gently taking her arm.

'Good heavens, no! I'm sure you have better things to do than waste your time doing that. I'll be all right in a minute or two.'

'We're not in any hurry,' Audrey murmured. 'We were really looking for a house; somewhere to rent,' she explained.

'If it's lodgings you're looking for,' the woman said, her face brightening, 'I may be able to help you. I have a boarding house, but it's completely empty at the moment.'

'Really! You're not thinking of renting it out, are you?' Megan asked eagerly.

'No, it's my family home, I wouldn't want to leave there. Anyway, I think you would find it rather too large. It has six bedrooms as well as two large reception rooms downstairs and a very big kitchen.'

'Really!' Megan's eyes lit up with interest. 'It sounds exactly the sort of place that I'm looking for,' she told the woman eagerly. 'Of course, it would depend where it's located.'

'That's probably one of the reasons why you wouldn't want it,' the young woman told them. 'My mother was left to bring me up single-handed after my father was killed in the First World War. She took this house near the docks with the idea of people staying there overnight while waiting to board a ship to continue to their destination. It served its purpose very well and provided her with both a home and an income while I was growing up. Unfortunately she died about a year ago but I have been trying to continue the business because I am now in more or less the same situation as she was.' She ran a hand over her extended stomach and smiled ruefully.

'Do you mean your husband has been killed in this war?' Audrey murmured sympathetically.

'Not exactly, but my situation is very similar. We were planning on being married next week, but unfortunately Hank has been sent overseas at a moment's notice and there is no chance now of us being married before our baby is born.'

'Hank? That's an unusual name.'

'Yes. Hank Jackson. He's an officer in the American army. One of the Yankee GIs who have come over to this country to help out.'

'I know him!' Megan said in astonishment. 'I met him at a dance about a week ago. Tall and slim and wearing a very smart uniform?'

'It certainly sounds like him,' the girl agreed. 'He was on duty at a dance about a week ago, shortly before they were sent abroad. The officers had to be there to make sure that none of the GIs got into any trouble. Although at the time none of them knew it, they were due to go overseas almost right away. Now I've no idea where he has been sent, only that he is no longer in this country.'

'It's terribly worrying, isn't it?' Audrey murmured, shaking her head. 'I know how you must feel because my cousin Martin has been visiting us and he was on embarkation leave, so I know exactly what you mean.'

'They are not told where they are going and of course no one knows how long they will be away from home.'

'How very true, and we all are left to wonder and worry about them,' the girl said ruefully.

'It must be very hard for you,' Megan said sympathetically. 'How are you going to manage?'

'I'm not sure. I don't think I'm going to be able to continue running the house as a boarding house, not for a few months anyway. That's one of the reasons why I've not booked anyone in for the next few weeks. I'm not interested in selling, but if you want somewhere to live for a few weeks then I would be quite happy to accommodate you, providing you looked after yourself.'

'Perhaps I should tell you what I am proposing to do,' Megan told her. 'I am going to open up a shelter for girls who have become pregnant and then deserted by Yankee soldiers or sailors, and even our own soldiers. Girls who have been left destitute because their families have turned them out as they feel it is a disgrace that they are pregnant.'

'That sounds very commendable,' the girl murmured. 'It's going to take an awful lot of work and resources though.'

'I know. I do have some money, but not enough to buy the sort of property I would like to have. It's going to be very much a question of make do with what I can afford to rent. I am hoping that perhaps some of the girls will be able to afford to pay while they are with me, or at least to give something towards their keep and care.'

'It certainly sounds a worthwhile project,' the girl said admiringly. 'Perhaps you should take look at my house and then, if it is suitable, you might be able to make a start there and give yourself a chance to find out if it is feasible or not before you commit yourself to renting anything bigger. Perhaps we could reach an agreement that you use it for, say, six months?'

Megan looked astonished.

'You'd be prepared to let me do that?' she said in amazement.

'Why not? I can't run the place as a boarding house until after the baby is born, and I'll probably need a few months' respite after that to get used to looking after it. If

44

you took over the house for that time then at least I would be able to go on living there. I would help you all I could, of course, but the main responsibility would be yours.'

'It sounds the perfect answer to my dreams,' Megan breathed. 'Where did you say your house was?'

'Chapel Gardens. It's not far from here.'

'It sounds perfect. By the way, I don't even know your name. I'm Megan Lloyd and this is Audrey Wilson. Audrey is a schoolteacher here in Liverpool and I come from Wales, from Beddgelert.'

'My name is Sandra Peterson, and I hope that in the not too distant future it will be Sandra Jackson,' she told them with a smile.

Chapter Six

Sandra Peterson took the turning off Scotland Road that led into Chapel Gardens. Although it still showed signs of bomb damage there was nowhere near as much devastation as there was in Scotland Road itself.

Sandra's house was midway along the street. The centre of a row of terraced houses, she had told them it was three storeys high. Half of the house on one side of it had been partly demolished but the rest of it had been shored up and most of the rubble swept away into an orderly pile in the back garden.

Most of the other houses in the street were partially boarded up or had strips of brown adhesive tape across the broken windows to secure them.

'Here we are,' Sandra said as she led them up the two stone steps and pushed open the paint-scarred dark green front door that had obviously been left on the latch because she didn't use a key.

As they entered the hallway a middle-aged woman appeared from the back of the house. She was stout, broad-shouldered and wearing a blue flannel blouse and a voluminous grey skirt. Her face was weather-beaten and wrinkled but her hard blue eyes were sharp and alert. When she spoke her accent was a mixture of Liverpudlian and Irish brogue.

'And where do you think you've been traipsing off to then, and you in your condition and like as not to drop that babe at any moment?' she greeted Sandra.

Megan was sure that the woman was a servant of some sort and she felt taken aback at the way she addressed Sandra. She waited for Sandra to reprove her. She knew what would have happened if any of their servants back home in Beddgelert had spoken to her mother like that.

To her astonishment Sandra only laughed.

'Shush! Nelly, don't make such a fuss. I've brought some friends home with me and they're simply dying for a cup of tea and some of your special scones.'

'Are they now, me darlin' girl. Then in that case I'll go back in my kitchen and see to it. Take yourselves into the sitting room and make yourselves comfortable,' she added, addressing Megan and Audrey. 'You go and sit down as well,' she ordered, looking at Sandra, 'and put your feet up or you'll have ankles like balloons before tonight.'

It was a large pleasant room with a bay window overlooking the street they had just come along. It was comfortably furnished with two sofas upholstered in dark red velvet and three matching armchairs. There was a coffee table in the centre of the room, bookshelves down one wall and a writing bureau in one corner by the big window.

'Do sit down and make yourselves comfortable,' Sandra invited as she sat down on one of the sofas and put her feet up. 'While we have a cup of tea we can go into more detail of what you are proposing to do and you can tell me how I can help.'

'You live here all on your own?' Megan asked in amazement.

'Yes, I do now since my mother died, apart from Nelly Flynn. She has lived with us ever since I was a small child and she cleans and cooks and bullies me, as you probably noticed. She has been with us for so many years that she now thinks of it as her home and I certainly wouldn't dream of turning her out.'

'She sounds something of a treasure,' Megan said with a smile.

'She is; in fact I don't know how I would manage without her. She could certainly be a great asset to us if we go ahead with your idea about taking in pregnant girls.

'While we are waiting for her to bring in the tea perhaps you would like to see the rest of the house,' Sandra suggested, getting up off the sofa and walking towards the door. 'That will give you some idea of the amount of space there is here.'

As well as the large sitting room there was a spacious dining room and at the rear of the house there was a very big working kitchen with another room almost as large that seemed to be used as a utility and junk room. On the first floor there were four bedrooms; two in the front of the house, both of them large and airy, and two smaller ones at the back. On the same floor there was a family bathroom and a separate toilet.

Sandra was puffing with the exertion of climbing the narrow stairs that led up to the top floor where there were two more bedrooms. They were much smaller and had very tiny windows. There was also a small bathroom and lavatory combined.

'Nelly has one of these as her bedroom,' Sandra told them. 'It's the one that runs across the front of the house and it's almost as large as the front bedrooms downstairs, only it has a sloping ceiling. Nelly loves it; she says that it reminds her of the room she had at her home back in Ireland when she was a child.'

To Megan the entire set-up of the house in Chapel Gardens seemed absolutely perfect for the purpose she intended. She could hardly believe her luck that they had met Sandra and that she was willing to cooperate and allow her to offer shelter to young mothers there. She couldn't wait for them to discuss all the details and see how they could formulate plans to do this.

By the time they arrived back in the sitting room Nelly Flynn had brought in a tray of tea things and set them down on the low table. She poured out the tea for them and then disappeared again back into the kitchen, leaving them to help themselves to the home-made scones and free to discuss the matter in hand.

Audrey said very little, leaving Megan to do all the talking. Sandra listened intently, nodding in agreement from time to time.

'Did you have all this in mind when you came here to Liverpool?' Sandra asked, her intelligent green eyes alive with interest.

'No, I simply wanted to do war work of some kind and I thought there was more possibility of finding the right role here in Liverpool than there was in the remote part of Wales where I was living.'

'Well, I think it's a wonderful idea,' said Sandra.

Megan let out an audible sigh of relief.

'It's going to cost quite a lot of money though to set up and run such an establishment,' Sandra mused.

'I have some money that was left to me and I am prepared to use it,' Megan told her. 'It will save me considerable outlay if I don't have to rent a house and furnish it, so that means that what money I have will go a great deal further.'

Sandra nodded. 'Well, as you know, most of the rooms already have a bed and furniture in them so there will be no expense involved there. Our initial expense will be feeding the girls and paying someone to help look after them. Nelly will do what she can, but I think we'll also need other help.'

'There will also be fees to pay for midwives or if you need to call out a doctor, and possibly for medicines. You will also probably have to supply nappies and clothes for the babies and even shawls to wrap them in,' Audrey reminded them.

'Surely the young mothers will have prepared clothes themselves for the coming babies?'

'Some of them might have done, but certainly not all of them will have thought about it. They mightn't even have the money to do so.'

Sandra nodded. 'It's really very challenging, isn't it! I was beginning to feel that I wasn't going to be able to do anything to help the war effort once my baby arrived, but if I'm helping you to run things then I will certainly be doing my bit.'

'Nelly might object to you taking on a venture of this sort,' Audrey warned her.

Sandra shook her head. 'No, she tries to make sure I take care of myself, especially at the moment, but she knows better than to interfere in anything I decide to do.'

'I will take great care to see that you don't overdo it,' Megan promised. 'You will have your baby to take care of as well, and that will take up a great deal of your time anyway,' she pointed out.

'I can't wait to write and tell Hank what we're planning to do. I'm sure he'll be delighted when he hears about it, especially when I tell him how it all started from a conversation he had with you.'

'Yes, it's amazing what a chance remark can lead to. I'm sure he never thought for one moment that someone would act on what he said,' Megan agreed.

While they drank their tea and tucked into the delicious home-made scones that Nelly Flynn had brought in they finalized some more of the details.

'It will all be so much easier once you move in,' Sandra said thoughtfully.

'When can I move in?' Megan asked.

'As soon as you like,' Sandra answered with a smile. 'I take it that you will have to go back to your home in Wales to explain to your family what you are doing and to collect your clothes and so on.'

'No, that won't be necessary. I've already left home and I'm staying at Audrey's house.'

'So you could move in immediately?'

'Yes, right away, if that's all right with you.'

'Today?'

'Yes, today!' Megan answered with a laugh. She looked across at Audrey. 'That's OK with you, isn't it?'

'Of course. We'll go back to my place and collect your belongings and come straight back if Sandra's in agreement.'

Sandra stood up and went across the room to her writing bureau, opened the drawer and took out a door key. 'Here,' she said, holding it out to Megan. 'Welcome to Chapel Gardens.'

'Thank you.' Megan took the key from her and turned it over and over in her hand.

'Would you like to see your room? I suggest you have the one on the first floor next to mine; it's quite large and the door has a lock on it so all your belongings will be safe in there.'

'I think that's important,' she went on when she saw Megan raise her eyebrows in surprise, 'because we have no idea of the type of girls we will be taking in; we are here to help them have their baby in comfort and not to concern ourselves with their morals or their background, aren't we?'

'She's right, Megan.' Audrey nodded her head in agreement with Sandra's words.

Sandra took them both back upstairs and opened the bedroom door next to hers. As she had told them it was a large room furnished with a double bed and oak bedroom furniture consisting of a double wardrobe, dressing table, and a chest of drawers. There was a bedside cabinet beside the bed. It was so light and airy and had such a welcoming feel to it that Megan immediately felt at home.

'This is lovely,' Megan breathed as she looked round the room. She went over to the window and peeked through the lace curtains at the street below and then turned back to Sandra with a broad smile.

'Right. Go and collect your belongings. I'll tell Nelly that you are moving in and that you will be back here in time for supper,' Sandra said enthusiastically.

'I should be back in about an hour if that's all right.'

'Don't rush,' Sandra told her. 'Let's say an hour and a half. It will give Nelly time to make sure that dinner is waiting for you when you get here.'

Chapter Seven

'You've been gone so long that I thought you had changed your mind,' Sandra greeted them when Megan knocked on the door some two hours later.

'I know, I know,' Megan said. 'It took us far longer to put all my stuff together than we expected and then we had to wait for a taxi. Audrey's in a hurry because she has to be somewhere in half an hour, so can I just dump everything in the hallway and take it up to my room later?'

'Of course you can; I'll help,' Sandra told her.

They formed a human chain from the taxi to the hall and in less than fifteen minutes the car was unloaded and Audrey heading on her way home in the cab, waves and good wishes ringing in their ears.

Nelly served supper almost immediately, grumbling that it was their fault not hers if it had dried up through being kept waiting.

'Take no notice of her,' Sandra said with a laugh. 'Enjoy your meal.'

The food was good and Megan commented on what a good cook Nelly was.

'Good plain wholesome food is her speciality. Nothing fancy, I'm afraid,' Sandra told her.

Left on their own after Nelly had cleared away the dishes Megan began to carry the various cases and bundles upstairs to the bedroom Sandra had told her was to be hers. Sandra tried to help with some of the lighter items but after two trips up the stairs she was breathless and had to give up.

'Could you go and ask Nelly to bring us a cup of tea,' Sandra gasped as she puffed her way into the sitting room and collapsed into a chair.

'Of course.'

Nelly looked quite annoyed when Megan made the request and explained what had happened.

'You shouldn't have let her help you to do something like that, not in her condition,' she scolded.

'She offered and I never thought any more about it,' Megan stated defensively. 'I thought she was feeling OK.'

'She struggled to help, that's the way she is,' Nelly retorted. 'Go back and stay with her and I'll bring the tea in as soon as it's brewed.'

Feeling rather like a naughty schoolgirl Megan went back to the sitting room. She found Sandra curled up in a heap and moaning softly. She had one hand held to the side of her bulging stomach and was obviously in pain.

Not waiting to ask her for details, Megan turned and rushed back into the kitchen to call Nelly.

'Out of my way, out of my way.' Nelly pushed Megan roughly to one side as she bustled out of the kitchen and hurried to the sitting room. Megan followed as fast as she could. When they reached the sitting room Nelly immediately took charge.

'You go and ring the doctor – the number is on the pad by the side of the phone,' she told Megan. 'When you've done that, come back and give me a hand to get her upstairs to her bed.'

'What do you want me to tell the doctor?' Megan asked.

'Tell him? What the divil do you think you ought to tell him? Tell him that Miss Sandra has gone into labour, of course, that's what you tell him.'

With a feeling of alarm Megan rushed to do as she had been told. A woman answered the phone and Megan explained what had happened, repeating her story over again to make sure the woman understood the urgency of the call.

'Dr Stott isn't here at the moment, but you can assure Miss Peterson that I will put out a call to him and inform him that it is an emergency,' the woman told her.

'I hope you told her how serious it was and that he must come as soon as he can,' Nelly tut-tutted when Megan reported back to her.

'Of course I did,' Megan insisted, annoyed by Nelly's querulous manner.

'Well, let's hope that woman at the other end of the phone understands it is urgent,' Nelly muttered. 'Come on, we'd best try and get her upstairs.'

'Perhaps it would be best if we left her where she was until the doctor gets here,' Megan said uncertainly.

'Her bed is the best place for her,' Nelly countered firmly. 'Take an arm and I'll take the other, and be as gentle as you can.'

It was quite a struggle but between them, moving very slowly, they managed to get Sandra up to her bedroom and on to her bed where she collapsed in a heap. Lying on her side with her knees drawn up she began groaning in pain and became so breathless that she was unable to speak.

'You'd best go back downstairs and let the doctor in when he arrives,' Nelly ordered as she mopped at Sandra's brow with a wet face flannel.

Dr Stott had obviously realized the seriousness of the situation and was there within ten minutes. As she opened the door to let him in, Megan was surprised at how young he seemed. Tall, with a shock of short fair hair, a clean-shaven chiselled face and piercing blue eyes, he looked extremely stern and authoritative.

His arrival calmed Sandra and she managed to tell him how bad the pains were and how frequently the contractions were coming.

An hour and a half later, the baby, a little girl, was born. There was a feeling of relief all round and Megan in particular felt that a weight had been taken off her shoulders because she was quite sure that if anything had gone wrong then Nelly would have blamed her.

Before Dr Stott arrived Nelly had been full of dire warnings about what might happen. Sandra, she claimed, had gone into premature labour because she had been helping Megan to bring her belongings upstairs and that it was more than likely that there would be complications with the birth as a result.

When Megan went into the room, however, she found Sandra propped up in bed, her new baby cradled in her arms. Her fair hair had been combed back from her face and she was wearing a pretty blue nightdress and matching silk bed jacket and she looked radiant; a picture of happiness.

'Now, more than ever, I understand why you are so eager to do something for the young unmarried mothers, especially if the baby's father is not with them when the child is born,' she told Megan.

'I'm sure you do,' Megan agreed.

'Why don't you fetch a notebook and we'll start planning right away,' Sandra suggested.

'No, you must rest now and for the remainder of the week,' Megan told her firmly. 'I'm sure Dr Stott wouldn't approve if he came back and found you working.'

'Perhaps you're right, and I must say I feel extremely tired, even though I'm sure I'm too excited to sleep,' Sandra admitted.

'Time enough for us to start drawing up plans when you are feeling strong again; when you are back on your feet and into your new routine.'

'Yes, I think that would be best,' Sandra said smothering a yawn. 'I do feel tired, I must admit. When you have made yourself comfortable in your room then perhaps you would like to put down some ideas on paper. As soon as I am feeling a little bit stronger we can go through them together and I can see if I can add anything of value to what you have suggested.'

'That sounds like a sensible idea,' Megan agreed. She bent over the bed, kissed Sandra on the brow and smiled down at the sleeping bundle in Sandra's arms before she left the room.

It was well over a week before Sandra felt strong enough to start talking about the plans Megan had drawn up for converting the house into rooms for the girls they planned to help.

Dr Stott called each day to check on Sandra's progress and to make sure the baby was settling in as well as it should. He was extremely interested when Sandra told him what she and Megan were proposing to do.

'Let me know as soon as you are ready to take someone in, because I know of a young girl who is living under great duress in her parents' home and she would certainly like to avail herself of such an opportunity. Her boyfriend, an American GI, has been sent overseas just like Hank Jackson. They wanted to marry but her parents objected so much that they kept putting it off. Finally when they discovered that she was expecting a baby they decided to marry without telling her parents until afterwards and then they planned to announce that they were not only married but that she was expecting a baby.

'Before they could do that he was sent overseas. Now that her parents have discovered she's pregnant they are horrified and at the moment her father is refusing to even speak to her. She tells me that if it had not been for her mother's intervention then her father would have turned her out on to the street.

'The atmosphere in the house is so bad that she is desperately unhappy and feels that she cannot go on living there very much longer. She would be more than happy to move into your house. At the moment she is quite fit and I am sure she'd be willing to help you organize things.'

'She certainly sounds an ideal candidate.' Megan smiled when Sandra related the conversation to her.

'Shall we say that she can come to us then?' Sandra asked.

'Why not! With Nelly's help I can get one of the back bedrooms ready for her in a matter of a day or two.'

'From the way Dr Stott spoke she is not hard up, so possibly she will be able to help contribute something towards her keep,' Sandra said hopefully.

'At the moment it doesn't really matter, because I have enough money to cover all our expenses.'

'Yes, I know that, Megan, but the sooner we can get money in the better. I would like to think we could keep some of your money in reserve for emergencies.'

'Yes, that would be a great advantage,' Megan agreed. 'We certainly don't know what expenses lie ahead.'

'No, but I have been promised by Dr Stott that he will come any time we send for him even if the girl in labour is not on his patient list or even if she comes from outside the area.'

'That is very reassuring,' Megan agreed.

'Yes it is, and of course we always have Nelly here to act as midwife if for some reason he is unable to get here.'

'Is Nelly qualified to do that?' Megan asked in surprise.

'Not officially, but she does know what she's doing and has assisted at so many births in the past that she probably knows more about what to do than the doctor, only don't tell Harvey Stott that I said that.'

'Is he quite happy about Nelly assisting?'

'Well, he didn't object to her helping me just now, did he?' Sandra smiled. 'I think perhaps it's better to simply take it for granted that he does approve rather than make an issue of the matter.'

–

The next couple of weeks were very busy ones for Megan. Although Sandra was now up and about she still tired easily and Nelly was insistent that she rested every afternoon. Megan could fully understand this and didn't argue about it.

The girl Harvey Stott had suggested should come there had already arrived and was installed in one of the back bedrooms on the first floor.

Jennifer White was in her late teens. She was a very delicate looking girl with dark hair, hazel eyes and a thin-lipped mouth. She was bright and helpful and willing to do almost anything Megan asked of her.

When she said that she had clerical experience Megan asked her to compile a record of the names of the girls they took in and any other information she could find out about them. She also asked her if she would like her to keep a record of all costs incurred each week in the running of the place.

Jennifer accepted the task with alacrity. She didn't need Megan to explain how she was to go about it; she knew instinctively what to do. Within a week she had produced record books and charts that were simple to follow yet packed with information.

Sandra was thrilled when Megan told her what had happened and immediately reported back to Harvey Stott and told him how delighted they were that he had recommended Jennifer White to come and stay with them.

'You do know that her father is one of the partners in a shipping line, so she can well afford to pay her way,' he reminded them.

'I think we should be the ones paying her,' Sandra said with a laugh. 'She seems to have produced a set of books that will save us hours of trying to devise them ourselves.'

'So you are now up and ready for business,' Harvey laughed. 'I'm on permanent standby, remember; you will have Nelly on full-time duty and now you have a resident bookkeeper. So what are you and Megan going to be doing?' he joked.

'We'll have plenty to do organizing everything else once it becomes busy. I'm sure that as soon as word gets round that shelter can be found here we will be inundated with young girls, especially now that most of the Yanks have been sent overseas and many of the girls they've left behind here are pregnant.'

'Yes, you are probably right,' Harvey Stott agreed. 'There are also many young girls left behind by our own boys who are in the forces and who have been sent overseas. Don't forget about them.'

'We won't,' Megan assured him. 'Any young girl who is pregnant is welcome to come here if we have room for her. We won't ask about their religion or their politics, or comment about their nationality or their colour or that of their child. We won't even ask them their reason for coming to us unless they wish to tell us. All we want to do is provide a haven for girls who are in trouble.'

Chapter Eight

It didn't take long for news of what was happening at Sandra Peterson's house in Chapel Gardens to spread by word of mouth.

Every time Megan saw a pregnant woman pause outside and stare up at the house she felt tempted to rush down and see if she could help her. Common sense told her that this would be foolish; it was up to the girls to make the first move and approach them, not for them to invite the girls in.

They already had almost a houseful anyway. Since Dr Stott had introduced Jennifer White, they had taken in Lulu Banks, a black girl whose baby was due at any moment, if the dates she had given them were correct.

There was also Mavis Jenkins, a short, dark-haired, Welsh girl in her early twenties from Cardiff. Her father, a miner, was a strict chapel-going man who had refused to acknowledge that Mavis was pregnant when she refused to tell him who the father was.

He had turned her out and for several months she had been living in Cardiff's Tiger Bay, eking out a living by cleaning and any other menial work she could find.

When the man friend she was sharing a room with said he was moving to Liverpool, Mavis had decided to come with him, hoping that perhaps they could both start a new life there. However, as the train pulled into Lime

Street station her friend had said that he was going into the gents and then he had disappeared. Although she waited in Lime Street station for several hours in the hope he would come back, he never did.

By chance Mavis had found her way to Chapel Gardens and obtained refuge with Sandra and Megan.

The latest to join them was Betsy Hagan from Ireland, a very innocent young girl who didn't seem to understand what had happened to her, only that she was getting fatter and fatter. She had come to Liverpool with a young man she'd known all her life who told her he was going to become a sailor and when he left her at the dockside he promised he would come back again for her one day.

Nelly Flynn immediately took Betsy under her wing and even insisted on letting the young girl share her bedroom. It turned out that they both came from the same village in Ireland – although, of course, Nelly hadn't been back there for years, since she was a young woman, but it was an important link back to home for both of them.

'She's just a child, so she is,' she defended when Megan advised her not to do that. 'I'll be telling her what it's all about, this business of having a baby, so I will, and show her how to care for it when it's born.'

Megan said no more, although she didn't approve. She felt it would be better to leave it until Nelly had suffered a few sleepless nights after the baby arrived and then she might be able to make her see sense, she reasoned.

It was several weeks before Megan contacted Audrey Wilson to let her know all that was happening.

'I thought it might take you a little while to settle in, and of course if Sandra has had her baby that must have also put an extra strain on things.'

'Everything is fine,' Megan assured her. 'You must come round some time and see Sandra's baby.'

'Thank you, I'd like to do that, but something awful has happened. You remember my cousin Martin, who you met the night you left home and came to our house? Well, I'm afraid he's been killed in action.'

'I'm so sorry to hear that, I thought he was extremely nice,' Megan said softly.

'He was, and it has upset both my parents very much. He was Dad's sister's only child and she has been quite ill ever since the news arrived. She's a widow and lives in Rochdale. We're thinking of moving up that way. Dad wants be near her so I've applied for a transfer to a school in the area.'

'Wouldn't it be easier if she moved down to Liverpool?'

'Yes, but she doesn't want to do that. Her husband died in Rochdale and is buried there and she visits his grave every week.'

Megan didn't know what to say. She thought it was crazy of Audrey to give up a school where she was happy and settled and move away somewhere else.

'Well, keep in touch and let me know what happens. Good luck for the future if you do decide to move, and please let's not lose contact with each other...' Megan felt sad that her one link with home and her new life in Liverpool was leaving, but she needed to learn to stand on her own two feet, especially now that she'd met Sandra and embarked on their new adventure together.

—

All the young mothers-to-be were fascinated by Sandra's baby. She had named her Hope and they took an avid interest in her daily routine and progress. They were always eager to help Sandra when it came to bathing her, although most of them squirmed at the thought of changing her dirty nappies.

'You'll have to get used to doing it when your own baby is born,' Sandra told them. 'It's not as bad as you think.'

Sandra herself was back into taking part in all that was going on and anxious to help Megan in every way she could. With Jennifer White undertaking all the clerical work it left both Sandra and Megan free to organize newcomers as they arrived and make them comfortable.

A timetable for the forthcoming births was drawn up and although they all knew that no one could be 100 per cent sure of when each new baby would arrive, it forecast a busy future ahead.

The war was still at its height and even though there were no American servicemen left in Liverpool, the area around the Pier Head was packed with men in uniform. Some of them were on their way overseas; others were sailors on short stays in Liverpool while their boats were repaired or reloaded with provisions and troops.

Fortunately the bombing in and around Liverpool had abated, but the devastation visible in every road and street was depressing and a constant reminder that the war was still going on.

Sandra and Megan were worried for quite another reason. They had no idea what they would do with the babies when they arrived if the girls didn't want to keep them.

So far no one had said that they were willing to bring up their baby when it was born. The main reason for this appeared to be because none of them had a home they could go to. Because they were well advanced into their pregnancies they were not working and they had no savings, so they had no money to keep the baby or themselves.

It was a problem that Megan and Sandra talked over and over without finding any solution.

'Why don't you ask Dr Stott if he has any ideas?' Megan suggested.

The next time that Harvey Stott called, Sandra did just that.

'This is surely something you should have thought about before you set up a home for these girls,' he said brusquely.

'Actually we were hoping that the girls would want to keep their babies once they arrived. I don't know how they can bring themselves to part with them once they have held them in their arms,' Sandra said, a doting smile on her face as she looked down at the little bundle she was cradling in her own arms.

'Your case is completely different from theirs,' Harvey Stott pointed out. 'You have a house, warmth and food, a comfortable bed and friends to help you.'

'Yes, you are right, Harvey. I know that I am very fortunate. Furthermore I have no one to reprimand me for being an unmarried mother. In addition, of course, I do know that Hank is coming back to marry me once this wretched war ends.'

'That still leaves the question of what do we do with any unwanted babies?' Megan repeated.

'Exactly, and we were wondering if you could help us, Harvey?' Sandra explained, giving him a hopeful smile.

'I can't help you myself, but I can put you in touch with someone who can probably do so,' he told them.

'We don't want the babies to go to nuns or Dr Barnardo's or any other sort of institution like that,' Sandra told him quickly.

'No, this is a lady who acts independently. Her name is Angela Burton. She is middle-aged, well-to-do and a tremendous organizer. She has a great many contacts and will be able to advise you on the best way of dealing with unwanted babies. Would you like me to ask her to call and see you?'

Sandra and Megan exchanged glances.

'I suppose she could be the answer to our problem. Is she some kind of do-gooder?' Sandra asked.

'I don't think she would like to be referred to as such,' Harvey said with a brief smile. 'As I said, she is very well connected and she will certainly know how it would be possible to get the babies adopted privately. They would go to good homes, I can assure you.'

Both Megan and Sandra agreed that it sounded as though Angela Burton could be a valuable contact and that Harvey should ask her to come and see them.

When Angela Burton did come to see them a few days later they were both immensely impressed by her appearance.

As Harvey had said she was middle-aged and very organized. She was carrying a monogrammed brown leather briefcase in one hand and a black leather handbag on her arm. Under her black fur coat she was wearing a smartly tailored pale grey suit with a blue cashmere jumper. At the neckline was a double row of pearls complemented by matching pearl earrings.

For the first time since she had been at Chapel Gardens Megan felt dowdy. She was always so busy that she rarely thought about what she was wearing. Now, as she compared her serviceable tweed skirt and grey jumper with Angela Burton's fashionable attire, she felt drab. She thought wistfully of all the clothes she had left behind when she'd left home. Then, with a brief sigh, she brought her mind back to the present, to Angela Burton.

Her manner was brisk but friendly and she listened in attentive silence as between them Sandra and Megan outlined their concern about the forthcoming babies.

'You have certainly taken a lot on your shoulders providing lodgings for these young expectant mothers,' she said admiringly.

'Yes, but the problem is most of these young girls are not in a position to keep their babies even if they wanted to. Finding a good home for the baby is of paramount importance both to the girls themselves and to us,' Megan said firmly.

'We won't feel we have done our duty by them if we simply hand the new baby over to some institution or other. What we would like to do is find a good home and know that the baby will be loved and cared for and brought up as if it was one of their own,' Sandra added.

'Do you think we are being overprotective, or overambitious?' Megan asked.

'You are doing only what I would expect you to do, and what I would want to do if I was in your shoes,' Angela Burton told them.

She picked up the briefcase that she had placed on the floor beside her and put it on the table, opened it and took out a file.

'You do realize, of course, that once I have placed a child for adoption then the natural mother must not be told where the child has gone and certainly will not be able to see it ever again.'

'That will be very hard for some of the girls, but a great relief for many of them,' Megan said wryly.

'Yes, some of the girls will be heartbroken at the thought of never seeing their baby again, but I am sure they will understand that it is for the child's best interest,' Sandra said with a sigh.

'It's a sacrifice they have to make,' Angela Burton pointed out. 'Furthermore you must make it abundantly clear to them that that is the situation. Once they have handed over their baby and signed the appropriate forms then that is the last contact they will have with the child,' she concluded, her voice hard and businesslike.

Opening the file in front of her she poised her pen ready to write. 'How many babies do you have waiting for adoption at the moment? I thought I heard one crying as I came in.'

'You probably did, but it is mine, and it is not up for adoption,' Sandra said with a laugh.

'We'll probably have one or possibly two within the next couple of weeks,' Megan told her. 'We will let you know as soon as they are born.'

'Yes, do that. I will need to know the sex and weight of the baby and any other details you may feel are necessary. I should point out that black babies or those of another nationality are sometimes difficult to place. The demand is for full-term healthy white babies of either sex, although many people do prefer boys.'

'What about if there are twins?' Megan frowned. 'Do you separate them?'

'Not if I can find someone willing to take both babies. If that is not possible then yes, it is necessary to separate them, but since they will never know that they were one of a twin it doesn't really cause any problems.'

By the time Angela Burton left, both Megan and Sandra felt dazed by all the information they had been given and all the questions they had been asked.

'There's no doubt about it, we'll have to devise forms for our own use before we part with any of the babies,' Megan stated, pushing her dark hair back from her brow.

'Yes, and the form will have to be very detailed. I had thought a simple form that merely stated the name of the baby and date it was handed over for adoption would do but now, after listening to all Angela Burton has told us, I think it needs a great deal more detail.'

'Yes, I agree, and I think we are going to have to look into how we register the babies in our permanent records so that we have every possibility noted. We need to include details about the father where these are known in case the girl ever needs proof that her baby has gone for adoption.'

'This is equally important if the girl has decided to keep the baby and is struggling to bring it up single-handed. If the father has been serving overseas then the child may be as much as two years old when they return and they may find it hard to accept that it is theirs,' Sandra said with a sigh.

'That's all going to take a great deal of time. Will you do it, or shall I? Or shall we do it together?' Megan asked, pulling a pad of blank paper towards her.

'I have a much better idea,' Sandra said with a triumphant smile. 'Why don't we let Jennifer White draw up the relevant forms, then we can check that they contain everything we feel is necessary and amend them if we find any points have been overlooked. She has a very good brain and is excellent for this sort of job, and I am sure she will do it better than we would.'

'Great idea!' Megan agreed. 'It's a pity she didn't sit in on our meeting with Angela Burton, then we wouldn't even have to brief her.'

'That won't be much of a problem, because she has a very analytical approach to such issues,' Sandra pointed out. 'Fortunately we have already taken down the details of the girls who have been admitted so far, so that will be a good starting point.'

'We could always get Angela Burton to check over our forms and see if they comply with the regulations as she knows them,' Megan said thoughtfully.

'We could, but I'd rather not do that. I'd like to think that we are capable of running our own show in our own way. We don't want any more outside intervention than we have to,' Sandra said firmly.

Chapter Nine

The first of the girls to go into labour was Mavis Jenkins early in December, and it stirred the entire household into a bustle of activity. The only person who appeared to be calm and unflustered was Nelly Flynn.

'It was to be expected if the dates she gave us were the right ones; she was due before any of you others,' Nelly muttered as she prepared Mavis's bed in readiness.

'Will a couple of you help Mavis upstairs as quickly as you can and get her into bed,' Megan asked, 'and I'll phone for Dr Stott.'

'Tell him there's no great hurry but to come as soon as he can,' Nelly told her philosophically.

Lulu and Betsy offered to do as Megan had requested. Mavis was gasping and moaning as they shepherded her up to her bedroom and then tried to help her undress.

At first Mavis refused to lie down on her bed but walked round and round the room, complaining bitterly that no one was helping her.

Nelly, wearing a big white apron over her dark skirt, came bustling in and took charge, issuing orders like a sergeant major.

'You get yourself into that bed, my darlin' girl, and do what we say. It will all be over in a couple of hours, so it will, and then you'll be holding a lovely little baby in your arms.'

'A couple of hours!' Mavis's protest ended in a sharp scream as another searing pain seized her body, making her catch her breath and double over.

'Come on, me darlin' girl. Stop making so much fuss. Things will be easier if you do what I tell you. Now lie down on that bed and let's be having no more nonsense,' Nelly said in a firm but cajoling voice as she bustled around the room getting things in order.

'Lulu, you come and stand at this side of the bed and let Mavis hold on to your hand. Betsy, you come and stand on the other side of the bed and use this damp face flannel to wipe her brow and keep her cool,' Nelly instructed. 'Stay by her side and talk to her; try and comfort her.'

She then sent Jennifer White, who had heard the commotion and came to find out what was happening, to fetch towels from the kitchen and, at the same time, tell Megan and Sandra that Mavis was progressing well.

Megan, looking rather dishevelled, came rushing upstairs, anxious to make sure that Mavis was being well looked after.

'Sandra is feeding her baby and said she would come as soon as she has finished and can put little Hope down to sleep,' she explained when Nelly met her on the landing.

'Mavis is doing fine, so she is,' Nelly told her. 'There's nothing for you to worry about at all. Everything is going as it should do and I have everything in hand.' She laid a reassuring hand on Megan's arm as screams of agony came from the bedroom.

'Lulu and Betsy are in there with her, there's nothing else we can do; nature has to take its course. I'll call you if we need you.'

By the time Harvey Stott arrived half an hour later, the room was full of women, all trying to help but unable to do anything to calm the hysterical cries of pain coming from Mavis as she twisted and writhed in anguish.

Harvey Stott immediately took over responsibility and ordered Betsy and Lulu out of the room.

'I'm sure you both find it upsetting witnessing something like this, in your condition,' he told them brusquely. 'Wait outside and I'll call you if I need any further assistance,' he ordered.

The screams, protests and groans that Mavis was making had completely unleveraged both Lulu and Betsy. They were both anxious to leave the room the moment he said they could make their escape.

They huddled together on the landing outside the bedroom door, clutching each other, breathing heavily, their eyes wide with fear every time they heard Mavis scream.

'Do you think we will be in terrible pain like that when our time comes?' Lulu asked.

'I hope not. Anyway, I'll make sure that I won't be screaming like she is,' Betsy said indignantly.

'I suppose we should go back in there and see if we can do anything to help,' Lulu murmured. 'Nelly told me to hold Mavis's hand but she held on to mine so tightly that I thought she was going to break every bone there is in it and I made her let go. I suppose that was a bit mean of me, wasn't it?' she added guiltily.

'Come on,' Betsy took her by the shoulder and propelled her towards the door. 'We'll both go back in there whatever Dr Stott says and take it in turns to hold her hand and do anything else we are asked to do. Remember, we will be wanting people to do the same for us when our time comes, so it's only fair that we do our bit for poor Mavis.'

Lulu hesitated, her eyes wide. 'Dr Stott told us to leave the room; in fact he ordered us to do so,' she pointed out.

'Only because he could see that we were upset,' Betsy said dismissively.

The scene inside the bedroom had changed very little. In between her screams Mavis was still moaning and groaning and bewailing the situation she found herself in. Then suddenly she let out a long ear-shattering scream that had Betsy and Lulu clinging to each other in alarm.

'Push, now, me darlin' girl. For sure, it is the right time for you to push,' Nelly urged Mavis. 'One more big push, me darlin' girl, and it will all be over and your lovely little baby will be born.'

'You've said that before, you silly old woman,' Mavis yelled back at Nelly. 'Can't one of you just cut me open and get it out? I can't stand this pain any longer. If I ever meet up with the bugger who did this to me I'll cut his bloody throat.'

'Mavis, Mavis, please try and control yourself,' Sandra begged in a shocked tone of voice as she heard the bitterness in Mavis's voice.

The painful process had advanced so much by now that all Mavis could do was gasp exhaustedly. Then, with a huge effort, she gave a final violent push as the baby made its entry into the world.

For a moment there was a stunned silence, and then it was quickly followed by gasps and exclamations of astonishment. The baby was black; a boy who not merely had a mop of tight black curly hair but every inch of his skin was black as well.

Even Harvey Stott looked slightly taken aback and held up a hand to delay Nelly passing the child to its mother until after she had cleaned it up and wrapped it in a soft white blanket.

'You have a little boy, Mavis,' he said in a low voice. Then, after a brief pause he added, 'Your baby is black. Does that come as a surprise to you?'

'It would be an even bigger surprise if it was any other colour,' Mavis groaned, passing a hand over her flushed face.

The women around the bed exchanged looks with each other. Sandra shook her head as though completely dismayed by the turn of events.

'Nelly, perhaps you would go and make us a pot of tea to celebrate the baby's safe arrival,' she instructed. 'I'm sure Mavis would like one after all she's been through.'

'I'd love a cuppa, but not to celebrate his arrival,' Mavis told them as she pushed the baby to one side and sat up straighter in the bed. 'I'm celebrating it's all over and now I can get rid of the little bastard and get on with my own life once again.'

'Don't you want to keep him now you've seen him and held him in your arms?' Betsy asked in astonishment. 'I dream all the time about the day when I will be holding my baby in my arms.'

'Keep him!' Mavis laughed derisively and pushed her thick, sweat-drenched hair away from her face. 'Of course I don't. I'd never be able to go back home again if I was carrying a black baby in my arms. My father would slam the door in my face and then denounce me from the pulpit.'

'If he is a religious man as you imply, then surely he would take pity on the child and forgive you even if he thinks you have sinned,' Sandra murmured.

'Not him! A bible basher of the worst kind but all the same he is still my dad and I want to go back home again as soon as I can. I can't leave here soon enough. I'm grateful to you for taking me in because I had nowhere to go, but now I've had the baby I want to get rid of it as soon as possible so that I can go back to Cardiff. I want to live my own life again and forget all this ever happened. It's been like one of those nightmares; the ones where you are running and running to get away from something evil and can't. Well, now I have.'

'What about your baby?' Megan interposed gently. 'You can't simply abandon it, *cariad*.'

'You told me that you'd arrange to have it adopted,' Mavis reminded her.

'Well… yes, I agree we did say that, but then we didn't know—'

'That it would be black,' Mavis interrupted contemptuously. 'No one wants to adopt a black baby, is that it?'

'Well, I don't know about that,' Megan parried. 'I am sure there are people who will, but it may be more difficult…'

It was something she would have to discuss with Angela Burton, and somehow she knew they wouldn't find it easy, certainly not as simple as finding a home for a white child.

'You shouldn't have let him live, should you?' Mavis said, turning to face Harvey Stott.

'What are you talking about?' he frowned. 'What do you mean by that?'

'You didn't have to slap him and make him breathe,' Mavis said bitterly. 'You could have let him die and thrown him out with the trash. You didn't, so now it's up to you lot to get rid of him the best way you can. I want nothing at all to do with him.'

'What about his father?' Megan asked. 'Shouldn't he have a say in what happens to the child, *cariad*?' she persisted.

'That black bugger! A one-night stand! I never saw him again; I don't even know his name. I know, it was my own fault, but I was drunk. That's what happens when you are brought up strictly teetotal; you have no head for drink. I had two port and lemons and then I was up for anything. He was an American GI, a smooth talker and as black as the night. That's all I can tell you about him.'

'Perhaps if your parents, especially your mother, saw your dear little baby, he would touch their hearts and they would accept him,' Sandra said softly. 'After all, Mavis, he is their grandchild.'

'They would still be horrified and refuse to let me go back home. They wouldn't welcome a grandchild unless I was married, and they'd be mortified by a black one.'

'They might feel differently once they saw him, so why not give it a chance, *cariad*,' Megan urged.

'Even though they know that there's every nationality under the sun living in Cardiff's Tiger Bay, they won't,' Mavis assured them. She laughed derisively. 'There's Whites, Negroes and Indians and no one takes any notice, but for a white girl like me to turn up with a black baby, now that would bring disgrace on my family. I have two younger sisters and they would be shunned as well as me. No, I am not going to take that baby home. If you don't want him then I'll dump him somewhere on my way to the train station when I leave here or throw him into the Mersey.'

'Shush, shush, *cariad*,' Megan soothed. 'That's a terrible thing to say. You are overwrought; a good night's sleep and you may feel differently about things.'

'No, I won't,' Mavis shouted. 'And stop calling me *cariad*. I know we're both Welsh and that it's a term of endearment, but I don't want sympathy from you or anyone else. I've had the baby and as I keep telling you I simply want to go back home and get on with my life and forget that any of this ever happened.'

'We all feel like that when we make a mistake, but we've got to face up to the fact that it has happened and take responsibility for the result,' Jennifer White said quietly.

'We're not all as perfect as you,' Mavis told her bitterly.

'Come, girls, there's no need for us all to quarrel,' Megan interposed as she saw a bright red flush flare up on Jennifer's cheeks. 'I think we should leave Mavis to drink her tea and then settle down for a sleep. We'll take our tea downstairs.'

'Good idea,' Mavis muttered. She picked up the baby which was lying on the bed beside her. 'Here—' she held him out to Megan '—take this squalling brat with you and don't ever bring him back, I never want to see him again.'

Chapter Ten

The pitiful crying of Mavis's baby roused Megan very early the next morning. She slipped out of bed, put on her dressing gown and went to see if she could help in any way.

The door to Mavis's room was ajar and with a feeling of apprehension Megan pushed it open. The room was empty except for the baby, which was lying in the middle of the unmade bed screaming lustily. There was no sign of Mavis.

Megan sighed. She knew that tracing her would be impossible. She suspected that the address Mavis had given them was a false one and to try and find her in Cardiff's Tiger Bay would be virtually impossible.

Megan picked up the screaming baby, cradling it in her arms and trying to soothe it as she made her way to the bathroom in case Mavis might be in there.

On her way downstairs she met Nelly, who had also heard the child crying and was on her way up to see what was the matter.

'Is Mavis having trouble getting it to feed?' Nelly asked, pushing back her straggling grey hair and smothering a yawn.

'Mavis has gone. Her room is empty,' Megan told her.

'You sure? That girl was in no fit state to leave. Perhaps she's in the bathroom,' Nelly persisted.

'No, she's not. I've already checked in there. All her clothes and belongings are gone as well, but she's left her baby,' Megan said sadly.

'Her family will never take her back,' Nelly said worriedly. 'She's told me all about them, and I know the sort of man her father is. A bigoted man who always knows what is right. He's very religious and he regards Mavis as a "fallen woman".'

'Then let's hope she has friends in Tiger Bay or wherever she's gone who will give her a home and help her to get back on her feet,' Megan said, shaking her head sadly. 'Now, if you will take this baby and see if you can get him to feed from a bottle, Nelly, I will see what arrangements I can make about finding him a home.'

'You won't find that easy to do,' Nelly murmured as Megan put the baby into her arms.

'Until he is taken away for adoption, do you think you will be able to look after him, Nelly? I'm sure that Lulu and probably Betsy will be willing to help you.'

Megan's phone call to Angela Burton later that morning did not go as smoothly as it might have done. Angela was on the point of going out for lunch but she said she would call round afterwards.

She instructed Megan to have the baby ready for collection and that she would have her own special carrycot in the car to take him away.

When she did arrive matters became even more complicated. She was delighted that they had a baby for her; that was until she saw it.

'You never mentioned that it was black,' she said caustically. 'Black babies are not easy to place; there are very few black families in need of a baby and white families don't want them as a general rule. I think he will have to go into a home if I can find one willing to take him. I'm afraid you will have to keep him here until I've managed to find one.'

Megan felt taken aback. This wasn't the arrangement as she recalled it, but she merely murmured her thanks and said no more. She didn't mind the baby staying with them for a few more days, but she was concerned about what its eventual fate was going to be.

Nelly seemed to accept the news without question. 'Poor little mite,' she muttered. 'Sure and I'd keep him myself if I was a few years younger. We'd better give him a name though.'

'Perhaps Lulu should be the one to do that, because she seems to be the one who cares about him the most,' Megan suggested.

Lulu was delighted at the idea. 'I think we should call him Moses,' she stated.

'Moses?' Megan thought about it but could find no reason why the baby shouldn't be called that and anyway, she told herself, he would probably be given a quite different name once he was adopted, so it might as well be Moses as anything else.

Having been the one to name him, Lulu immediately took over the responsibility for looking after Moses. She had plenty of help from the others. There was always someone ready to mix his feed and sit in the armchair nursing him while he took his bottle.

He was a contented baby and usually slept right through the night provided that his last feed was around ten o'clock. Lulu seemed to be happy enough to under-take to do this and to settle him for the night in the small cot that had been moved into her room.

Sandra left all this organizing to Megan. Most of her own time was now taken up with looking after her own baby; Hope was not nearly as placid as Moses.

Little Hope was a fretful baby, demanding a great deal of attention. Megan felt the child would have been better if she had not been fussed over quite so much but she was too tactful to say anything.

After all, she told herself, it was Sandra's house, and although they were more or less partners, it was not up to her to interfere over what Sandra wanted to do when it came to looking after Hope. If Sandra wanted to take advice from Nelly then that was a different matter altogether, since she seemed to regard Nelly almost like a surrogate mother.

They all had other things on their minds anyway. Christmas was less than a week away and they were trying hard to find extra food to make it as special an occasion as possible.

Nelly had quite a few contacts and she was also well known in Paddy's Market at the top end of Scotland Road. The stallholders there often saved things for her and she made a point of reminding them how many she was going to have to feed over Christmas.

Megan and Sandra made up stockings for each of the girls almost as if they were still children. A few shiny coins, a small bar of chocolate, a pair of lisle stockings, a lipstick, a tablet of scented soap and a cheap magazine went into each one.

For Nelly, knowing how much she felt the cold when she went shopping, they decided on a thick woollen scarf and matching gloves.

The menu for Christmas Day included a capon that the butcher had kept for Nelly and a Christmas pudding to be served with custard.

The girls were delighted by their presents and by the festive feast. They sang carols and chattered happily about the Christmases they had known in the past.

Megan felt homesick remembering the Christmas festivities she had enjoyed at Yr Glaslyn. She wondered if her parents were missing her as much as she was missing them. Once or twice during the day she was tempted to phone them but managed to put the thought from her mind, afraid it might show a sense of weakness on her part.

She had made her decision to stand on her own feet and she had made a new life for herself here in Liverpool. She felt she was doing something worthwhile; her own special war work.

The war was still being fiercely fought in Europe and had now been extended to North Africa, where the British had captured Tobruk, as well as to Burma, and many of the troops had been sent there. It was where Sandra feared Hank might be fighting.

Shortly before Christmas they had heard that the British had bombed Eindhoven in the Netherlands and the Americans had bombed Naples, and the Allies had clashed with the Japanese. It seemed to Megan as she read the headlines that the whole world was at war and casualties mounting daily. It all seemed so senseless.

As the year came to an end, however, things looked brighter for the Allies: Rommel was trapped in Tunisia and the Germans were encircled at Stalingrad.

Early in 1943 two other girls moved in. Hilda Heath, who was a big strapping twenty-year-old with red hair and a broad freckled face, and Sally Ainsworth, who was small and childlike and who laughed nervously or giggled at everything that was said to her.

They both came from Birmingham and when Megan asked them what they were doing in Liverpool they were very evasive. Hilda muttered something about being given a lift by a lorry driver bringing stuff down to the Liverpool docks. Sally merely giggled. She appeared to be dominated by Hilda and looked at her for guidance before answering any questions or speaking at all.

Neither of them had any luggage and neither of them had their ration books or clothing coupons; nothing, in fact, but the clothes they stood up in and no money at all.

It was going to be an extra drain on their already meagre rations, and as Megan had feared there was a great deal of grumbling from Nelly when it came to planning their meals for the coming week.

Nevertheless, Megan felt she couldn't turn them away. From their appearance, Megan judged that their babies were due within a few weeks but they both still seemed fit and well and assured her that they were willing to help in whatever way they could.

When Megan warned Nelly not to allow them to do any really heavy work, Nelly merely laughed at her.

'Them two,' she scoffed. 'They could lift a three-ton lorry and think nothing of it. Still, if that's your orders, then I'll try and remember.'

Their arrival meant that the house was now so packed that Betsy would need to be in Nelly's room permanently, so that the two newcomers could each have a room of their own.

'Are you sure you'll both be happy about that?' Megan asked Betsy.

'Oh, Nelly won't mind. We're both from the same part of Ireland, sure we are, and we'll get on like a house on fire.'

When Megan tentatively spoke to Nelly about it she found that Nelly was in complete agreement.

'There's just one thing; a bit of a change I'd like to make if it's all right with you. I would sooner have the room next door to the kitchen as my bedroom.'

Megan frowned. 'You mean the utility room that we use as a storeroom or lumber room?'

'That's right,' Nelly said forcefully. 'It's bigger and it would be far more convenient. I'm that tired when I finish at night that having to drag myself up the stairs puts years on me. Now if I could just walk the few yards and be in me own quarters then that sure would be fine. It would free up another room for the girls, too, sure it would. Put those two Brummies up on the top floor; they'll be less trouble up there and it's my opinion that they could be a rowdy pair and cause disruption amongst the other girls.'

'Well, Nelly, if you're quite sure,' Megan said hesitantly.

'Of course I'm sure; I've said so, haven't I! There'll be more room, too, for Betsy, especially when she has the baby and that's in with us as well.'

It sounded almost too good to be true to have solved their problem so easily and, as it turned out, it was. Two days later a hatchet-faced, middle-aged man from Liverpool Council called to ask if he could inspect the place because it had been reported to them that they were living in an overcrowded situation.

Megan felt angry. She was doing her bit to help the war effort and she didn't want interference from any officials.

When she demurred about letting him in, he glowered at her and threatened to get a court order.

'Then I'll be back with a policeman and you'll have to let me in, so you may as do it quietly now,' he told her.

Reluctantly she let him in and took him through the house, apologizing to each of the girls when she was forced to tap on their door and ask if they minded if he looked into their room.

When the inspection was over the official said he was sorry for disturbing them all.

'From information we received concerning all the girls who come and go here at all hours of the day someone had the impression that it was a brothel,' he explained. 'As it hadn't been registered as such, we were forced to check what was going on and assure ourselves that it wasn't overcrowded.'

'I wouldn't have thought you'd be so particular about overcrowding when half the homes in this city have been bombed and families made homeless so that they have to move in with relatives for shelter,' Megan said frostily.

'It's nothing to do with me, miss, I'm just the man they send out to check on these things.'

'Well, I hope you're satisfied and that they accept your report.'

'They will, there's nothing amiss here.' He smiled awkwardly. 'I am a bit confused, however, by all the very pregnant young ladies all living under one roof. Is it some sort of commune you've set up here?'

Briefly Megan explained what she was doing.

He gave her a look of respect. 'That's wonderful work, miss. Dreadful the way these Yanks came here, made so many of our girls pregnant and have now vanished completely.'

'You don't think that they will return as soon as they can and claim the girls they have promised to marry and be delighted to meet their children?'

'Not them Yanks! They're like the sailors; a fresh girl in every port, and if the girl gets pregnant then it is up to her to sort things out,' he said.

'You sound very bitter,' Megan murmured.

'My own daughter was trapped like that, and now me and my wife have to help our girl to bring up the child. Lovely little lad but we are far too old for that sort of lark, I can tell you.'

'Well, I'm glad you didn't disown her or throw her out into the street to fend for herself,' Megan murmured.

'No,' he shook his head. 'I was tempted to do so when she first told us about it, but she's our own flesh and blood and we should have protected her more.' He sighed lugubriously. 'Hindsight is a wonderful thing. You do what you think is best at the time.'

Chapter Eleven

Megan was roused the next morning by a loud banging on the front door. She peered at her bedside clock and saw that it was only twenty past six. As the knocking was repeated, she pulled on her dressing gown and went downstairs to see what was going on.

As she reached the hall Nelly came stumbling out of the room she had taken over as her bedroom. She was wearing an old coat over her nightdress and her grey hair hung around her shoulders like a dingy grey curtain.

'What on God's earth is going on? Who's hammering on the door at this time of the morning?'

'I don't know,' Megan told her. 'Wait here and I'll see who it is.'

As she undid the locks and opened the door a few inches, a stout middle-aged man hastily put his foot over the threshold so that she couldn't close it again.

'Is she here?' he demanded hoarsely, trying to push past Megan. 'My daughter, is she here?'

'I don't know, what is your daughter's name?' Megan said, trying to block his way even though she knew it was impossible because he was far more heavily built than she was.

'She's only a child,' he said accusingly as he pushed his way into the hall. 'I'll have the law on you,' he went on, ignoring Megan's question.

'Tell me her name,' Megan persisted.

'Sally. Sally Ainsworth, and she's only a child, I'm telling you, and she doesn't know what she's doing.'

'And she's pregnant,' Megan said dryly.

'So she is here. You have her. You're planning to sell her baby when it's born.'

Megan drew herself up and clutched tightly at her dressing gown. 'I must warn you to watch what you are saying, Mr Ainsworth, or I will be the one having the law on you,' she said angrily.

'Your daughter is here,' Megan went on more calmly. 'She arrived a few days ago accompanied by an older girl called Hilda Heath. You probably know her as well.'

'Know her, I'll say I know her! She's the one who led my little Sally astray and got her into trouble. She's been a bad influence on Sally ever since the first day they met. Time and again I've told my missus to do something about it and stop our Sally seeing that Hilda Heath. I even told young Sally that I'd throw her out if she didn't stop going round with Hilda.'

'Well now, it seems she has taken you at your word and left home,' Megan told him.

Suddenly all the fight seemed to go out of Sally's father. He mopped at his brow and his shoulders sagged. He looked so beaten that Megan felt sorry for him and suggested he had better come and sit down so that they could discuss the matter in a more civil manner.

Turning to where Nelly was lurking in the shadows and listening to all that was going on, Megan said, 'Why don't you make us a pot of tea, Nelly, while I have a chat with Mr Ainsworth.'

Megan wished she could go and get dressed because she felt at a disadvantage in her dressing gown but, deciding that was impossible, she tried to behave in as dignified a manner as she could.

Instead of inviting him into the sitting room to sit down in one of the comfortable armchairs she took him into the dining room. 'We'll both sit here at the dining table, Mr Ainsworth,' she said in an authoritative manner.

He complied without question and as Megan took a seat facing him Nelly appeared with their tea.

'Milk and sugar?' Megan asked as she picked up the teapot.

'Yes please. Three sugars if you can spare them, I've a very sweet tooth.'

Megan gave a tight smile and said nothing as she complied with his request. Mentally she was thinking how this would deplete their meagre rations, especially since Sally hadn't brought her ration book with her.

As they sipped their tea Mr Ainsworth told Megan a harrowing story of how Sally had been led astray by Hilda Heath from the very first day she had gone to work and the two girls had met.

'Hilda Heath was a charge hand at the factory and she dominated our Sally from day one,' he said bitterly. 'I'd heard her name mentioned long before Sally met her because she'd dabbled in the black market and drugs from the day the war started.'

He took a gulp of tea and then wiped his mouth with the back of his hand. 'Led our Sally on to do the same. Then the pair of them started going out with the soldiers who were billeted nearby. Traded themselves for what they could get; nylon stockings, chocolate and, in Hilda's case, for cigarettes. Sally doesn't smoke, but that Hilda has smoked like a trooper ever since she was about ten years old, or so I understand.'

'You tried to stop Sally seeing the soldiers, of course,' Megan murmured.

'Aye! We did everything we could. We even locked her in her room but she climbed out through the window, helped, of course, by that Hilda Heath,' he said bitterly.

'The wife and me were at our wits' end and then when she fell pregnant...' He paused and mopped at his brow with a red handkerchief that he pulled out of the top pocket of his jacket. 'I thought it would be the death of my wife. Took to her bed for three days crying non-stop, said it was all her fault for not watching over the girl more than she did.'

He took another mouthful of tea. 'Seeing as how she did everything any mortal person could do to protect our Sally it was ridiculous for her to take on like that. In the end I had strong words with her and told her that she needed to pull herself together, we needed all our strength to deal with the situation. I reminded her that Sally had no husband, nor was likely to have one now, so it would be up to us to bring the child up.'

'Your wife accepted this?'

'Aye, she's a sensible woman, I'll say that much for her. She knew what I was saying was true.'

'So why did Sally run away? Why did she come here to Liverpool?'

'She was persuaded to do so by that Hilda, I suppose. She was pregnant too, only she knew that her family wouldn't do anything to help her when the baby arrived, and it was probably her idea to get away from Birmingham. What with one thing and another the place was getting too hot for her and she wanted to go somewhere where she weren't known.'

'Why involve Sally? Why persuade your daughter to go with her, Mr Ainsworth?' Megan asked, frowning.

'Probably hadn't the guts to do it on her own,' he said angrily.

'You think they intended to start a new life after they'd had their babies?'

'That's right. She'd have our Sally look after the kids and she'd be off doing her own thing. You can bet your boots it would be somewhere where there were plenty of soldiers,' he said bitterly. 'Hilda was always telling Sally that the Yanks were the ones to go for because they were well paid and generous and furthermore they supplied things like nylon stockings and cigarettes.'

'So why did they come to Liverpool, and to our house here in Chapel Gardens?' Megan asked with a frown.

'Can't say, don't know why they did that. Are there any Yanks stationed nearby?'

'There were, but as far as I know they've all gone overseas, which is one of the reasons why Sandra Peterson and I have set up this house as a refuge for unmarried girls expecting babies.'

'They talk about coming over here to help us and all they do is give us a load of trouble,' Mr Ainsworth said angrily.

'Yes, the Yanks are responsible for a great many of the girls who now find themselves in trouble and deserted, not knowing which way to turn. Many of them are hoping that when the war is over the men they knew will come back and marry them as they have promised to do and accept their ready-made family. In a great many instances, however, we know that the girls will never see or hear from them again. Some of the girls we help are planning to keep their babies; others are offering them for adoption.

'I suppose it shows how caring and responsible Hilda and Sally are if they are planning to find lodgings together and bring up their babies,' Megan added thoughtfully.

Mr Ainsworth ran a hand through his thinning grey hair, pushing it back from his furrowed brow in a gesture of frustration and despair. 'No! They're naïve and Sally should have stayed with her family. But it doesn't matter one way or the other anyway,' he stated. 'I'm here to take Sally back home. Her baby, it will have a good home with us and so will she once she sees the error of her ways. Now, can I see her?' he asked forcefully.

'Of course. I'll ask Nelly to call her.'

'Don't tell her that I'm here,' Mr Ainsworth cautioned.

'Very well, I won't say why I need her,' Megan agreed.

As they waited for Sally to join them Megan wondered what would happen. She hoped there would not be an unpleasant scene. She understood Mr Ainsworth's concern for his young daughter. She could well see that Hilda could be a dominating influence and obviously not one for the best.

Sally's gasp of surprise when she came into the room and saw her father sitting there was followed by a burst of joy as she flung herself into his arms, wrapping her own arms around his neck as she hugged and kissed him.

The warmth in her voice as she asked anxiously, 'How is Mum?' confirmed Megan's suspicions that Sally was homesick.

'Missing you very much,' her father told her. 'I've come to take you home.'

Sally pulled away from him. 'I can't come home,' she said in a whisper. 'It would make Mum so unhappy when the neighbours and her friends find out I'm having a baby.'

'What utter rubbish,' her father said dismissively. 'Most of them know anyway and wonder where you are. We told them you were gone on a little holiday and most of them said we shouldn't have let you go gallivanting off in your condition. Come on now, don't waste time, get your things together and we'll be on the next train back to Birmingham.'

Sally hesitated, looking at Megan for support. 'Will that be all right, Miss Lloyd?' she asked.

'Of course it will, Sally. I am more than pleased to know that you will be back with your family and that they will be taking care of you.'

'Go and get your things then,' her father urged.

'I haven't anything to collect. I only have what I stand up in,' Sally said shamefacedly, tears filling her large blue eyes.

'Then we'll be off,' her father stated, standing up and holding out his hand to Megan. 'Thank you for taking care of my daughter.'

Sally still seemed to be reluctant. 'What about Hilda?' she blurted out. 'I ought to tell her I'm going home.'

'You'll do nothing of the sort,' her father told her in a severe voice. 'One word with her and she'll be trying to get you to stay here and go ahead with her madcap plan for a so-called new life.'

'No,' Sally said with a sweet smile. 'I've had enough of trying to have a new life. I really do want to come home again, Dad.'

'That's good to hear,' he said, putting an arm around her shoulder and squeezing it affectionately.

'Don't worry about Hilda, I'll tell her what you have decided to do,' Megan promised with a smile.

'Right then, now we really will be off,' Mr Ainsworth said. He pulled out his wallet and extracted a five-pound note. 'It's all I can spare at the moment, but I'll send another when I get back home,' he said in a rather embarrassed voice.

Megan hesitated to take it, then remembering all the bills that were mounting up, held out her hand. 'Thank you, Mr Ainsworth, that is very kind of you.'

Hilda Heath was extremely angry when Megan broke the news that Sally had gone home with her father. She stormed and raved and grabbed Megan by the shoulders, threatening what she would do and shaking her until Megan's teeth chattered.

Hearing the commotion Nelly came out of the kitchen to find out what was going on. Grabbing hold of Hilda's shock of red hair, she dragged her backwards off Megan and then bundled her towards the door, pushing her out into the street and telling her to clear off and to go back to Birmingham herself before slamming the door shut.

'Are you all right?' Nelly asked anxiously, turning her attention to Megan, who was breathing heavily and holding both hands to her head as if in pain. 'Shall I send for Dr Stott?'

'No, no, of course not! I'll be all right in a minute,' Megan gasped. She ran a hand over her hair and straightened her dressing gown. 'I wouldn't like to run into her on a dark night,' she said in a shaky voice.

'Nor at any other time,' Nelly agreed. 'I told you the moment I set eyes on her that she was going to be trouble. Has the other one gone home with her dad?'

'Yes, Mr Ainsworth has taken Sally home; we needn't worry about her any more. He and his wife will take care of her and the baby,' Megan murmured. 'I thought he was being overprotective when he said that Sally was bullied by Hilda Heath, but now I can see that he had every reason to be worried by their friendship.'

For the next ten minutes Hilda Heath banged on the front door, calling them every imaginable name. Then all was quiet and from where they were watching from the sitting-room window, Megan and Nelly saw Hilda thumbing a lift.

Megan gave a sigh of relief when she saw a car stop and a man lean out. After speaking to Hilda, he opened the passenger door.

As Hilda climbed inside, Megan momentarily felt concern.

'We really shouldn't let her go off like that with a perfect stranger, anything could happen to her,' she said contritely as she rushed to the door to try and stop her.

'No, perhaps not, but she's gone now and so there's nothing we can do about it, is there?' Nelly said complacently. 'Let's hope we never hear from her again,' she added, a look of relief on her lined face.

Chapter Twelve

It was an eventful day. As soon as Mr Ainsworth and Sally had left and Hilda Heath had been driven away, Megan started to go upstairs to get dressed.

'Don't wait for me, I want to take a shower and wash my hair,' she called to Nelly, who had gone back into the kitchen to prepare breakfast.

She was halfway up the stairs when Nelly came bustling out into the hallway, wiping her hands on a towel.

'Why don't you sit down for a few minutes and get your breath back,' Nelly said. 'You still look shaken up by that attack from Hilda Heath.'

'I do feel shaken up,' Megan admitted. 'What's more my head really hurts. She had a really tight grip on my hair and when she started shaking me it felt as though a mad dog was savaging me.'

'Nasty piece of work that one, I thought so the first time I set eyes on her,' Nelly said again. 'Never mind, I gave her a touch of her own medicine. If your head hurts then hers must be hurting three times as much,' she added consolingly.

'What I would really like is a strong cup of coffee, if you can spare the coffee. Something to settle my nerves.'

'You go on into the sitting room and I'll bring it in to you with a slice of freshly made toast,' Nelly promised.

Within a few minutes Sandra joined her, wanting to know what all the noise and disruption had been about.

'Well, I for one am not sorry to see the back of those two girls. I sensed they'd be trouble from the moment they crossed the doorstep.'

'Hilda Heath yes, but not little Sally Ainsworth. She was so childlike.'

'Yes, and vulnerable too, and that Hilda would have used her as a tool to demand all sorts of things if they had stayed on here. No, this is good news, so stop worrying about it. Sally has gone back home and from what I have heard from you of her father it's a warm and loving home and they'll keep the baby and help Sally to bring it up. Pity there aren't a few more families like that. Now,' Sandra said with a smile, 'I must go and give my little Hope her bath and feed her. Being a mother is a full-time job, I can tell you.'

Megan smiled understandingly. She felt a little worried because Sandra certainly did seem to be spending more and more time with the baby to the exclusion of every-thing else. Her whole life seemed to be centred around Hope and lately she had discouraged any of the girls doing anything at all to help her with the child.

Megan sat for quite some time after Sandra had left the room. She knew that she ought to go and have her shower and wash her hair and then get on with her daily tasks. She should be getting the accounts up to date and checking with Nelly that everything was running smoothly. After the upheaval of the early morning though, she was enjoying the peace and quiet of having the sitting room to herself.

She felt a trifle guilty at more or less turning Hilda Heath out but she knew that Nelly and Sandra were right and it had been the best thing to do. Hilda had all the hallmarks of a troublemaker and might well have caused upsets in the future.

She wondered if she ought to record the details about the two girls and their brief stay with them in case they were questioned by the authorities at some later date. She would have liked to forget all about them, but she decided that perhaps it was the sensible thing to do.

At the moment everything was crystal clear in her mind, but in a few months' time she was quite sure the details would be blurred. It wouldn't take her long because there was very little to record apart from their names and the dates they arrived and left.

They still had a fairly full house and she was particularly concerned about baby Moses. There had still been no word from Angela Burton about any adoption plans for him and she was fearful that it meant little Moses would have to go into a home.

She had just risen from her comfortable chair and walked across to the bureau that stood in the far corner of the room to make a note about Hilda Heath and Sally Ainsworth when Nelly burst into the room looking very agitated and flustered.

'You'd better come as quick as you can, Miss Megan,' she stated. 'Young Lulu has had a fall and she's bleeding badly. To make matters worse I think she's started her labour.'

'Where is she?'

'She's lying on the landing floor right outside the door of her room. I left her there because I was afraid to move her. I didn't want to disturb Miss Sandra because I know she's attending to little Hope so I've asked one of the girls to let Dr Stott know what has happened.'

Megan felt apprehensive as she accompanied Nelly to where Lulu was lying. As Nelly had said she was haemorrhaging badly and groaning in between crying out with pain.

'We can't let her lie there,' Megan said worriedly. 'Perhaps with Jennifer and Betsy to help we could manage to get her on to her bed. I'm sure she's not very heavy.'

Nelly shook her head. 'I don't think we should risk moving her, not with her in that state. I think we ought to wait until Dr Stott gets here,' she insisted.

'He may not be able to get here for ages,' Megan demurred.

Nelly's mouth tightened into a firm line. 'I'd still sooner leave her where she is,' she said firmly. 'We can make her comfortable; put a pillow under her head and a blanket over her if she's feeling cold.'

Megan decided it was pointless arguing. Nelly had been present at far more births than she had and if Nelly thought it was dangerous to move Lulu then it probably was.

'Whatever you think is best,' she agreed. 'I'm off to quickly get dressed. I won't have a shower now, so I'll only be a couple of minutes.'

Chapter Thirteen

The rest of the morning passed in a series of comings and goings. As soon as she was dressed Megan stayed with Lulu most of the time but she was very relieved when Harvey Stott finally arrived and took charge.

He agreed that Nelly had done the best thing in leaving Lulu where she was and he confirmed that the birth was imminent. Because of where Lulu was lying it was not easy for any of them to administer help and Lulu did not have the strength to push.

'I think we'll have to get her on to her bed,' he said at last. 'I've examined her pretty thoroughly and she doesn't seem to have broken any bones so I don't think it will hurt to move her as long as it is done carefully. Have you a board or something similar that we can slip underneath her?'

Nelly searched the kitchen diligently but there was nothing they could use. Then she had the bright idea of using the ironing board.

'If we keep it folded up flat it should serve the purpose,' Dr Stott agreed. 'Find some string, Nelly, so that we can tie it so that it doesn't start to open up when we lift it up with Lulu on it.'

It was a very ungainly contraption but it served the purpose. With the help of a couple of the girls they gently rolled Lulu on to her side, slipped the board underneath and then rolled her back so that she was lying on it.

With Nelly lifting at one end, Dr Stott at the other and a girl on each side to make sure Lulu didn't slip off, they carried her from the landing into her bedroom and gently transferred her on to the bed.

Although, as Dr Stott had said, Lulu wasn't hurt apart from bruising, she was very weak and exhausted. She had great difficulty in managing to push down when the contractions came. Her delivery was long and arduous and it was almost evening before her baby was born.

It was very small and despite all Dr Stott and Nelly's efforts it would not breathe. Eventually, with a deep sigh, Harvey Stott pronounced that it was stillborn.

At first Lulu cried uncontrollably, refusing to be comforted; crying until she was so completely exhausted that she fell into a sleep that was so deep that Megan began to worry in case she, too, never woke up.

Lulu's state of depression lasted for almost a week. Megan and Nelly did their best to rouse her out of it, making sure that someone stayed with her night and day.

The girls shared a good deal of this watchfulness. They sat there, talking to Lulu or trying to get her to eat and drink. For most of the time though she simply lay there, her eyes closed and her breathing so slow and shallow that sometimes they were afraid that she had stopped breathing altogether.

It was Betsy who hit on the idea of taking Moses in to Lulu and seeing if that might rouse her and bring her back to normality. At first Megan was against the idea; she felt it would only make losing her own baby even more harrowing for Lulu.

Secretly, against Megan's wishes, Betsy took Moses to see Lulu.

At first Lulu clapped her hands over her ears and buried her head under the quilt. Then, very slowly, she pulled the quilt back and stared at Moses. Finally, she held out her arms to him.

Gently Betsy settled the fat little black baby into the crook of Lulu's arms and then stood back, leaving her to stare down at the enchanting little face and the big dark eyes that stared up at her.

Betsy left them together for about ten minutes and then went to take Moses away.

'No, leave him here with me,' Lulu begged.

'I can't. It's time for his feed and I have to put him to bed.'

'Bring him back again tomorrow morning then.'

When triumphantly Betsy told Megan what she had done and that she had promised Lulu she would take Moses back to her the next day Megan felt uneasy.

'You might have made things much worse for Lulu,' she told her rather crossly.

'How have I done that? It's the first time she's shown any interest in anything.'

'I know, Betsy, but remember I'm already making arrangements for Moses to be adopted. If Mrs Burton turns up today or tomorrow to collect him then poor Lulu will feel more bereft than ever.'

Megan need not have worried. When Angela Burton did turn up a couple of days later it was to say that she had not managed to find anyone willing to adopt Moses and that she was making enquiries to see if there was a home where they would consider taking him.

'Meanwhile, I'm afraid you will have to keep Moses at Chapel Gardens for a little while longer,' she told Megan.

When the news of what had transpired reached Lulu she was most indignant.

'It's because he's black, isn't it? Well, if no one wants to adopt him then I will,' she declared. 'What's more I'll not merely look after him but I'll think of him as mine. Mavis left him and went back to Cardiff as if her baby had never existed. I'll be a better mother to him than anyone else!'

'Do you really mean you will actually adopt him, Lulu?' Megan said in astonishment.

'As far as I'm concerned he is my baby,' Lulu said, stroking the baby's face and kissing him on the brow. 'No one outside these four walls need know anything different. I've just given birth and this is *my* baby. Who's to know that he isn't mine? Who's going to concern themselves anyway?'

Megan and Sandra discussed the matter in detail and then took Harvey Stott into their confidence.

He looked rather grave. 'I'm not quite sure what is involved here?' he said frowning. 'Are you asking me to say that Moses is Lulu's baby?'

'Mavis abandoned him to us here at The Haven so she has no hold over him, and it is certainly what Lulu wants,' Megan told him. 'Angela Burton can't find a home for Moses and it does solve the problem of what is to happen to him,' she added.

Harvey Stott pursed his lips in a silent whistle. 'Maybe it does, and it is certainly a solution to your problem over adoption, but I'm afraid that would be very irregular; it might even be considered a criminal offence.'

'Lulu claims that her family wants her back and they are prepared to overlook what has happened and they want to give a home to her baby,' Megan said.

'Unless we tell them they are not to know that Moses isn't her baby. They never met the father and she doesn't think that he will ever come back to Liverpool again, so what harm is there in it?' Sandra persisted.

'If Lulu doesn't take Moses then Angela Burton says he will have to go into a home,' Megan pointed out. 'What sort of life is a little black child going to have in one of those places?'

They argued about the matter for a long time. Eventually Harvey Stott shook his head, still unconvinced that it was the right thing to do although he could see that their reasons were excellent.

'What about when eventually Angela Burton comes back to collect him? What are you going to tell her?'

There was an uneasy silence, then Megan said slowly, 'We'll tell her that the mother has decided to keep Moses.'

'When you start telling lies they only lead to more and more lies,' Harvey Stott warned with a sigh.

'Do you have a better story?' Sandra asked.

He shook his head. 'No, I'm afraid I haven't.'

'Well then, as Megan has pointed out, poor little Moses would have a far better life with Lulu and her family than in a home.'

'So why not agree to let us treat him as Lulu's baby?' Megan pressed.

Later that day, when Megan spoke to Angela Burton and said that the mother of the black baby had decided to keep him, Mrs Burton was obviously relieved.

'Far the best outcome,' she said lightly. 'Let's hope you don't have any more problems like that for me. Now, when is the next baby due?'

'Probably any day now,' Megan told her.

'Good, I have quite a waiting list so I do hope they are all going to be white babies, because that is what people want. I hope I shall be hearing from you very soon, very soon indeed,' she added cheerfully.

Chapter Fourteen

Three other babies were born over the next few weeks and were promptly given up and taken away by Angela Burton for adoption, but their mothers were still at Chapel Gardens.

Brenda Sutter, a Lancashire girl in her late twenties, had been relieved to know that her guilty secret had been dealt with so discreetly and was determined to forget it had ever happened.

Claire Parker, a pretty eighteen-year-old from a nearby road off Scotland Road, also vowed she would never forget the experience and she would never let another man touch her as long as she lived. She, too, had been completely uninterested in what happened to her baby once it had been born.

Angela Burton had been quite shocked by Claire's attitude when she had told her that she must not try and trace the baby's whereabouts once it was put up for adoption and that she must sign a paper to that effect.

'Don't you worry your head about that, luv,' Claire laughed. 'I can't wait to get rid of it; I didn't even want to know if it was a boy or a girl when it was born. As long as you take it away you can do whatever you like with it and I'll sign whatever I have to.'

The other young mother, Janet Williams, a soft-spoken, fair-haired girl with a round baby face, was full of tears and remorse at having to part with her baby.

'I wish I could keep him,' she said wistfully, 'but my mother is a widow and there are still six children at home and she's finding it a real struggle. I couldn't ask her to bring him up and I must go back to work to help her; she counts on my wages,' she explained.

'I ought to go home right away but I feel I need a bit of time away from them to pull myself together,' she added tearfully.

Since it was so bitterly cold, both Megan and Sandra felt that it would be heartless to send the girls away when they had only just had their babies.

'You can stay on for another week as long as you are prepared to share a room if any new girls arrive,' Megan told them.

The girls seemed to welcome the arrangement.

–

Betsy Hagan's baby, a little girl she called Mary, was born early in the spring while gales raged outside.

Angela Burton said there was nothing she could do about placing it for adoption until the weather calmed down, so Megan had no option but to let Betsy stay on.

They already shared a room, but now that the baby had been born Megan fully expected Nelly to complain about the baby keeping her awake at nights with its crying, which was loud and persistent. To Megan's surprise Nelly made no comment at all and actually seemed to be enjoying both Betsy's company and that of the baby.

Relieved, Megan turned her attention to another problem that was very much more important. She had thought that she was running the house in Chapel Gardens in a very efficient way, but at the end of the month her bank statement showed that the money she had inherited was rapidly dwindling away.

There had, of course, been several major outlays in the first few weeks for cots and bedding in order to make sure that all the bedrooms were adequately equipped.

Sandra had pointed out right from the start that she was willing to pay her share of the general running costs but that she couldn't afford to buy anything else, because she was no longer working and earning money.

At the time Megan had felt confident that she could afford to meet any extras that might be needed. She had, however, found that everything seemed to be far more expensive than she had thought it would be. Even though most of their cots and bedding had been bought either from pawnbrokers or from Paddy's Market and were either 'seconds' or second-hand, the outlay had been considerable.

Megan had quickly realized that their budget was limited. They also shopped for their food at Paddy's Market, buying the very cheapest they could find. Again, because they had no ration cards for any of the girls, they were forced into buying what she knew was black market produce, for which they had to pay high prices.

There were times when Megan felt quite guilty about this but then she salved her conscience by telling herself that it was justified because she was helping girls who were in trouble.

None of the girls had offered any kind of contribution towards their keep. Except for the five-pound note that Mr Ainsworth had given, there had been no other donations.

Angela Burton hadn't mentioned any payment either, although Megan was quite sure that those people who took babies from her were asked to pay a fee for her services.

It was all very worrying but Megan hesitated to mention it to Sandra because she felt so indebted to her for her cooperation. Sandra had kindly given up the privacy of her home, they were living there rent-free and Sandra was paying the rates and so far she had not asked for any contribution towards the heating, lighting and general running costs of the house.

No, Megan decided, it was a problem she had to solve herself. She tried to think what her father would have done in such a situation. He was an astute businessman who had been running the slate mine and their estate in North Wales for countless years and she had never once heard him complain that he was short of money. He did have good returns from the slate quarry, of course, but he had to find the wages for all the men he employed there.

The upkeep of Yr Glaslyn, their large country mansion, must have been a drain on his resources, yet neither her father nor her mother ever seemed to be short of money and were always very generous whenever money was needed for local affairs.

She stood up and walked over to the window and stared out, not seeing the dereliction, but instead remembering the peace and beauty of her home in North Wales.

Then she pulled herself together; that was all in the past, and there was no way she could ask her father for advice or help, she reminded herself.

So whom could she ask? At once her thoughts flew to Harvey Stott. He was always so clear-thinking and sensible whenever she approached him on medical matters concerning the girls, but could she trouble him with her own personal problems?

Finally, in desperation Megan did ask Harvey Stott for advice. He was the only person, she thought, who might be able to make suggestions as to how to solve the dilemma she found herself in.

His handsome face became extremely grave when he heard how things were organized.

'You can't possibly carry on funding everything out of your own pocket,' he told her firmly.

'I know,' she agreed ruefully, 'I'm at my wits' end because my money is almost exhausted. Yet how can I earn any money?'

'Well, for a start you must register this place as a charity.'

Megan looked at him in astonishment, her dark eyes wide with apprehension. 'What do you mean? It already is a charity. The girls can't afford to pay anything, most of them are destitute when they arrive at our door,' she pointed out. 'Half of them have only the clothes they stand up in.'

'All the more reason for you to register it as a charity immediately, and then you'll be able to raise funds.'

'That sounds like begging,' Megan said scornfully, her mouth tightening into a thin line as she looked at him reproachfully.

'No, it's not! If it's a fully registered charity then you are legally entitled to organize events and raise money. No,' he said, holding up a hand to silence her when she was about to protest. 'I know what you are going to say, but it is not begging, most definitely not. While the girls are with you awaiting the birth of their babies, why don't you set them to work to make things and then from time to time have a craft sale and make a profit from their endeavours.'

'What sort of things?' Megan frowned.

'I'm sure you'll find that they all have skills of some kind. They can probably all knit or sew, and some may even be competent at other things like painting pictures, making gift cards, rug making or cane work.'

Megan's dubious expression changed to one of interest and she looked at him admiringly. 'That's certainly a possible idea,' she admitted.

'You make the most of their talents and then organize a craft fair and plough back the takings into the funds for running the place.'

'You make it sound easy,' Megan said thoughtfully, 'but would they be prepared to cooperate?'

'They'd probably enjoy it, and since they will have different skills they'll egg each other on and then you will have a variety of items to sell.'

'It's certainly something to think about,' Megan agreed.

'Also, it will bring this place and what you are doing here to the attention of the general public. When you have a sale of the work the girls have produced, always make sure that you invite along a reporter from the local Liverpool newspaper to give you a write-up. There'll always be people who attend or read about it and whose heartstrings will be touched and who will then make a contribution.'

Emboldened by all his suggestions, Megan said tentatively, 'I keep wondering if we ought to ask Angela Burton to make some sort of contribution each time she takes a baby for adoption.'

'You mean she's not paying you anything?' he said in surprise, his blue eyes narrowing.

'No, she has never mentioned money. I can understand there would be no money involved when the baby has to go into a home, but when it is placed with couples who want to adopt…' Her voice trailed off and she found the colour rushing to her face. It all sounded so mercenary, as if she was trying to sell the babies.

'She should be making a contribution of some kind,' he said firmly. 'You should have come to some arrangement with her long before this.'

'Perhaps then I should make it a late new year resolution to do so,' Megan agreed with a smile.

'You need to go further than that; you need to ask her for payments for the babies you have already handed over to her.'

He began listing them, but Megan interrupted him to remind him that Lulu had taken Moses and that Betsy's baby was also still with them. If Megan was being honest, it seemed that Betsy and Nelly were so attached and fond of each other that Betsy and Mary might end up being permanent members of the household. In fact, Betsy was very helpful in settling in the new girls, and she shared Nelly's room, so it seemed to suit them all for the moment.

'Make those the exception, but there have still been three or four others that Angela Burton has placed,' he reminded her.

'There's also the question of your fee for attending all the deliveries,' Megan pointed out. 'You've never presented us with a bill.'

Harvey Stott looked uncomfortable. 'Initially I did it because I was a friend of Sandra's,' he stated.

'And now?'

'Well, I'm still a friend of Sandra's, but there is another reason why I am happy to come here whenever I am needed.' He looked directly at her. 'It means I have a chance to see you.'

'See me!' Megan flushed, the hot blood rushing to her cheeks and her dark eyes opening wide with a mixture of astonishment and pleasure.

'Does that surprise you, Megan?'

'Well, yes,' she murmured shyly, clenching her lower lip with her teeth as their eyes met. 'I have come to think of you as a very good friend,' she added hastily.

'Nothing more?'

'We barely know each other, apart from when you come to attend one of the girls,' she said awkwardly.

'True, and that is something I think we should put right as soon as possible. Will you have dinner with me tonight?'

Megan's heart started beating faster. Was she dreaming, she wondered, or was Harvey Stott really asking her out on a date? She was about to accept, then some inner caution warned her not to rush things.

'I can't manage tonight,' she said hesitantly.

'Tomorrow night then?'

'Yes, I'd like that,' she said with a warm smile.

'Good! I'll pick you up at seven o'clock.'

Without waiting for an answer he stood up ready to leave.

'Until tomorrow night then,' he said as he headed for the door.

Megan stayed where she was for several minutes, going over in her mind what had just taken place. She could hardly believe that Harvey Stott had asked her to go out with him. She admired him and liked him a great deal and as their friendship had grown she knew she could trust him, but she had always regarded him as Sandra's friend.

She also thought about the suggestions he had made concerning funding the running of the place. They were good, but it would be some time before she could organize enough craft items to make a sale a feasible possibility.

Registering their place as a charity sounded sensible, but it would mean they would have to give it a name of some sort. Sandra would have to be consulted about this and that meant she would have to explain to Sandra why it was necessary, and so far she had tried not to worry her about their financial status.

They would need to make it sound like a worthwhile project, one that didn't carry any stigma about the unmarried mothers; perhaps they could call it Chapel Garden Homes? She rather liked the sound of that.

Since it had to be done then there was no time like the present, Megan decided. She looked at the clock; with any luck Sandra would have finished feeding little Hope and would have put her down to sleep. Now might be an admirable time. She'd ask Nelly to bring a tray of tea into the sitting room and make sure that they weren't disturbed for the next hour.

Sandra was alarmed when Megan related the financial situation they were now in.

'You shouldn't have borne all this worry on your own,' she told Megan reprovingly. 'When we decided to set up this place I thought it was in partnership, and if there were any concerns of any kind then we would discuss them and try and solve them between us.'

She listened in silence as Megan related the advice she'd been given by Harvey Stott.

'It all sounds very sensible,' she agreed, 'but it will take quite some time to organize. We could put this on the agenda for the coming year. If we have enough items then we could have a sale in the summer; failing that, we could stockpile anything that is made and have a sale shortly before Christmas.'

'We're going to need money long before that,' Megan pointed out.

'Yes, I realize that,' Sandra agreed. 'I think registering ourselves as a charity is a good idea though, and that we should do so as soon as possible. I'm sure what Harvey had in the back of his mind was that he could then approach some of his more well-off patients and see if they would make a donation.'

'You really think he would do that?' Megan asked in surprise.

'To impress you he most probably would,' Sandra said dryly.

'What do you mean?' Megan asked, the colour rushing to her cheeks.

'Oh, come, Megan, you must have noticed how attentive he always is when you speak to him.'

'He's certainly always ready to help,' Megan admitted.

'Harvey has a crush on you; anyone can see that! I would have thought you would have realized it long ago.'

Megan smiled, her eyes dancing with mischief as she said, 'Perhaps that's why he's taking me out for dinner tomorrow night.'

'Really!' Sandra gave a beaming smile. 'That's wonderful news. What a terrific start for the spring.'

'You don't mind?'

'Mind, why should I mind? I'm absolutely delighted for you. My two favourite people getting together is tremendous news,' Sandra told her happily.

Megan took a deep breath of relief. For the first time she felt light-hearted about the feelings that she was slowly developing for Harvey Stott. Until that moment she had not realized that in some ways she had been holding back because she felt he belonged to Sandra, even though she knew Sandra was desperately in love with Hank. Now that it was all out in the open and Sandra actually approved, it brought such a feeling of relief that she wanted to shout about it from the rooftops and let everyone know how happy she was.

Chapter Fifteen

It took a load off Megan's mind knowing that Sandra was in agreement about them registering as a charity but, like Sandra, she had no idea how they should go about it.

'Now that I know you're as keen as I am then I'll try and find out what we have to do,' Megan told her.

'I believe that there is an association called the Charity Commission or something that governs all charities, so perhaps if you can get in touch with them they will be able to guide me along the right lines.'

When she started to make enquiries Megan found that there was a great deal more involved than she had expected. It took her some time to accumulate and collate all the information that appeared relevant. She then found that the forms that had to be filled in were not only intricate but extremely confusing, so in the end she suggested to Sandra that they took Jennifer White into their confidence and told her what they were planning to do.

'Jennifer is brilliant when it comes to filling in forms,' Megan said as she handed one of the forms to Sandra so that she could see for herself how arduous it was.

'I agree, and yes, we should ask her to help,' Sandra agreed with a nod as she handed the forms back to Megan. 'They certainly look complicated, and I'm sure it's important to fill them in correctly.'

'There is one problem,' Megan said hesitantly. 'Jennifer's baby is due any day now, so do you think it's fair to trouble her with a task like this?'

'I don't see why not,' Sandra said. 'It will help to take her mind off what is ahead.'

'That sounds a bit harsh,' Megan laughed, 'but I know what you mean.'

Jennifer seemed pleased to be asked to deal with the forms. She spent an afternoon and evening going through the papers that Megan had obtained and told them that before they could start to do anything it would be necessary to give the place a name.

'I was thinking we could call it Chapel Gardens Home,' Megan said thoughtfully.

'Does Sandra agree with that?'

'I haven't asked her yet.'

'Then perhaps we should do that first.'

Sandra had several objections. 'In the first place,' she said, 'some of the people in Chapel Gardens might object. Also it sounds far too institutional, and anyway I don't particularly like it as a name.'

'So what do you want to call it?' Megan asked.

'I really don't know, but I think it should be something that identifies the actual house, and I don't want it to be called a home. That sounds far too much like a charitable institution.'

'Well, isn't that what it is?' Megan said dryly.

'Yes, but what I mean is it sounds somehow wrong, almost as if we are a charity home. I can't quite explain what I mean, but it doesn't feel right.'

'Have you any ideas, Jennifer?' Megan asked, turning to look at the girl.

'I think it would be rather nice to call it The Haven.'

There was a moment's silence as Megan and Sandra exchanged looks. Jennifer coloured up and looked embarrassed. 'It's only my idea,' she explained, 'but it is a haven.'

Megan's face softened. 'Is that the way you look at it?' she asked.

'I do, and so do most of the other girls here. Where else would you be able to find somewhere where you could spend the last few days or weeks before your baby was born and know that you would be safe and well looked after?'

There was a moment's silence as if no one knew what to say, although Megan felt pleased by what Jennifer had said. It was good to know that she was obviously succeeding in doing what she had hoped to do.

'What is more important to many of the girls who come here is the fact that the baby will be adopted if you are unable to take it home or you know you are going to be unable to bring it up. That is a terrific bonus and one that really does turn this place into a haven.'

'That's a wonderful tribute to what we are trying to do,' Sandra said. 'Thank you, Jennifer.'

'I agree, a wonderful tribute,' Megan murmured. 'Very well, that's settled, so we will go ahead and see if we can register it as a charitable undertaking called The Haven.'

It took Megan and Jennifer White almost a week to fill in the relevant forms and make sure they provided an accurate description of what went on at The Haven.

Both of them breathed a sigh of relief after Megan finally sealed the bulky envelope containing all the information that seemed to be needed and took it to the post office so that she could register the package to make sure that it didn't go astray.

'All we can do now is sit back and wait for the results,' she said when she returned.

'Let's hope we have given them all the details they want and that it will be plain sailing from now on.'

'I hope it will,' Jennifer agreed. 'I don't know whether it's because I've been sitting at the desk for so long or whether it's that I am starting labour, but my backache has turned into sharp pains.'

She broke off and gave a gasp as her whole body shook and she clenched her teeth to stop herself crying out.

'I think there's no doubt that you are in labour,' Megan agreed. 'Come on, let's see if we can get you upstairs to your room and then I'll send someone to fetch Nelly. She'll know whether or not we ought to phone Dr Stott and let him know what's happening.'

It was a long hard labour for Jennifer. Her baby, a little boy, was born in the early hours of the following morning.

Jennifer was utterly exhausted and slept for most of the day.

When Harvey Stott called back in the evening to check if she was all right he was so worried about her he ordered complete bed rest for a couple of days.

She was still spending most of her time in bed a week later when the letter arrived informing them that The Haven was now officially registered as a charity.

'Unfortunately we can't make a toast in the traditional way, but we have brought a cup of milky cocoa to celebrate our victory,' Megan and Sandra told her as they came together to break the news to her.

Although she drank the cocoa with them Jennifer was still so pale and listless that Harvey Stott became more concerned than ever.

'Is she showing any interest at all in the baby?' he asked.

'That's one of the main problems; she won't let us take it out of the room.'

'Have you any idea why that is?' he asked with a frown.

'She's afraid we may send it for adoption. She doesn't want to have it adopted and she simply won't believe us when we tell her that we have no intention of doing anything without her consent.'

'You mean that she's going to try and bring it up herself, single-handed?' he asked, his jaw tightening and his bright blue eyes widening with astonishment.

'I think that's what she's hoping to do, but I really can't see how it will be possible. She has nowhere to go and she has no job. Having the baby adopted would be the best thing for both of them.'

'Would it, though? I think you may be wrong about that. I have known the family for a long time and I am dismayed that they have rejected her.'

'Well, there's not very much we can do about that now, is there!' Megan said resignedly.

'I'm not so sure,' Harvey Stott said thoughtfully. 'I'm wondering if perhaps I should let Joshua White know that he is now a grandfather.'

'Surely that would be going against Jennifer's wishes,' Megan said briskly.

'Again, I'm not so sure. You see, it was her mother who was so adamant that Jennifer should leave the family home before anyone was aware of the fact that she was pregnant. Mrs White moves in a very grand circle of ladies and adverse gossip of any kind about Jennifer would mortify her.'

'In those sort of cases isn't it usual for the girl to be sent to stay with relatives in some obscure part of the country and when it is all over she returns home and says she has been on holiday?' Megan said.

'In some families, yes, but in this instance I understand that Jennifer wouldn't agree to such a subterfuge.'

'I see. In that case the decision of whether to inform her father or not must rest with you. I certainly couldn't break my promise to her,' Megan said stiffly.

'I'll think about it,' Harvey Stott said thoughtfully as he took his leave.

Megan wondered whether to mention it to Sandra, but in the end decided to keep her own counsel. She felt confident that Harvey would handle the matter in the best possible way, but nevertheless it worried her that it was betraying Jennifer's trust.

As it happened she had no need to be alarmed. Harvey Stott did phone Joshua White at his office only to find that he and his wife were both away on holiday.

'I understand they won't be back for at least a week,' he told Megan the next time he visited The Haven. 'I did leave a message to let him know that Jennifer had had her baby. I said nothing else so it's now a question of waiting to see what he does. Meanwhile, we must do all we can to get Jennifer back to full health. Can you try and get her involved again in this business of registering The Haven as a charity?'

'It's already been done, and we have had a letter confirming this and allocating us with the number of our registration,' Megan told him with a beaming smile.

'Great news! I think that perhaps I ought to take you out to dinner tonight to celebrate. I would ask Sandra to come as well,' he said teasingly, 'but I doubt if she would leave her baby for an entire evening.'

He promised to pick her up at seven that evening and said he would book a table at the Adelphi.

'That's very grand,' she commented with a smile.

'It's a very special celebration,' he countered.

The Adelphi was like another world. Although there was a war on it had not stopped them from putting on a wonderful meal. As she tucked into delicious delicacies that were beyond most people's reach Megan felt relaxed and happy.

As she caught sight of their reflection in the mirrored walls she thought what a good-looking couple they made and wished that everything was normal so that she could take him home to meet her parents.

Pushing such thoughts to the back of her mind she began to tell him about how Jennifer had helped them with all the form filling entailed in registering their undertaking.

'Splendid! Now I can begin to mention the project to some of the organizations and businesses that I'm involved with and send them details about what you're doing. Have you done a press release or planned any fundraising events?'

'No, we've done nothing at all yet. I'm not too sure what you mean by a press release,' she said in a puzzled tone.

'I mean a detailed description of what you are doing and one or two case histories. Something to send out to individuals and companies to gain their support.'

'I see.' Megan concentrated on the food on her plate. She still wasn't too sure what Harvey meant.

'Now that's something that Jennifer White would be good at,' he went on. 'I'm sure she's had experience of

PR work when she was working for her father. Why don't you have a word with her?'

'Do you think she's strong enough to undertake a commitment as arduous as that?'

'I think it may be the challenge she needs; something to take her mind off the hard time she's had and stop her worrying about the future of her baby.'

'Well, if you think so,' Megan said with a feeling of relief. 'It would certainly save me a headache; in fact I'm not too sure what is actually required in a press release.'

'Don't give it another thought; Jennifer will know exactly what to do, so leave it to her. She'll probably be very pleased to be asked to do it.'

Harvey was right; Jennifer was delighted.

'Can you bring me up all the relevant paperwork,' she said, sitting upright in bed and pushing the pillows behind her back to support her. 'I'll read through them and then make notes of exactly what we want to say. When I've done that you and Sandra can read them through and see if you approve.'

It took Jennifer less than a day to give them a rough outline of what she proposed to say in the press release. Megan and Sandra looked at each other in astonishment as they read through the lucid details she produced.

'You've certainly made it sound like a worthwhile project, Jennifer,' Sandra said admiringly.

'Well, it is,' Jennifer said with a smile. 'I owe you both a great deal. I am more than grateful.'

'It was Dr Stott who drew my attention to our need for a press release. Do you think we should let him have a look at it before we have it printed off?' Megan asked.

'I do. It would be a very good idea to let someone else read it to make sure I've included everything and not gone over the top,' Jennifer agreed.

Harvey thought she had done an extremely good job and asked them to let him have about twenty copies as soon as they were printed. He even recommended the printer they should use.

'He's quite right,' Jennifer confirmed. 'They are the firm that our company uses when we are having contracts or business proposals printed.'

Writing the press release seemed to bring Jennifer back into the real world as Harvey had hoped it would. She still looked very pale but the listlessness had gone. She was still emphatic, however, about having the baby with her all the time. He was progressing satisfactorily, fed well, but nevertheless she watched over him every moment of the day.

Megan and Sandra were worried about her. At the same time, they found her extremely helpful and would have been more than happy to employ her full-time had they been able to afford to do so.

'It would be wonderful if she could stay on because she could organize campaigns to raise funds for us,' Sandra pointed out.

'Yes, that's very true, but until we have some money we can't afford to pay for help of that kind.'

'Yet, at the same time, we need expert promotion in order to interest the right people who will want to provide us with funds.'

It was a dilemma that neither of them knew how to resolve in a satisfactory way no matter how hard they tried. There had been some response from people to whom Harvey Stott had sent the press release. Mostly they were enquiries or letters of approval, but so far there had been no monetary help.

'Early days yet,' Megan said a few days later when she had been sorting out the post and Sandra had come in to ask if anything specific had turned up.

'We must have patience, I suppose,' Sandra said with a deep sigh.

Suddenly a loud knocking on the front door disturbed them. They heard Nelly go along the hallway to answer it, followed by the murmur of her voice mingled with that of a man. The next minute Nelly was tapping on the door of the sitting room and saying, 'There's a gentleman here asking for you, Miss Megan.'

Frowning, Megan went to see who it was. A very tall, broad-shouldered man with thick grey hair and a neatly trimmed grey beard was standing there. He was very well dressed in a navy blue striped suit, white shirt with a stiff collar and dark blue tie and with a black alpaca overcoat and black trilby.

'Are you Megan Lloyd?' he demanded.

He looked so authoritative that Megan's pulse raced. She was afraid that he was some sort of official come to interrogate them about what went on at The Haven.

'Yes I am, how can I help you?' she asked, squaring her shoulders.

'Am I right in thinking that you have my daughter here?'

'Your daughter?' Megan took a deep breath. 'What is her name?' she asked, playing for time.

'Jennifer. Jennifer White.'

'There is a girl of that name here, but—'

Before she could finish he interrupted. 'Good! I am her father, Joshua White. My friend, Dr Harvey Stott, informed me that she is here and, what is more, that I am a grandfather. Is this correct?'

'Jennifer White has had her baby,' Megan admitted.

'Then can I see it? Jennifer as well, of course.'

Megan hesitated. She was unsure what to do. Jennifer had told her how her parents had turned her out and told her never to come back. She also recalled that Harvey had told her that it was Mrs White who had been so adamant that Jennifer could not remain at home in her condition.

Megan was anxious not to upset Jennifer by doing the wrong thing. But she knew Jennifer wanted to keep her baby, and if her father was here asking to see them both then surely that meant he had forgiven her. It also possibly meant that he would be prepared to provide some sort of home for them both, Megan reasoned. Even if he and his wife didn't want her to go back to her home he might be prepared to provide her with a flat or house where she could bring up the baby.

'Come on, come on, what's the problem?' he asked impatiently.

'If you will step in here, Mr White,' Megan invited, backing into the sitting room, 'and take a seat I will ask someone to bring you a cup of coffee while I go and ask Jennifer if she is willing to see you.'

'Willing to see me! What utter nonsense! Of course she'll see me, she's my daughter!'

'Yes, Mr White, I hope she will see you, but she has been under my care for quite some time now, so I must warn you I have no intention of going against her wishes.'

Chapter Sixteen

Jennifer looked shocked when Megan told her that her father was downstairs and asking to see her and the baby.

'You mean he's come here?' she gasped, the colour draining from her face, making her look as scared as a naughty child. Megan felt sorry for her and wished she'd sent him on his way or even told him that Jennifer was no longer there.

'Yes, he's in the sitting room waiting to see you.'

Jennifer hesitated for a moment then threw back the bedclothes and stood up. 'I'd better see him, I suppose,' she said with a deep sigh. She picked up the baby sleeping in the crib alongside her bed and wrapped him carefully in the blanket that had been covering him. 'I'm ready!'

'You can't go down like that in your nightgown,' Megan said gently. 'Shall I hold the baby while you get dressed?'

Again Jennifer hesitated, then without a word she held the shawl-wrapped bundle out to Megan, picked up her clothes from the chair beside her bed and began to put them on.

She looked so young and vulnerable that Megan's heart ached for her.

As they went out on to the landing Jennifer was shaking so much that Megan insisted on carrying the baby down the stairs.

'I'll hand him over to you outside the sitting-room door,' she promised when Jennifer started to protest.

In the hallway outside the sitting room Megan carefully handed the baby back to Jennifer. 'I'll go in and tell him that you're here,' she whispered.

Jennifer took a deep breath and again squared her thin shoulders. 'Nothing else, mind!'

'Very well.'

'I've had a shock, now it's time for him to have one,' Jennifer said, trying to smile but failing to do so.

'Sorry to have kept you waiting,' Megan said as she went into the room. 'Jennifer is waiting outside the door, Mr White, if you would like to see her.'

'She is?' He looked perplexed for a moment. 'Then why doesn't she come in?' he asked curtly.

There was no need for Megan to reply. Jennifer had heard what he had said, pushed open the door and came into the room.

There was a moment of uneasy silence as they stared at each other almost like two strangers meeting for the first time. Then Joshua White strode across the room, arms outstretched, ready to embrace her.

Jennifer pulled back quickly, one hand held up as if warding him off.

Her father stiffened as if afraid that she was rejecting him. Then he saw what she was holding in her arms and instead placed his hands on her shoulders.

The frozen look on his face softened as he stared down at the miniature replica of himself that she was carrying in her arms. Murmuring softly he stroked the baby's cheek with his forefinger. Then he reached out to take the child from his daughter and hold it in his own arms.

For a brief second Jennifer hesitated. Then very gently she passed her precious bundle into his care.

Megan felt a lump rising in her throat and tears pricking her own eyes as she saw the joyous look on the girl's face and the proud look on her father's face as he nursed the baby.

'My grandson,' he exclaimed possessively. 'Another Joshua to carry on the family business.' He looked up questioningly at Jennifer. 'You have called him Joshua?'

'I've called him Joe,' she said quietly.

'Well, from this moment on he is Joshua, Joshua White,' her father stated firmly.

Megan felt relieved that the meeting between the two of them was so amenable because she was sure that it meant that Jennifer's problems, for the moment at least, were at an end. If she went home to her family then her future and that of the baby would be settled and safe.

She would miss Jennifer, but this wonderful reconciliation she had witnessed was more than she had ever dreamed could happen.

'So how did you find me?' Jennifer asked as her father handed the baby back to her.

'Harvey Stott left a message for me at the office, letting me know that you'd had a baby boy and that I could locate you at this address.'

'I see.'

'I couldn't believe it was the right address so I thought I ought to check it out and make sure that you really were here before I mentioned it to your mother.'

'I see,' Jennifer repeated in a non-committal voice.

'I didn't want to raise her hopes until I had made sure that it was you.' He gave a beaming smile. 'She'll be so relieved when I take you back home with me.'

'Hold on!' Jennifer exclaimed. 'I'm not prepared to do that.'

Her father stared at her in surprise, his mouth tightening. 'Of course you must come home; I want you to come back with me right now,' he said forcefully.

She shook her head defiantly. 'I desperately want to come home, but I'm not prepared to do so until I am quite certain that Mother wants me to be there.'

'Please, Jennifer, don't let the altercation we had all those months ago stand in the way of our being reunited as a family.'

'Not until I am quite sure that it's what Mother wants.'

'Of course she does,' he stated irritably. 'She's been terribly worried about you.'

'In that case why didn't she come here with you today?'

'Apart from the fact that I didn't tell her anything about Harvey Stott's message, your mother is not well, Jennifer. She's suffering from some sort of heart problem. I want her to visit a specialist but she refuses to do so. Maybe you will be able to persuade her how important it is that she does.'

'I'm sorry she's not well, but I am not coming home until she has spoken to me and told me she has forgiven me,' Jennifer said stubbornly. 'If she isn't well enough to come over here to see me then tell her to telephone, and Miss Lloyd will let me speak to her.'

Joshua White stood up and pulled himself up to his full height, shaking his head in dismay.

'I tell you what I'll do, Jennifer, I will go home and tell her I have seen you and the baby, and then I will ask her to invite you to dinner so that the two of you can discuss the matter and you can be sure that she has forgiven you. Will that do?'

Jennifer nodded cautiously. 'Can I bring Miss Lloyd with me?'

'Excellent idea! We'll invite Harvey Stott as well, since it is thanks to him that I have found you again.'

–

Two days later Megan received a very formal letter inviting her to the Whites' home in Warren Drive, Wallasey and requesting that Miss Jennifer White should accompany her.

Megan read it through several times; each time she did so she thought how cold and impersonal it was. She knew that there had been a letter for Jennifer with a Wallasey postmark and she hoped that Jennifer's invitation was couched in a warmer manner than hers.

Later in the day Megan received a telephone call from Harvey Stott asking her if she had received the invitation and promising that he would pick them up in his car at six thirty the following evening.

Jennifer merely shrugged when Megan told her this.

'Would you like to see if there is anything in my wardrobe that you would like to wear for the occasion?' Megan asked, knowing how limited Jennifer's choice of clothes was.

'No thank you. I shall wear my skirt and I'll wash and iron my blouse so that I look clean and tidy,' she stated.

'What about a warm coat then? It has turned chilly again over the last few days.'

'The coat I came here in will do. We'll be in Dr Stott's car so I won't feel cold,' Jennifer insisted.

Megan sat in front alongside Harvey, Jennifer in the back, nursing the baby in her arms. Harvey tried to make conversation with them both but Jennifer didn't respond. She sat rocking the baby and crooning to it even though it was sound asleep.

Megan was on edge wondering what sort of a reception they would get. She longed to ask Harvey details about Mrs White but she wasn't sure if Jennifer could overhear what they were saying or not so she kept quiet.

The Whites' house was very large and imposing. It was a double-fronted red brick edifice with a gabled roof and high bay windows both upstairs and down. They parked in the wide gravel drive and the front door was opened before they were out of the car.

Joshua White hurried forward to take the baby from Jennifer, but as soon as she was out of the car she reached out and took it back from him. He greeted both Megan and Harvey with a handshake and then led the way into the house.

Mrs White, a short, plump, dark-haired woman was waiting in the hallway. She was wearing a black velvet dress and an exquisite gold and pearl necklace was her only jewellery. She greeted Megan and Harvey very effusively and invited them into a lavishly furnished sitting room where a log fire was burning brightly.

Megan was aware that Jennifer had hung back and she suspected that Jennifer wanted the rest of them out of the way before she greeted her mother.

As she sat next to Harvey on the green velvet settee in the sitting room Megan waited anxiously for Jennifer and her parents to join them. She could hear the murmur of their voices; Jennifer's sounded petulant, her mother's forceful and the deeper voice of Joshua White sounded as if he was acting as mediator between Jennifer and her mother.

After several minutes Joshua White came into the sitting room and offered them a glass of sherry. He talked of mundane matters but like Megan and Harvey he seemed to be half listening to what was happening on the other side of the door.

When, about five minutes later, Jennifer and her mother came into the room Megan noticed with relief that it was Margaret White who was carrying the baby.

Megan exchanged looks with Harvey and he gave a slight nod, as if he agreed with her that it surely indicated that peace had been restored between Jennifer and her mother.

The rest of the evening passed very pleasantly. Their meal was excellent. Delicious food and wine and the conversation was kept to general subjects.

Afterwards, though, when they were preparing to take their leave, problems arose. Joshua White brought in their coats and helped Megan into hers. Mrs White looked astonished when Jennifer began wrapping the baby up in its blanket and then asked for her coat.

'Surely you're not leaving, are you, Jennifer? You can't! We've made our peace. I thought you were back home for good.'

Jennifer took a deep breath. 'All I want to do is come back home, Mother; you have no idea how homesick I've been. It's simply that I can't do so right away. Now that The Haven is registered as a charity I must finish the fundraising work that I've undertaken to do for Megan.'

Joshua White frowned deeply. He looked across at Megan, but before he could speak Megan said quickly, 'No, no, Jennifer. You don't have to do that. Stay home, now. You must think of your own future and that of your baby, not of helping us.'

'You can carry on helping them from here, from home,' her father intervened. 'In fact, there will be far better facilities for you to do it here than there. You can call on the fully trained staff at my office to help you. They can send out your press releases and requests for donations and deal with all the correspondence that comes in. I am sure Miss Lloyd will agree to them doing that.'

He turned to face Megan. 'Please, let my company take over the administration for you and deal with all the correspondence that organizing a charity entails.'

'It is extremely kind of you, Mr White, but are you sure you want to take on so much extra work?'

'It will be a pleasure.' He smiled. 'That is the least I can do in gratitude for all the help and care you have given my daughter and baby grandson.'

Joshua White turned to his daughter and held out his arms again for the baby. 'I'll send someone from the office to pick up any papers and documents relating to this charity work. We'll sort them all out in the next few days,' he promised Megan.

'My offices are in Old Hall Street, which is not so very far away from you, so call in any time you or Miss Peterson have anything to pass on to Jennifer and they will see I get it and I'll bring it back home for her to attend to.'

Megan nodded understandingly. She was going to miss Jennifer, but at the same time she was delighted that the girl was reunited with her own family.

As Joshua White, his wife and Jennifer said goodbye Megan was sad that Jennifer was leaving them but happy about the outcome for her.

'All in all, this arrangement with the Whites should work out very well,' Harvey commented as they drove away. 'Let's hope they're as successful when it comes to interesting people in what you are doing here and in raising adequate funds for you to carry on at The Haven as they are in running their shipping business.'

'Yes, l943 has turned out even better than we thought possible. Let's hope the rest of the year will be as good.'

'I have a feeling it will,' Harvey said. 'Joshua is already talking about a write-up in the *Liverpool Echo*.'

'Well, I hope that turns out to be good publicity, we don't want people protesting about what we are doing or turning up on our doorstep and causing trouble,' Megan murmured.

'No, they won't,' Harvey said confidently. '1943 is going to continue to be a good year for all of us; it might even prove to be a very special year,' he said with a smile.

'Now,' he added, 'since we're not far from the promenades, what about a drive along there?'

'We won't be able to see very much in the dark,' she protested.

'True, but it'll be nice and secluded and you say that you have never been there before,' he said with a low laugh, giving Megan a meaningful look that brought the colour rushing to her face.

'I'd certainly like to, but it is very late,' she demurred. 'Perhaps some other time.'

'Very well, what about Sunday afternoon?'

'I'd like that very much!'

'Good!'

'Tell me something about New Brighton,' Megan said as they headed back to Liverpool.

'In winter it's pretty deserted,' Harvey replied. 'In summer it's so packed that it is a place to avoid. Trippers come from the Midlands and of course from Liverpool.

For them it is a ride on the ferry boat which only takes about twenty minutes.'

'So what else is there at New Brighton?' Megan questioned.

'The Tower Ballroom, which is quite famous and a favourite with dancers worldwide. There are also swings and roundabouts and sideshows of all kind. There's a variety theatre that has shows running all through the summer season. There used to be a menagerie in the Tower grounds but I'm not sure if they've managed to keep it going. Finding food for some of the animals became difficult once the war started.'

'And hotels?'

'A few; but mostly the accommodation for visitors is in boarding houses. There's also an excellent open-air swimming pool and a long wide promenade with a sea wall to protect you from the Mersey.'

'Oh!' Megan tried to envisage the scene but failed.

'The comings and goings on the Mersey are also very entertaining since there is everything from small craft like the ferry boats that travel constantly back and forth to Liverpool throughout the day, up to huge cargo boats and big ocean-going liners. Sometimes you see these waiting out at the bar at the mouth of the Mersey until the tide is safe for them to enter or leave on their way to and from all parts of the world,' Harvey went on.

'Have you always lived by the Mersey?' Megan asked, regarding him with renewed interest.

'Yes. My parents lived over here in Wallasey. You could see the Mersey from our house in Warren Drive. My father was part-owner of a major shipping line.'

'Is that why you know the Whites so well?'

'My father and Joshua White were very well acquainted and attended a lot of functions together. I used to stand for hours at my bedroom window watching for the liners carrying a flag bearing the emblem of his company up the Mersey.'

'Is he retired now?' Megan questioned.

There was a moment's silence and she saw the sadness come into Harvey's eyes and his jaw stiffen. She suspected a trauma of some kind and wished she had not asked.

'Like countless others on Merseyside both my parents were killed when our house received a direct hit a couple of years ago,' he said in a clipped voice.

'Oh, I'm so sorry.' Megan reached out and touched his arm.

One of Harvey's hands covered hers briefly but he said nothing; it was as though he couldn't bear to talk about it.

'So I'll see you on Sunday,' he said as they reached The Haven and he got out of the car and walked to the door with her.

'I'll be over here about half past ten, or is that too early for you?' he asked teasingly.

'I'll be ready on time, so don't be late,' she told him.

'Good! Wear something warm and sensible shoes because I intend to make you walk from Seacombe to Leasowe; that's the entire length of the promenade,' he warned her.

'How far is that?'

'Wait and see, but make sure you wear comfortable shoes,' he advised.

'Will we have to walk all the way back or can we catch a bus or a train?'

'We walk both ways,' he told her firmly.

'What happens if I can't walk all that way, will you carry me?' she teased.

'No,' he told her gravely, 'I will help you to the nearest shelter and leave you there. Until Sunday then,' he murmured as he gave her a hug and a kiss that seemed to go on forever. 'I love you, Megan Lloyd,' he whispered, his voice husky, as finally they broke apart.

It was a long time before Megan dropped off to sleep. She went over every detail of their evening together after they had left the Whites' house. And the prospect of going to New Brighton with Harvey on Sunday was very exciting.

It was quite true she had never been to any seaside resort before. Her father didn't feel there was any need for them to go on holiday since they lived in a beautiful mountain area. The sea was not far from them but for some reason they never went there. Now she found it exhilarating and she looked forward to her walk with Harvey.

It was a long promenade and although she was blissfully happy walking along hand-in-hand with Harvey, by the time they reached Leasowe she was very tired. Far too tired to resist when he suggested a rest in one of the shelters dotted along the promenade.

For a few moments they sat there in silence, enjoying the sounds of the sea and the tranquillity that enshrouded them. She made no resistance when his arm went around her waist, pulling her closer. The warmth from his body enveloped her like a warm cloak and when he pulled her even closer into his arms she melted into his embrace, raising her face so that their lips met.

An hour later, when they broke apart and Harvey said it was time they were getting back, her tiredness seemed to have vanished. This time however he didn't walk very far along the promenade before turning up a side street that led them directly to Wallasey village and back home.

Chapter Seventeen

News that there was a new enterprise called The Haven in Chapel Gardens and that it was for unmarried mothers spread rapidly and brought mixed reactions. Some people sent them donations, others wrote requesting more details or asking if they could visit.

They were also visited by local clergy of almost all denominations as well as a battery of do-gooders concerned about the moral status of the girls who came there and anxious to educate them and show them a better way of life.

When Megan suggested that if they were so interested in the welfare of these girls then why had they not set up a retreat for them themselves, a place where they could have their babies, she received frosty looks.

In some cases they explained that they had no facilities for providing accommodation for such people and looked angrily at Megan when she suggested that they could always have taken one or two girls into their own home.

Gradually visits from such callers diminished and they were left to run The Haven in peace.

They had so many applications from pregnant girls, however, that they were forced to introduce restrictions about which girls they ought to take in and which ones they reluctantly were forced to turn away.

'We really haven't room for girls who are only a few months pregnant and looking for somewhere where they can stay for three or four months,' Sandra pointed out. 'We really must confine ourselves in future to only taking in girls who are in the final stages of their pregnancy.'

Although Megan agreed with Sandra because she knew she was right she found it much harder to turn girls away when they came to the door pleading for shelter than Sandra did.

'I hate to think how many homeless people you will take into our home when we have one,' Harvey teased when he heard about this.

'I won't want to have anyone there except you,' Megan assured him.

'Well, that's a relief,' he said with a smile. 'Now,' he went on, 'I have some very special news for you. Apparently Joshua White's wife, Margaret, has a heart problem and he has finally agreed to consult a specialist. She has asked me to persuade my uncle who is a leading heart specialist to come to see her.'

'I'm sorry to hear about Margaret, but surely if she is seeing a specialist she will have to go to his consulting rooms,' Megan said with a frown.

'In the ordinary way she would.' Harvey smiled. 'In this instance, however, my uncle practises in Glasgow. She isn't well enough to travel there so I am arranging for to him come here to see her.'

'And he has agreed?'

'Yes. By lucky coincidence he is going on holiday next week to visit an old school friend in North Wales and he has agreed to come on here afterwards. He will be staying overnight so I hope you will be able to meet him.'

'Oh dear, that's going to be quite nerve wracking,' Megan said anxiously.

'Not at all.' Harvey assured her. 'You'll like him. He is in his early sixties but he has a very lively mind.'

'He might disapprove of me,' she countered with a nervous smile.

'Not a chance! He has an eye for the ladies and he is a widower so I will have to watch that he doesn't captivate your heart and take you from me.'

As he spoke, Harvey drew her into his arms, kissing her on the brow and then, placing a hand under her chin, raised her face so that his next kiss was full on her lips.

Megan sighed blissfully as she melted into his embrace and returned his kisses with equal passion.

Throughout the following week they were so busy installing two new girls into The Haven that Megan had no time to worry about her forthcoming meeting with Harvey's uncle.

The two newcomers, Susan Harris and Alice Fletcher, were both local girls. Susan Harris came from one of the better areas in Wallasey and it was obvious from her expression when she was shown into the small attic bedroom that she was horrified by what she had been reduced to accepting.

Too well brought up to make any comment she listened in silence as Megan told her the simple house rules and showed her where the bathroom and lavatory were situated.

The other girl, Alice Fletcher, came from Seacombe. She was not quite so well dressed as Susan Harris and it was obvious that the accommodation she was being offered did not in any way distress her.

Both girls were within days of having their babies and Megan was so busy making the necessary arrangements for this that she had no time to think about the coming meeting with Harvey's uncle and she was therefore taken by surprise when Harvey said his uncle had arrived in Liverpool.

'Joshua White has invited Uncle Marcus and his friend to dinner tonight and apparently he's told him that he was inviting us as well.'

'Oh, dear!' Megan hesitated.

'Come on, you've been over there before. It's an excellent opportunity to break the ice with Uncle Marcus, seeing that you are so nervous about meeting him.'

'Even more importantly it would be a chance to see Jennifer again and make sure she's settled in,' Megan ventured.

'Right, that's settled then. Be ready at six thirty.'

'Are you taking your uncle?'

'No, he and his friend will be making their own way there.'

Jennifer White came to the door to welcome them. She was wearing a pretty dress and looked well and happy, eager to take Megan to the nursery to see baby Joshua.

'My word he's grown,' Megan enthused. 'Is everything all right for you now, Jennifer?' she asked. 'You certainly look well.'

'Everything is great. Both Mother and Father adore Joshua and they… they…' She giggled. 'They seem to have grown up; they are so very much more understanding these days.'

'They might possibly think the same about you,' Megan said with a smile.

'Are you happy with the publicity we are getting for The Haven?' Jennifer said, changing the subject. 'We still have several ideas for new campaigns.'

'You've done wonders,' Megan assured her. 'If I don't get the opportunity to thank your father for all he has done to help us, will you tell him for me, please.'

'Of course! I suppose we should join him and his guests,' she murmured as she straightened the covers on Joshua's cot.

'You're right. Come on, lead the way.'

Once more Megan found herself in the Whites' luxurious sitting room and she felt happy for Jennifer that things had turned out so well and that she was back in the heart of her family.

'We were beginning to think you'd got lost,' Harvey said, coming over to them. Taking Megan by the arm, he led her over to where Joshua White was talking to two well-dressed older men.

'This is Megan Lloyd who is one of the founders of The Haven,' Harvey stated, pulling her forward. 'Megan, this is my uncle, Marcus Millward.'

Megan found her hand being shaken by a tall, distinguished man in his early sixties. His thatch of grey hair was brushed back revealing a high forehead and clean-shaven face with a strong jawline and a wide mouth. His eyes were a deep blue and his penetrating appraisal of her brought the colour to her cheeks.

'By heaven, that's a coincidence,' he exclaimed with a booming laugh. 'The friend I brought with me is also called Lloyd.'

For the first time Megan looked at the man who was standing beside Marcus Millward and drew in her breath sharply. She couldn't believe her eyes. The man standing there was her father.

She could hear Harvey speaking to her but she took no notice. She stared again, wondering if she was imagining things, but there was no mistake at all. It was her father, Lewis Lloyd, who was standing there.

He looked slightly older than she remembered but as their eyes met and she saw the shock and hesitancy in them as he stared at her, it made her heart pound.

Overwhelmed by the unbearable homesickness that she had tried so hard to push to the back of her mind for the past few months and unable to stop herself, she flung herself into his arms.

'Dad, Dad!' she whispered. 'How wonderful to see you. I've missed you so much.'

He held her close, stroking her hair and murmuring his delight at seeing her again.

'Mother? How is she?' she asked, pulling back a little so that she could stare into his eyes.

He looked grave. 'I'm afraid that she is not very well at all. She misses you and worries about you a great deal. She'll be so relieved when I tell her I have found you. Will you come home, Megan?' he asked, his voice pleading.

'I'll come for a visit,' she agreed. 'My work is here though, there is so much to be done.'

'Marcus read about it in the paper and told us about it when he came to see us this weekend. When he said his nephew was involved and that he was coming to Liverpool to meet him I decided to come with him and find out if it really was you behind the scheme.' He squeezed her arm. 'I am so proud of you. It is a wonderful effort.'

'It's my war work,' she told him quietly.

He nodded. 'It's an extremely worthwhile project,' he said quietly. 'Can we come and look round The Haven?'

'Of course you can. I'd very much like you to see it.'

'Tomorrow? Before I go back to North Wales?'

'That would be wonderful. Will you be bringing Mr Millward with you?'

'Yes, we'll both come. I know he's extremely interested in what you are doing.'

'What time will you come?'

'That will be up to Marcus to decide. I'll go along with whatever he wants to do. Does it matter?'

'No, of course it doesn't. I want to make sure that Sandra Peterson, the woman who has let me use her house, is there to meet you as well, that's all.'

–

As it happened Lewis Lloyd arrived half an hour after Harvey, with Megan's help, had delivered Alice Fletcher's baby.

As Harvey and Megan came out of the room where Alice Fletcher was now resting, the baby in a crib at the side of her bed, Megan still in her bloodstained overall, her hair untidy and her face damp with sweat from her exertions, both of them were taken by surprise when they found Lewis Lloyd and Marcus Millward waiting for them on the landing.

'Heavens above, I didn't expect to meet you like this,' Harvey said in a startled voice as he passed a hand over his brow, pushing back his dampened hair.

'The housekeeper – Nelly, I think she said her name was – let us in and when I told her that I was a doctor she didn't ask any questions but sent us up here to find you,' his uncle told them.

Megan introduced her father and Marcus to Sandra and left them to enjoy a chat and a cup of coffee in the sitting room while she and Harvey went to get cleaned up. Then they took them on a tour of The Haven.

Both Marcus Millward and Lewis Lloyd were impressed by what they saw.

'So you've spent all your inheritance, have you?' Megan's father said with a smile. 'In that case then, I think I ought to reinstate your allowance, only make sure that you spend it on yourself, not on others.'

He held up a hand, as she was about to demur. 'You won't need it for The Haven,' he told her. 'I will make sure you get adequate funds for that when I get back to North Wales. There are a good many wealthy business people in the area, as you very well know, and they have no idea of the appalling conditions the people in and around Liverpool have suffered since this war started. They live in a different world but I shall make it my business to let them know what has been happening to so many young girls and I am confident that they will give generously.'

That evening they all went for dinner at the Adelphi Hotel, where her father and Marcus Millward were staying. As their taxi took them through some of the poorer areas of Liverpool, Megan felt her father's hand tighten on her arm.

'It really is a different world,' he murmured with a deep sigh. 'I can't ever remember seeing so much poverty or people living in such squalid conditions. The Haven is like a beacon of hope for the young girls who find their way there.'

His words brought a smile to Megan's face. She felt that at last he understood her aims and would no longer oppose what she wanted to do. Knowing that, she loved him even more.

The splendid meal they enjoyed at the Adelphi made her realize how right he was and what a divide there was between those who lived in comfort and those who struggled to exist.

Before they left she promised her father that at the first opportunity she would come home on a visit.

'You are very welcome to bring Harvey Stott with you,' he told her solemnly. 'The poor boy looks as though he could do with a break. From what Marcus tells me, he is under great pressure and hasn't had a holiday since the war started.'

'Perhaps I will,' she agreed. 'Anyway I'll tell him what you said, but I think he probably has too many commitments to take a holiday.'

'Rubbish! He needs to recharge his batteries before he has a breakdown,' her father said crisply. 'What's more, I know his welfare matters to you every bit as much as the welfare of those poor girls you are trying to help. You make a first-class team,' he added proudly.

Chapter Eighteen

It was six months and eight babies later before Harvey and Megan could manage to take a break and visit Megan's family in North Wales.

In the meantime Megan had kept in touch with them and it was her mother's repeated requests for her to come on a visit that finally Megan decided she ought to try and do so.

Harvey was in full agreement. 'Great idea! It will give me a chance to ask your father's permission,' he said.

'Permission? Permission for what?'

'Permission to marry you, of course.'

Megan stared at him in astonishment. 'You really ought to ask me first if I want to marry you,' she told him, trying hard not to smile as she said it.

Harvey pulled her into his arms. 'I know I don't need to do that. You've been waiting for me to propose for the last few months and I have always known what your answer would be.'

Megan wriggled free of his embrace. 'You really are very sure of yourself, Dr Harvey Stott,' she told him, tossing her head in assumed disdain.

'I know,' he replied with a confident grin. 'I want us to be married as much as you do, and as soon as possible. I still think though that the correct thing to do is to ask your father for your hand.'

'What will you do if he refuses?' Megan teased.

'Marry you just the same,' he laughed. 'Now, have you any objections to that?'

'None at all,' she told him, 'and as you say the sooner we can get married the happier we will be.'

It was November before they were finally able to take a long weekend to spend with Megan's family in North Wales. They travelled by train and although it was lovely being together, the journey seemed to take them an awfully long time. Harvey kept looking out of the window and each time they drew into a station he would look enquiringly at Megan and ask, 'Are we there yet?'

When she shook her head he would frown and question whether she was right or not.

'I'll certainly know when we're there,' she told him laughing when he looked doubtful. 'It's my home we're going to, remember?'

'I know that, but none of the stations are marked, so how can you be so sure? This business of taking down all the nameplates is so confusing. I know it's been done because of the war so that the enemy won't be able to find their way around if we are invaded but I have no idea how far it is.'

'Don't worry, I'll recognize it when we get there,' she told him confidently.

Her father was waiting at the station for them. 'Come on, my car's outside; you must be weary after that journey. Ten minutes and we'll be home; there's a meal waiting and a glass of Madeira, so that will put new life into both of you.'

Megan was amused by the look of amazement on Harvey's face as they drove up the gravel drive that led from the main road up to Yr Glaslyn.

'Here we are, home at last,' she said with a rapturous smile.

'This is some place you've got here,' Harvey said admiringly. 'It's almost like a mediaeval castle.'

'Yes, my ancestors were granted permission to have castellated walls,' Lewis Lloyd stated proudly.

'You also have a turret. Do you use it?'

'Not to watch out for the enemy approaching, but I have my study in there and Megan used to have the top room as her playroom when she was a child.'

'The view is outstanding,' Megan said. 'I'll show you tomorrow when I take you on a tour of the whole place.'

Bronwyn Lloyd, Megan's mother, was waiting at the door for them. Megan was dismayed to see how frail she looked. Surely six months couldn't have made all that difference to her, Megan thought worriedly.

As they embraced Megan was even more concerned when she felt how thin and birdlike her mother was when she put her arms around her. It seemed as though she had wasted away. Surely worrying about me hasn't done this to her? Megan thought guiltily.

Over their delicious meal of lamb with mint sauce, croquette potatoes, roast parsnips, carrots and peas, Megan tried to explain to her mother the sort of work she was doing in Liverpool.

'It sounds very fulfilling, but couldn't you come back home and do something similar here?' Mrs Lloyd asked in a pleading tone.

'No, Mother, I'm afraid not,' Megan said gently. 'Many of the girls who come to us for help are from very squalid backgrounds; they are very poor and a great many of them have been bombed out of their homes.'

'All of them?' Her mother exclaimed in surprise.

'Well, no, not quite all of them,' Megan admitted.

'Most of them have been turned out by their parents because they are pregnant,' Harvey explained.

'Oh, my goodness, what a terrible thing to happen!' Bronwyn Lloyd exclaimed, her hand flying up to her mouth in horror. 'Why do they do that?'

'Because they feel the girls have brought shame on their families. None of these girls are married, you see, Mother. In fact, most of them are planning to get rid of their babies the moment they are born. They know they won't be able to support them since they have no jobs and no homes or anything, so they either abandon their babies, give them up for adoption, or put them into a charitable institution of some sort.'

'I've only known of one young girl around here who got herself into such a predicament and she committed suicide before the baby was born,' Mrs Lloyd said, shaking her head sadly.

'I am afraid there are a great many more than that in Liverpool,' Harvey told her. 'Of course it is a seaport, and visiting sailors...'

Bronwyn Lloyd clapped her hands to her ears and shook her head. 'Please, young man, don't tell me any more, it is far too harrowing.' She turned and looked directly at Megan. 'Are these the sort of girls you are trying to help?'

'Yes, Mother. Girls who have been left pregnant by the Yanks or the sailors who have been in Liverpool because of the war.'

'That is such a shocking state of affairs,' Bronwyn Lloyd said and shuddered. 'I really do think it is a dangerous environment for you to be in.'

Megan, knowing that it was pointless to argue with her mother, decided to change the subject.

For the rest of the evening they talked about local affairs and her mother related all she knew about what was happening in the village of Beddgelert.

After a stroll round the garden just before dusk, accompanied by her parents and Harvey, Megan said she was going to bed.

'It's been a long day and tomorrow I am going to take Harvey up Moel Hebog.'

'You do pick the most unsuitable places to go,' her mother scolded. 'I'm quite sure he doesn't want to climb up a mountain, do you?' she asked, directing her question at Harvey.

'Well, I have never climbed one yet, so it could be quite a challenge,' he countered.

'We'll only be gone for a couple of hours, and we'll be back again before lunchtime,' Megan told her mother.

The walk up Moel Hebog was, as Harvey had predicted, something of a challenge.

'I take it that this is the mountain that dominates the skyline from here,' Harvey said as they set out.

'Yes, it's 2,750 feet high, not quite as high as Snowdon. The name Moel Hebog means the Hill of the Hawk and it is where Owen Glendower is said to have hidden from the English,' Megan told him.

She made short work of the climb but Harvey was breathing heavily. To give him a chance to get his breath back, Megan paused on a patch of rocky ground.

'Do we have to go much further?' Harvey gasped, straining his neck to look up at the summit.

'No, it's not far now,' Megan assured him.

'I should hope not; we're already in low cloud.'

'Mist, not cloud,' Megan laughed.

'Perhaps we should turn back,' he said cautiously. 'I've heard about people finding themselves caught out by the mist coming down when they are on a mountain and losing all sense of where they are. We don't want that to happen to us, do we?'

'Don't worry, I know my way to the top and back down again blindfolded,' Megan replied with a laugh. 'I've been climbing Moel Hebog ever since I was ten years old. The mountain is an old friend to me and I couldn't get lost up here even if I wanted to.'

By the time they reached the summit the mist had cleared and the sun was out. From their vantage point they could see not only the rest of the Snowdon range but also right across to the Irish Sea.

'It's absolutely breathtaking,' Harvey exclaimed.

The journey back down Moel Hebog was less strenuous but they had to be careful because the ground, especially the grass, was extremely slippery.

By the time they arrived back at Yr Glaslyn, Harvey was exhausted and he readily welcomed the invitation to have a glass of sherry before they started lunch.

'I've been thinking over what you told me about life in Liverpool and I really do think that Megan should pack up working down there and come back home,' Megan's mother stated as she handed him a dry sherry.

'There's simply no knowing what she might pick up,' she went on. 'These girls are probably diseased and at best they will be full of lice and fleas. We didn't send her to university to end up spending her time amongst those sorts of people,' she murmured as they took their places at the table. 'I would like her to come back up here where things are far more civilized and where she has well-mannered, well-brought-up friends. If she really wants to work then let her father find her a job in his office.'

'Are you talking about me?' Megan asked as she came into the room and slipped into her place at the table.

'Yes, dear, I was explaining to Dr Stott how I would prefer you to be back here, not down in Liverpool, and that if you wanted to work then your father would find you something to do, wouldn't you, Lloyd?'

'I'm sure he would,' Megan said stiffly, 'but it is not the sort of work I want to do. Harvey will tell you that what I am doing is very important. I would have thought that you realized that after what we've told you about The Haven.'

'Your mother does know; she read the report in the newspaper I brought home after I came to visit you in Liverpool.'

'Yes, of course I did, but no one believes what they read in the newspaper,' her mother said forcefully.

The atmosphere became tense. To Megan's relief, Harvey changed the subject.

'Mr Lloyd,' he said in a firm but polite tone, 'I want to ask you something. It is one of the reasons why I came to see you this weekend. I want to ask if I can marry your daughter Megan.'

A hush descended over the room and for several minutes no one spoke. Then Lewis Lloyd cleared his throat. 'She is very young to be thinking of marriage,' he prevaricated.

'Young in years, maybe, but not in experience,' Harvey said with a smile.

'True!' Lewis Lloyd agreed. 'There is the question, however, of whether she is willing to marry you?' he went on in a speculative tone. 'I assume you've asked her?'

'I have, and she has said yes, but I still feel that I need your approval and permission.'

'Quite right, my boy, quite right,' Lewis Lloyd said approvingly. He looked directly at his wife. 'I have no objection. What about you, my dear?'

Bronwyn Lewis said nothing but delicately mopped at her eyes with a lace-trimmed handkerchief. Her husband picked up his glass and raised it in the air. 'A toast then, to welcome Harvey into our family and to say how much I approve of the fact that he and Megan are getting married.'

'Have you decided when it is to be and where?' he asked as he set his empty glass down on the table.

'It will be here, of course; Megan must be married in our local church and it must be officiated at by our own vicar,' Bronwyn Lewis said tremulously.

'Are you sure that's what you want, Mother?' Megan asked. 'If we do that then there will be an awful lot of people attending and you know you hate all that sort of thing.'

'You are our only child and it is only right that you should be married from the family home,' Bronwyn Lloyd said firmly. 'I couldn't bear it if you had one of those awful register office weddings with none of us present.'

Megan bit her lip. She had been on the point of telling them that it would be at a register office and that the wedding would take place in Liverpool but now, as she caught a quick nod of approval from Harvey, she knew it was best to go along with her mother's wishes.

'I do hope, though, that you are going to wait until the war is over,' Bronwyn Lloyd said firmly.

'Good heavens, no! None of us have any idea when that could be. We might have to wait years before we could get married if that is one of the conditions.'

'No, of course it isn't,' her father said decisively. 'I have given my approval and you can get married any time you like and wherever you like.'

He looked directly at his wife as he spoke. 'This is wartime, and we have to adjust accordingly. If these two want to get married in Liverpool then we must accept that, and if it means it has to be a register office, I quite understand.'

He frowned across at his wife as if defying her to contradict him. Bronwyn merely gave a slight shrug, knowing that he was the master and in control and if he was willing for their only daughter to marry without them being present then so be it. She knew there was nothing she could do to change it.

As they travelled back to Liverpool the next day, Harvey raised the subject with Megan.

'Well, what is the answer? Have you given any thought as to whether we get married at your parents' home or in Liverpool?'

'You heard what my father said; he is prepared for us to make our own minds up about it.'

'I know, that's why I'm asking you what you want to do.'

'I'm not at all sure,' Megan said thoughtfully. 'But I would very much like Jennifer White and Sandra to be at our wedding if it's at all possible, and I don't think they could travel to North Wales, not at the moment.'

'Then that makes it Liverpool,' Harvey said in a tone of relief. 'I'm sure your parents will come, so it's now up to us to set the date and let them know.'

'I rather think we'll have to consult Sandra and Jennifer to find out what's most convenient for them. We'll also have to check when our next babies are due before we can set a date,' Megan laughed.

'No, we'll make sure that Sandra and Jennifer are free, but as far as the girls are concerned we are not going to let any of them interfere with our plans,' Harvey told her firmly as he gathered her into his arms and kissed her.

'We might have to postpone the idea of going on honeymoon until after the war is over but we'll still be able to move in together once we have signed the register and I know that you really are my wife,' he murmured as his kisses became more fervent.

Chapter Nineteen

Sandra was delighted when Megan and Harvey told her that they were getting married.

'I was beginning to think that you two would never get around to it,' she laughed. 'It's certainly about time; Harvey has been running after you ever since the first day you met!'

'Rubbish! He thought I was a complete and utter idiot because I was so helpless and so inexperienced when it came to helping him to deliver a baby,' Megan said and grinned.

'You've proven to be a very apt pupil,' he told her, placing an arm around her and squeezing her shoulders affectionately.

'I've certainly had plenty of practice,' she agreed.

'So when and where is the wedding to be?' Sandra asked.

'There's a slight problem over that,' Harvey told her. 'We want both you and Jennifer White to come and perhaps her father as well, since he has been so very generous in helping us make The Haven a viable concern.'

'Well, in that case it will have to be in Liverpool, won't it?' Sandra said. 'How do your family feel about that, Megan?'

'My father is happy enough for us to get married wherever we think is most suitable, but my mother wants us to have a traditional wedding from my home with all the trimmings.'

'Surely that's out of the question? There is a war on! Think of all the problems about catering and all the clothing coupons you would need for a wedding dress.'

'True, and I think that's why she would like us to wait until the war is over and then we can do the whole thing in style. She is very much a traditionalist and she would like the entire village as well as all the employees from the slate mines to be part of the celebrations.'

'Everybody!' Sandra exclaimed in astonishment.

'You see, my father is held in high regard in Beddgelert and that's why she feels everyone must be invited.'

Sandra pursed her mouth in a silent whistle. 'The end of the war might be years ahead. At the moment we seem to be doing all right in Europe, but who can tell? The war has taken so many twists and turns since it started and although at the moment we appear to be making headway there's no guarantee that things won't change again and we'll all be back to square one.'

'Now don't say that,' Harvey said sternly. 'Things are looking up and they look brighter than they have done for years. Anyway, we don't want to wait until the war is over. I'd get married tomorrow if it was possible.'

'Well, it's certainly taken you both long enough to come to a decision,' Sandra said in a scolding tone, 'so don't delay things for too long.'

Harvey shrugged. 'You know how it is, you have to be certain about these things,' he said in a mocking tone.

'The man who never makes any mistakes never makes anything,' Sandra rejoined. 'Seriously though, when are you two planning to get married?'

'As soon as possible and preferably here in Liverpool,' Harvey confirmed. He looked at Megan questioningly. 'You are in agreement with that too, aren't you?'

'Anything you say,' Megan replied and smiled happily.

'That's not the way to deal with it, you should always make sure that it is your wishes that are paramount, not his, otherwise you will become a slave,' Sandra told her.

'I bet you wish you had the chance to be a slave,' Harvey joked. 'Have you heard from Hank lately?'

'No!' Sandra's face clouded over. 'I wish I had; it would be such a relief to know that he was safe and well.'

'No news is good news, or so they say,' Megan said quickly, sensing how worried Sandra was. 'You'll hear from him any day now, and with any luck he'll be back in time for our wedding.'

'Stop raising my hopes,' Sandra retorted with a sad little smile.

Megan's prediction came true quicker than any of them expected. A few days later Sandra did hear from Hank. It was disturbing news. He was back in England, but in hospital in Southport.

'Southport? Where's that?' Megan asked.

'A little bit further along the coast, not very far from here.'

'I see. Do you know what's wrong with him? Or the reason why he's been sent back to England? Has he been seriously injured?'

Sandra shook her head. 'I only know that he's back in England and in hospital in Southport.'

'You have no idea though what's wrong?'

'No, I'm going to ask Harvey to phone the hospital and find out.'

'Will they tell him? He's not a relation.'

'No, but he is a doctor, and I'm sure he'll be able to get far more information from them than I will.'

Sandra was right. Harvey was successful in finding out what was wrong with Hank and why he had been sent back to England.

'It's nothing too bad,' he assured them when he came off the phone. 'He has broken his leg and it has not healed well; in fact it sounds as though he has an infection in it. They've sent him back to England for specialized treatment at the military hospital in Southport.'

'So can I go and visit him?' Sandra asked.

'Yes, provided you have identification to prove who you are and that you are related to him.'

'That's impossible. We're not married or anything, so how can I prove who I am?'

'Perhaps you'd like me to take you over there?' Harvey offered. 'I'm sure that as a doctor it would be fairly easy for me to cut through any red tape.'

'That would be wonderful!' Sandra clapped her hands together in delight. 'When can we go?'

'Tomorrow, as soon as I've finished morning surgery.'

'Oh, I had hoped it would be today,' Sandra said in a disappointed voice.

Harvey frowned. 'Look, leave it with me. I'll phone again in a couple of hours' time and check if you can visit this evening,' he promised. 'It'll have to be after my evening surgery finishes, so that means it won't be until about eight o'clock.'

'That'd be fine!'

'That will be rather late for you to be taking Hope out and I suppose you will want to take her with you,' Megan mused.

'Of course I must take her. Hank hasn't even seen her yet!' Sandra exclaimed.

'It will be rather late but I don't suppose that upsetting her routine just for once is going to matter very much,' Megan agreed.

'It's not nearly so important as Hope meeting her father for the very first time and for Hank to see his little daughter.'

'Very well, unless you hear from me to the contrary I will be here to collect you at eight o'clock tonight, providing the hospital will allow such a late visit,' Harvey promised. He looked at Megan and asked, 'Are you coming with us?'

Megan looked questioningly at Sandra. 'Would you like me to look after Hope for you?'

'I've already said that I'm taking Hope with me,' Sandra said quickly.

'Do you think that's a good idea? For your first meeting, I mean?' Harvey said with a frown. 'Hank may not be feeling well enough.'

'Of course I must take her! Hank must be dying to see her. I can't wait to show her to him, he's going to be over the moon with excitement.'

'He may not be,' Harvey warned. 'I really think it would be a good idea for you to see him on your own first. What about Megan coming with us and staying outside in the corridor or in the waiting room with the baby until you've had a chance to be reunited with Hank? Once you've done that, then you could tell him that the baby is outside and if he's well enough to see Hope then you can collect her from Megan.'

'I think that would be a good idea,' Megan agreed.

Sandra thought about it for a moment before she consented. 'Yes, very well then, although I think you're being rather overprotective, Harvey. I'm quite sure that Hank will want to see Hope the moment we get there.'

As it turned out, Sandra was right. Hank's broken leg was heavily bandaged and he was unable to put any weight on it, but he was sitting in an armchair by the side of his bed with his leg supported on a stool.

Harvey gave them a few moments alone while he went back outside into the corridor where Megan was waiting with the baby and told her there was no reason why she shouldn't take Hope in to see Hank.

Hank's attention was focused on Hope and he barely glanced at Megan. She didn't recognize him immediately either; he looked much thinner than the soldier she had seen at the dance and not nearly so imposing out of his uniform.

As she placed the child in his arms and he looked down and saw his little daughter for the very first time it was as if he couldn't believe his eyes. The expression of wonderment on his face brought a lump to Megan's throat.

He kept looking from the baby to Sandra and then back again to the baby, his face wreathed in smiles. 'She is so beautiful,' he exclaimed huskily, 'so small and petite, I'm frightened I might crush her.'

'She'll soon let you know if you do that,' Sandra told him with a light laugh. 'She has a good pair of lungs on her.'

Harvey and Megan went for a walk around the hospital grounds so that Hank, Sandra and Hope could have time on their own. When they went back into the ward a nurse was already at the bedside admiring the little girl but telling Sandra it was time for her to leave.

'I'll be back tomorrow,' Sandra promised Hank as she kissed him goodbye.

'Are Megan and Harvey coming as well?' Hank asked.

'I'm not sure that we'll be able to spare the time,' Harvey explained. 'I have my patients to attend to and Megan has The Haven to run.'

'Yes, Sandra has been telling me all about it. I can't imagine how a chance comment from me could have inspired Megan to take on such a commitment. It sounds a fantastic undertaking.'

'I certainly wouldn't have been able to do it had it not been for Sandra's generosity in letting me have the use of her house,' Megan pointed out.

'That again was an incredible chance for both of you; I mean, meeting up in the street like you did.'

'Yes, it most certainly was,' Sandra agreed. 'I could hardly believe it when Megan said she had been talking to an American soldier called Hank and from her description I realized that it must be you,' she added with a smile.

'Incredible! To think that a chance remark that I made should have been the start of so much,' he repeated, shaking his head in bewilderment. 'I do hope you can both come tomorrow because I am eager to hear the full story.'

'We'll try,' Harvey promised.

'I also want to hear all about how you two met. I understand you're planning to be married in the very near future. As soon as they let me out of here I'll be doing the same thing. I want to marry Sandra as soon as I possibly can and make our darling little girl legal.'

'Perhaps we could make it a double event,' Megan said hopefully.

'Only if you make it very soon.'

'And in Liverpool,' Sandra said quickly. 'We can't wait until the war is over so that we can stage a grand event at your home.'

'Will you have to wait for the army to give you permission?' Harvey asked.

'I'm afraid so, and of course that may take quite some time,' Hank warned.

'Not all that long, surely?' Sandra exclaimed. 'I don't want Hope to be there as a bridesmaid walking down the aisle behind us,' she quipped.

'I'm quite sure they'll make me wait until I can get out of here before I can even apply for permission,' Hank answered with a sigh.

'Have you any idea when that will be?' Sandra asked.

'No idea at all. Once the infection has cleared up it may take a little time for me to regain my mobility. I will have to do that and also meet all the other regulations to ensure that I am fighting fit. And when I am fit enough to go back to my unit that might mean a posting overseas again,' he warned.

'Oh, no! Don't say that,' Sandra wailed. 'I want you home with me where I can be with you every day.'

'I want to be home as well,' Hank told her. 'By that I mean really at home, back in America. This war can't end soon enough for me. I want to be able to take you and my little daughter back home to America to meet my folks.'

'Well, that's certainly out of the question for the moment,' Megan told him. 'Even if you were discharged from the army I doubt if you would be able to get back to America. You probably stand more chance of that happening if you are still in the army.'

'Yes, I'm caught between the devil and a hard place.' Hank sighed. 'If they think I am no longer suitable for active service then they will probably ship me back to America and I won't be able to see Sandra or Hope for heaven knows how long. If I am passed as fit for active service then I can be sent anywhere, even to the Far East.'

Chapter Twenty

1943 had been a very traumatic year, Megan reflected as she made the final entries for the year in the logbook-style account she kept of what was happening at The Haven and in her own life.

All through 1943 there had been conflicting stories about the progress of the war. The Luftwaffe had recommenced their bombing of Britain at the beginning of the year and Megan had lived in dread that they would start coming to Liverpool again. This time, however, the Germans had concentrated on the more historic towns of York, Norwich, Exeter and Canterbury.

Towards the end of the year there had also been a small Blitz when Hitler had once again ordered the mass bombing of southern England and as a result, the Luftwaffe gathered some 500 aircraft to carry out this order. But the raids were not of the same scale or intensity as before, mainly because most of the experienced bomber crews had been lost over Russia and in other campaigns.

Britain had, of course, retaliated. The bombing of German cities, spearheaded by Bomber Harris and the men from Bomber Command, brought utter destruction. Regardless of the effect on the Germans, it did a great deal to hearten people in Britain who had seen London, Liverpool, Cardiff, Coventry and many other cities attacked and bombed and remembered the terrible resulting casualties.

In 1943, though, Megan reflected, many people in Germany still believed that they were going to be victorious in the war – primarily because of the propaganda they were fed and the punishments handed out to those labeled 'defeatist'.

Britain's '1,000 bomber' raid on Cologne had shown that mass bombing was inaccurate and not totally fruitful in terms of strategic gains. However, Harris, supported by Winston Churchill, still believed that a devastating attack on a symbolic target would push the Nazis into seeking a peace deal. Cologne, Dortmund and Dusseldorf had all been bombed. The most obvious other target of any symbolic importance to the Germans was Hamburg.

The first attack had been carried out in the early hours of a Sunday morning. It was reported that 1,000 tons of bombs were dropped which included 350,000 incendiary bombs. Some 15,000 people were killed and many more wounded.

In previous bombing raids, the RAF had sent in pathfinder planes to illuminate the target by dropping incendiary bombs. The main bulk of the attack followed on to what was now a burning target. For the attack on Hamburg, the RAF combined the use of high-explosive bombs and incendiary bombs, which were dropped together. The result made all but useless any form of firefighting.

The Americans had attacked on Monday 26th July and sustained heavy losses as a result of Luftwaffe attacks. An American attack on the Tuesday was called off due to poor weather.

The raid was resumed on the Wednesday. The 722 bombers were loaded with an extra 240 tons of incendiary bombs and dropped a total of 2,313 tons of bombs in just fifty minutes. The impact of this attack led to a firestorm with temperatures estimated to have reached 1,000 degrees centigrade. Bomber crews reported smoke reaching 20,000 feet. Winds on the ground reached 120 miles per hour.

While not exclusively a wooden city, Hamburg did have many old wooden houses and after a dry summer they easily burned. Even the tarmac on roads melted and anyone who had the chance of escape found they were stuck in the sticky mess that remained.

Megan recalled how Hank had told them that while he was in hospital wounded airmen had been brought in who told them that time and again they had seen burning people suddenly start to run and soon after, to fall. There was no way to save them. Some 30,000 died in this raid; the smoke blotted out the sunlight. It was 'the greatest crisis of the war for Germany'. Hamburg was cordoned off for the remainder of the war; such was the unnerving impact the raids had on the Nazi hierarchy.

Did the raids have any value? Megan wondered. There was little doubt that the reported impact of the raids did a great deal to lift morale in Britain. Many of the girls admitted to The Haven around that time were confident that it meant the war would be over any day. They saw it, together with the birth of their baby and the baby being placed for adoption, as the start of a new life for them.

The raids clearly had an impact on the Nazi government. Hitler refused to visit the city, possibly not wanting to see what his war had resulted in. Hamburg was the major port of the north and the work done by the port was disrupted.

Now, with 1943 coming to an end, the war was still raging, Megan thought sadly. Italy had declared war on Germany; the Americans had invaded the Solomon Islands; less than a month ago Churchill, Roosevelt and Stalin had met at Tehran to discuss policy and strategy; when and where would it all end?

With a sigh she turned back to check the register of babies. Fourteen had been born at The Haven in 1943. Two had died at birth but the remainder had either been adopted or kept by their mothers. Megan wondered what 1944 held for the babies; would they be loved and cherished or would they always bear the stigma of being unwanted?

What of her own life; what would 1944 bring her? Megan wondered. She and Harvey were still not married, nor, for that matter, were Hank and Sandra.

Their plans for a spring wedding had been postponed and she was uncertain about a new date. When they finally did get married, would it be here in Liverpool in a register office or would they be able to hold the sort of wedding her mother hankered after in the church in Beddgelert? That would be a white wedding with the organ playing, a marquee for the guests and all the villagers and men from the slate works in attendance.

Time alone would tell, she told herself. She no more knew if that was going to be possible than she knew how many pregnant girls would turn up on their doorstep seeking refuge and expecting her to take control of the future of the babies after they were born so that they could start a new life.

Hank had been allowed out of hospital very briefly over Christmas but he was now back in there and things were not good. His wound had turned out to be far more serious than he had led them to believe and the infection difficult to control. He had come to them for Christmas Day but it was obvious that as the day went on he was becoming increasingly uncomfortable and in considerable pain.

Sandra had wanted Harvey to give him something to control the pain but Harvey refused.

'I can't do that, it would be dangerous as well as unethical, seeing that he's already having medication from the hospital,' he explained.

'In that case, will you drive him back to Southport?' Sandra requested. 'I can't bear to see him in so much torment. I had no idea he was injured so badly.'

Two days later, when the three of them as well as little Hope had gone up to see him, they found that he was back in bed, not even allowed to sit in an armchair.

'I don't know what he got up to while he was with you,' the nurse scolded Sandra. 'Did you take him dancing or something? His leg is very swollen, the infection has flared up and he's in a lot of pain.'

'I think his leg must have been far worse than any of us thought,' Sandra told her.

The nurse raised a speculative eyebrow. 'If it doesn't respond to further treatment, he may have to have it amputated,' she warned.

–

Megan finished getting the records for The Haven completed and looked at the clock. She was utterly weary.

Within a few minutes it would be the start of 1944. She looked out of the window at the heavy dark sky. There was no moon, no stars, only a black space. At one time, before the war had started, there would have been a cacophony of sound at this time on New Year's Eve. Church bells would be ringing and here, in Liverpool, there would have been ships' hooters and klaxons sounding to welcome in the new year.

She felt so alone; after spending most of the day with Hank at the hospital in Southport, Sandra had said she was too tired even to eat. When Megan had insisted that she must have something because they couldn't afford for her to be ill, Sandra had managed a bowl of soup. It was thick and packed with vegetables, one of Nelly's special recipes. After she'd finished it, Sandra said she was going to feed Hope, give her a bath and put her to bed and then she was going to bed herself.

Which leaves me all on my own, Megan sighed. Even the three babies and their mothers in The Haven were sleeping. She wished Harvey was there to celebrate with her but he was at the bedside of a dying man.

She went to the sideboard and brought out the bottle of Bristol Cream Sherry that she had bought for Christmas and poured herself a glassful. She knew that traditionally it should have been scotch but she didn't really like the taste of whisky.

As she raised the glass to her lips she thought about her family at Yr Glaslyn and friends in Beddgelert and wondered if they were all celebrating the start of 1944 and when she would manage to see them again.

She took another sip of the sweet sherry and wondered what the new year would bring for her. Would she and

Harvey finally manage to get married, or would circumstances dictate that they would have to wait until the war was over? When would that be? If only Hitler would capitulate and all the men come back home. Even then it would probably take a long time for everything to return to normal, but at least the fear of bombings or of British and American soldiers being killed or injured would be at an end.

She drained her glass and decided that since it was now past midnight she might as well go to bed. She was halfway up the stairs when there was a knock on the front door. It sounded loud in the silence of the house and she felt so tired that she was on the point of ignoring it, but her conscience got the better of her.

Suppose it is a girl in trouble, she thought, and then reluctantly turned back down the stairs.

The girl on the doorstep was young, bedraggled and in tears. As Megan opened the door the girl tried to speak but a spasm of pain sieved through her and she doubled over gasping and tearful.

Without a word Megan helped her inside. It was obvious that the girl was in an advanced stage of labour.

Megan helped her into the only vacant bedroom they had and then on to the bed. Very gently she removed the threadbare coat the girl was wearing and the down-at-heel shoes.

The girl tried to protest and garbled an explanation about where she had come from but Megan hushed her to silence.

She knew enough now about childbirth to know the birth was imminent and that it was pointless sending for Harvey; even if he could leave the hospital he wouldn't arrive in time.

She was reluctant to disturb either Sandra or Nelly, who by now would both be sound asleep, so there was only one thing she could do, Megan decided, and that was to roll up her sleeves and act as midwife and deliver the baby herself.

Chapter Twenty-One

It was almost mid-morning before Harvey came to The Haven. Megan was still having breakfast. She felt utterly exhausted after the events of the night before.

'What's all this?' Harvey asked as he looked at her in surprise. 'Did you have a late night? Were you and Sandra up late celebrating?'

Megan shook her head. 'Not a chance! Sandra went to bed early and—'

'You stayed up and celebrated on your own, and now you have a first-class hangover,' Harvey said, giving her a critical look.

'If you sit down I'll pour you a cup of tea and then I'll tell you exactly what happened,' Megan muttered.

'Right, whatever you wish. Do you want me to talk in whispers?' he asked with a wicked grin as he pulled out a chair and sat down. He stirred the cup of tea that Megan passed to him and waited patiently for her to tell him about what had happened the night before.

'I was on my own so at midnight I decided I would go to bed. Yes, I did have a drink, a sweet sherry, but only the one. My mind was on what 1944 might bring for us and for The Haven.

'I was halfway up the stairs when I heard someone knocking on the front door. I thought about ignoring it but I couldn't. I went back down and there was a young girl so obviously in the final stages of labour that I simply hadn't the heart to turn her away.'

'Good heavens! Where is she?' He half rose from his chair, but Megan laid a restraining hand on his arm.

'Sit down and finish your tea; she is quite all right, and so is the baby.'

'The baby was born last night? Who delivered it?'

'I did, of course; I was the only one up.'

'Why the devil didn't you send for me?' Harvey said crossly.

'If I remember correctly you were unable to come round to see the new year in with me because you were sitting at the bedside of a dying man,' Megan reminded him.

'I was. Even so, in an emergency like that I would have come immediately. The man was dying, there was nothing I could do for him except to be with him, to give him some feeling of comfort. He was my very first patient when I started in practice in Liverpool and he lost his wife and two daughters when their home received a direct hit.

'At the time he was working in a munitions factory and knew nothing about it until his shift finished and he came home. He was never the same again after that and I felt I owed it to him to be with him in his final hours. Even so, I would have come straight here if I had known what was going on.'

'Well, we can't turn the clock back and fortunately everything went quite smoothly.'

'Did Nelly help you?'

'No, like Sandra, Nelly was fast asleep and I thought it was better not to wake her since I felt quite sure I could cope on my own.'

'You mean you dealt with everything single-handed?' he said in amazement.

'That's right!'

'Good heavens! You say everything went smoothly? The baby is all right?'

'I've already told you so,' Megan said in an exasperated voice. 'I had a good teacher, remember,' she added with a smile.

Harvey stood up. 'I think I ought to see this girl right away. I'm quite sure you did your best, but just to be on the safe side.'

'Of course.' She knew her voice was sharp but she was stung by his obvious doubt that she had been able to cope with the situation and she sensed his underlying disapproval that she had done so. 'I'll come with you.'

As they went up the stairs Harvey asked, 'Did you get her name?'

'No, I'm afraid I didn't. There was so much to do that I didn't even think to ask her and she didn't volunteer it. I haven't seen her this morning. I told Nelly about what had happened and asked her to look in on the girl and see if she wanted breakfast and asked her to let me know if everything was all right. When she reported that it was I decided to have my own breakfast before I went in to find out her history.'

'Perhaps you'd better go in first, since she knows you,' Harvey suggested when they reached the bedroom door.

'Very well.' Megan pushed open the door and as she did so the girl turned to smile at her. Then she saw Harvey standing behind Megan and slid back down under the bedclothes, pulling them up as high as she could, almost as if she wished to hide.

'Good Lord!' Harvey stared at the girl in the bed who was clenching her bottom lip between her teeth and trying to avoid his eyes.

'Josie Porter,' he said steamily, 'what on earth are you doing here? Does your mother know where you are?'

The girl made no reply, merely shook her head and turned her face away.

'You know her?' Megan said in astonishment.

'Oh yes; her mother is a patient of mine, and so is Josie.'

'You knew she was pregnant?'

Before Harvey could answer Nelly came rushing into the room looking very flustered. 'Sorry to disturb you, but there's a woman downstairs asking if we have her daughter here. She's in a terrible rage; I thought she was going to hit me.'

The next moment Nelly, who was standing in the doorway, was pushed to one side and a very stout woman in her early forties, wearing a bright red coat and with her shoulder-length, dark brown hair pinned back behind her ears, pushed her way into the bedroom.

'What the devil are you playing at running away from home and coming here?' she shouted angrily at the young girl in the bed. 'You're only fifteen, you're still a schoolkid.'

'I've heard all about you and what goes on here from Hilda Heath,' she continued in a loud belligerent voice, turning round to stare accusingly at Megan. 'She told me how you take in young girls and then snatch their babies from them the moment they're born and sell them. Well, you're not doing that with my kid's baby, so don't for one moment think that you are.'

As she stopped to draw breath she suddenly caught sight of Harvey Stott.

'What are you doing here then, Dr Stott? Surely you're not the doctor that Hilda Heath told me about. She said there was a doctor helping out at this place. I never dreamed it was you, of course. I can't believe that you're involved in baby farming like her,' she said scornfully, nodding her head in Megan's direction.

'I think it might be a good idea if you stopped talking for a moment, took a deep breath and calmed down, Mrs Porter,' Harvey said calmly. 'When you've done that and stopped making spurious accusations against Miss Lloyd you should be thanking her for not only taking your daughter in last night but for delivering her baby.'

'You mean my Josie's already had it?'

For a moment Mrs Porter stood mouth agape in surprise. 'Where is it? Let me see it, or have you already sold it?' she demanded angrily.

'Don't go on, Mam.' Josie Porter stretched out a hand towards her mother. 'I've had the baby, but I'm not coming home. You said you were going to get rid of it but I want to keep her, she's so sweet.'

'Ever so sweet,' Mrs Porter said in a mocking voice. 'You're going to keep her! Who's going to keep you, I'd like to know? That cocky young GI who got you pregnant isn't likely to come back here and take care of you now, is he!' she ranted.

'I don't care whether he does or doesn't, I'm keeping her,' Josie repeated stubbornly.

'Kids cost money; they don't live on fresh air, you know. Once she's off the titty then you'll have to buy real food for her, and where are you going to get the money to do that?'

Josie was crying too much to answer. Megan bent down and picked up the baby from the crib at the side of Josie's bed and held her out so that Mrs Porter could see her.

'This is your granddaughter, Mrs Porter. I suggested to Josie that she should be called Dawn because she was born so very early this morning that the dawn had not yet broken.'

Mrs Porter turned to look at the baby and then drew in her breath sharply as she gazed at the tiny face and perfectly formed little hand that lay outside the shawl that Megan had wrapped her in.

'She's lovely, Mam, she's so sweet, I can't give her away, I really can't,' Josie wept.

'So what do you want me to do? Bring her up as me own?'

'Well now, she very well could be yours, Mrs Porter,' Harvey Stott said quietly. 'She certainly looks like a minia-ture of Josie. She has the same dark hair and eyes and even her nose and chin look similar.'

'Bring her up as my own?' Mrs Porter stared at him in utter astonishment, then slowly the frown eased from her face leaving her looking thoughtful.

'Who's to know except you?' Harvey murmured.

Mrs Porter gave him a crafty look. 'Are you going to help me to do it?'

'What do you mean?'

'Well, you would have to keep your mouth shut for a start. I wouldn't want the neighbours to know what sort of game I was playing – it would give rise to too much gossip. I think I could do it though, that's if Josie wants me to.'

'I don't really know what you mean,' Josie said in a puzzled voice.

'What the doctor is saying, luv, is that I tell folks that little Dawn here is my baby and I bring her up as if she was your sister.'

'What about Dad? He'll know that's a lie!'

'No need for him to know the truth,' her mother defended. 'He's been away with the army in the desert for the past six months, so he isn't to know whether it's the truth or not.'

'He'll wonder why you never told him in any of your letters that you were expecting a baby,' Josie reasoned.

'Keeping it as a big surprise for him, wasn't I?' her mother told her with cynical laugh. 'As for the neighbours, well, the size I am these days they don't know if I'm pregnant or not.'

'You mean you're going through with the idea?' Megan asked in amazement.

'What I'll do,' Mrs Porter went on, ignoring Megan and speaking directly to Harvey Stott, 'I'll go away for two or three weeks, and then when I come back I'll be carrying the baby in my arms and no one need know the truth. She's tiny, so folks won't know whether she's three weeks or a month old now, will they?'

'It all sounds very plausible,' Harvey agreed. 'What do you think, Josie?'

'I suppose it's a good idea. I'll be able to see her grow up; I'll even be able to look after her.'

'Oh, you'll be looking after her all right, make no mistake about that,' her mother said with a hearty belly laugh. 'I'm too old and too set in my ways to be bothered getting up in the night when she cries or running round the park playing ball with her when she gets a couple of years older. No, you'll be the one looking after her all right, but she'll be at our house and as long as you keep your mouth shut no one need know the truth, that she's your kid, not mine.'

'Well, Megan, that seems to be settled in a very satis-factory manner,' Harvey Stott said, smiling at her smugly.

'Not quite so fast, you two,' Mrs Porter said. 'If I'm to go along with this plan then you've got to help; you've got to keep our Josie and the baby here until it's time for me to take them home. I want a bit of a holiday, a bit of time to enjoy myself, before I take on the burden of a young baby. Three weeks. Is that all right?'

Harvey and Megan exchanged glances and when Megan nodded her head in acceptance of the idea, Harvey nodded too and turned back to Mrs Porter.

'Very well, we'll keep Josie and the baby here while you take a holiday. Two weeks though, and no longer.'

'Yes, yes, whatever you say,' Mrs Porter agreed impa-tiently. 'You stay here and find out how to look after the baby,' she added as she reached the door and turned and waved a hand to Josie.

Harvey looked apologetically at Megan. 'It is an answer, I suppose,' he murmured.

'They're your patients, so it will be up to you to make sure it works,' she pointed out. 'I hope you realize that it is going to put an extra strain on us keeping Josie and Dawn for another few weeks.'

'Sorry about that,' Harvey said contritely. 'I promise I'll make it up to you… as well as for not being here last night when you needed me.'

Chapter Twenty-Two

'Do you think my mam really is going to keep her promise to let me take my baby home?' Josie Porter asked wistfully the morning her mother was due back from her holiday.

'Well, she said she would,' Megan reassured her as she helped Josie to pack up her few meagre belongings, a face flannel and a couple of spare nappies for Dawn and some baby formula, into a carrier bag to take home with her.

'She should be here any time soon, so then we'll know for certain,' she added as she looked at the clock.

Mrs Porter was already half an hour late and there had been no word from her all the time she had been on holiday, not even a postcard for Josie.

As the day wore on and there was still no sign of Mrs Porter, Josie seemed to be looking more and more miserable. Megan, too, was extremely worried because it certainly did look as though Mrs Porter didn't intend to keep her promise.

Megan wondered what the future would be like for Josie. She hadn't the stamina to bring up the baby single-handed and, as her mother had said, there was very little possibility of the baby's father ever showing up again in Liverpool. Also, Josie was still only fifteen, still a school-girl.

It was after eight o'clock in the evening when Mrs Porter finally came to collect Josie and baby Dawn. By then Harvey had finished at his surgery and was there with them. Like them he was dubious about whether Mrs Porter was going to keep her promise.

'I know I'm late, luv, but don't start moaning at me,' she gasped when Megan opened the door to her. 'I know I look a mess; as if I'd been pulled through a hedge backwards. I've run all the way up Water Street from the Pier Head lugging this damn suitcase because I knew our Josie would probably be bawling her eyes out and thinking that I wasn't coming,' she puffed as she put a brown fibre case down on the floor.

'The boat coming back from the Isle of Man was late leaving Douglas and the delay meant that it had to wait out at the Bar for over an hour before they could get into the usual berth here in Liverpool because there was already a liner there using it,' she explained breathlessly. 'Anyway, I'm here now. All's well that ends well, as they say. Is our Josie all packed and ready to go home?'

'Yes she is,' Megan assured her.

'Don't you want to take a peep at the baby before we go?' Josie asked.

'I'll see all I want to see of your kid when we get home. I'm gasping for a cuppa so get a move on, girl,' her mother said sharply.

'No, come and sit down for a minute, Mrs Porter, and I'll ask Nelly to make us a cup of tea and then we can talk things through,' Megan said, taking her arm and propelling her towards the sitting room. 'You come as well, Josie,' she said over her shoulder as Josie hung back.

'Talk things through! What is there to talk through? I've brought up one bloody kid so I don't need advice on how to bring up another. Anyway, it's Josie you should have been telling what there is to do because she's the one who's going to be looking after it, not me!'

'Are you still going to say that Dawn is your baby and that she's my sister?' Josie asked in a querulous tone of voice.

'Of course I bloody well am! I told you that from the start, before I went on holiday.'

'I know that's what you said then, Mam, but I've been thinking about it ever since, and I don't understand why we can't say that she's mine?' Josie persisted.

'Because you are only fifteen, and if we say it's your baby then we'll have the authorities poking their noses in on our affairs and all sorts of inspectors calling. What's more, some busybody or do-gooder will try and take it away from you and you don't want that now, do you?' Mrs Porter paused as Nelly brought in a tray loaded with cups and saucers, a teapot and a jug of milk and put them down on the coffee table.

'What's more,' she went on when Nelly had left the room, 'because you're still only fifteen the rozzers will probably turn up, say it's a bloody crime or something and take the kid away. Say it's mine and they can't do a damn thing. Now do you understand?'

'I suppose so,' Josie admitted reluctantly.

'Then get that tea down you and shut up. Let's get out of here and on our way,' she added as she drained her cup and put it back on the table.

'I'm not at all sure that we're doing the right thing, Harvey,' Megan said worriedly after they had helped the Porters into a taxi, and Harvey had paid the cabby, and they were waving them goodbye.

'What do you mean?' he asked, putting his arm around her shoulders and squeezing her tight. 'I thought you would be relieved that Mrs Porter kept her promise and finally turned up?'

'Oh, I am pleased about that,' Megan assured him. 'I mean about this business of pretending that Dawn is Mrs Porter's child instead of Josie's.'

'No, I agree it's a ruse that I don't like, but it is the best thing to do for the sake of Josie and the baby. As her mother says, Josie is breaking the law because she is still at school, or she was until Christmas. I don't suppose she will ever go back again. She'll be too busy looking after little Dawn.'

'Don't you think Mrs Porter will take over once they get home?'

'I very much doubt it. She's very lazy at the best of times. She might sit and nurse the baby while Josie does the housework, I suppose. Even then she'll either be eating, smoking or drinking and it probably won't be tea or coffee!'

'You never told me that she drank,' Megan said in alarm. 'That's terrible. Are you sure she's fit to bring up a young baby?'

'Don't worry yourself about them,' Harvey told her, kissing the top of her head affectionately. 'You've done all you can and I'll keep an eye on them. In any case, I'll certainly get a call from them if they have any problems, I don't doubt that for one moment,' he added with a laugh.

Nevertheless, Megan did worry about Josie. Over the next couple of weeks she regularly asked Harvey if he had seen them or had any news of them but he always assured her that they were fine and not to worry about them.

Megan's mind was finally set at rest when one day when she was shopping at Paddy's Market she met Josie, who was pushing an old but well-polished pram.

Josie greeted her enthusiastically and insisted she must stop and look at the baby and Megan was very impressed. Not only was the bedding spotlessly clean but also little Dawn had put on weight and looked the picture of health.

'She is lovely, isn't she?' Josie said, smiling happily as she pulled back the little blanket to display how plump and healthy the baby was.

'She certainly seems to be thriving,' Megan agreed. 'Are you finding that things are working out all right between you and your mother?'

'Oh yes,' Josie answered with a smile. 'We never mention whose baby it is any more. It was so kind of you and Dr Stott to buy this pram for me, it means that I can take Dawn out every day and it's lovely and safe for her to sleep in.'

Her mind set at rest that all was going well, Megan told Harvey that she had seen Josie and baby Dawn and that Josie seemed very pleased with the pram that they had given her. 'That was news to me, of course,' she added with a grin. 'You might have told me.'

'It must have slipped my mind.' He smiled back. 'Anyway, now you've seen her and the baby and you know that all is well perhaps you'll stop worrying about them. I'm sure there are plenty of other things happening at The Haven to merit your attention.'

Harvey was quite right. To start with, Hank had been given weekend leave. Sandra was highly elated because it meant that they had cleared up the infection and that once again he was back on the road to full health.

'Do we have a spare room?' she asked Megan.

'No, we don't have a spare room. Anyway, why do you need a spare room?'

'For Hank, of course! I was hoping he'd be able to stay here at The Haven, but if there isn't a room free then he will have to book into a hotel,' Sandra said in a disappointed voice.

'Why will he have to do that? He can sleep in your room, can't he?'

'I suppose he could, but he really needs to be in a bed, not making do on the sofa. I suppose I could sleep on the sofa and let him have my bed,' she said thoughtfully.

'What on earth do you want to do that for?' Megan said with a broad smile. 'What's wrong with you both sleeping in your bed?'

Sandra looked taken aback. 'You mean sleep together? Here?' she said in astonishment.

'Yes, sleep together! That is precisely what I mean. You already have a child and you are planning to be married as soon as possible, aren't you?'

'Of course we are, you know that perfectly well.'

'Then what's wrong with you sleeping together?'

Sandra looked at her wide-eyed, shaking her head slowly from side to side. 'Haven't you any morals at all, Megan Lloyd?' she said with mock severity. 'Yes, you're quite right, there's no reason at all why we shouldn't sleep together.'

'So that problem's solved, now can we move on to the next one?' Megan asked, trying not to laugh.

When Hank eventually turned up for the weekend he had other news to give them. Following his most recent medical, he had been told that he was no longer fit for active service. As a result of that, he was being sent back to America where in due course he would be employed in a clerical position at a recruiting centre.

'They think that I'll be a good ambassador because I've seen active service, been injured, and come out the other side more or less fine. Isn't that great!'

'It's certainly great that they think you are reasonably fit,' Sandra said, 'but where does that leave us? We'll be separated by the Atlantic Ocean. When will we see each other again?'

'Well, that's the other part of the good news; they say I can take my family with me.'

'They have!' Megan looked amazed.

'So many of our men have married English girls and this proviso is now standard,' Hank explained.

'You can take your family when you go back to America, but you haven't any family,' Sandra said in a bemused voice.

'I have you, and Hope,' Hank said, pulling her into his arms and hugging her. 'I want you to come back to America with me but, of course, in order to do that you will have to be my wife, so we need to be married. How soon can we do that? I only have about a week.'

'That's impossible, it takes months to arrange a wedding,' Sandra said with a groan.

'Not if you get married in a register office,' Megan pointed out.

'I thought your mother persuaded you to have a grand wedding ceremony at your home in North Wales? We were counting on it being a double wedding, if you remember.'

'That was then, this is now,' Hank drawled with a shrug of his broad shoulders. 'It's still wartime, so you have to live for the minute and take opportunities as they come.'

Sandra looked across at Megan helplessly. 'What do you think, Megan?'

'I agree with Hank, and since it's February why don't we settle for St Valentine's Day? That's only four days away.'

'You mean you'll get married on the same day?' Sandra gasped, her eyes wide with astonishment.

'Why not? We always said we would have a double wedding. Well, I'm sure we can do that at the register office.'

'What about your promise to your family?' Sandra asked uneasily.

'They'll understand, and then sometime in the future you can come back from America on holiday and we'll arrange the grand affair at the church in Beddgelert that my mother dreams about, if you still want to do that.'

'Can you do that... get married twice, I mean?' Sandra asked.

'I'm sure we'll be able to have some sort of ceremony,' Megan said airily.

The next few days were so hectic as they made their plans for their weddings that neither of them had time for anything else. They even turned away two girls because they were so caught up in their own affairs.

'I feel awful about that,' Sandra admitted, 'but we really can't take on anything else at the moment. I still have to pack what I want to take to America with me and there are all Hope's things to be sorted out as well.'

'Why don't you ask Nelly to help you? She'll see to all Hope's things and then you can concentrate on what you want to take,' Megan advised.

'Nelly is a treasure, isn't she?' Sandra sighed. 'I don't know how I'm going to manage without her. At least I won't have to worry about her future, though, will I, because she'll be here with you. Are you going to be able to cope here on your own with only Nelly to help out?' she asked worriedly.

'I won't be completely on my own,' Megan replied and smiled. 'Harvey will be here as well.'

'You mean he's going to move in and live here?'

'Of course! He's keeping the flat over the surgery for emergencies; if he's called out in the middle of the night then he can sleep there rather than come back here and disturb the entire household.'

'Lucky devil! You mean he's got a bolthole for when married life becomes too much for him,' Hank teased.

'Are you going to tell your parents what you've decided to do?' Sandra asked Megan.

'No.' Megan shook her head. 'Not much point, is there? It's such short notice. I don't think my mother would come this far anyway and I don't think my father would want to come on his own. No, I'll tell them the next time we go up to see them.'

'They'll be terribly disappointed,' Sandra murmured.

'I'm not so sure. I think my mother may be relieved to know that Harvey has made an honest woman of me. She still has Victorian values, remember, and I'm sure she suspects we may be sleeping together.'

–

Although they had very little time to make any elaborate preparations, Megan and Sandra managed to dress up for the occasion. They both wore smart dresses with short matching coats over them and pretty hats. They looked radiant on what was a rather dull overcast February day.

Hank looked very smart in his American officer's uniform and Harvey chose a dark grey suit with a crisp white shirt and striped grey and red tie.

When the brief ceremony was over, they took a taxi to the Adelphi for a celebratory meal. They toasted each other in champagne and vowed a lifetime of friendship no matter what part of the world they eventually ended up in.

Chapter Twenty-Three

Sandra, Hank and little Hope were up early, their cases packed, ready to leave The Haven on the first stage of their journey to America. They had said their goodbyes to Nelly and were on the point of kissing Megan goodbye when a dispatch rider arrived with a message for Hank.

His face blanched as he read it.

'What's wrong?' Sandra demanded.

'It's not good, you're not going to like this,' he said, shaking his head.

'Why? What's the matter?'

'We're not travelling by boat; they're flying me back. I have to leave immediately.'

'We're flying with you, how thrilling!' Sandra exclaimed excitedly. Then her expression of animation faded. 'They are flying Hope and me out as well?'

'No, I'm afraid you'll have to stay on here in England and wait until they start to ship wives back to America sometime in the future. There are over four thousand wives to be transported but they promise you will be on the very first ship.'

Sandra stared at him blankly. 'I don't want to wait for a ship, I want to come with you. It was a promise they made; they said that your family would be able to accompany you to America when they sent you back. We took it that they meant together.'

'I know, I know.' He ran a hand through his hair. 'It distresses me, sweetheart, just as much as it upsets you, but there is absolutely nothing we can do about it. I'm still a soldier and orders are orders and you simply have to jump-to and carry them out.' He looked at his watch. 'I must go right now, they're sending a car for me immediately. It's probably outside waiting for me now,' he added as he went to look out of the window.

'It is,' he affirmed. 'I'll have to go.'

He took Sandra in his arms and kissed her, wiping away her tears with the ball of his thumb. Then he picked up little Hope and kissed her. 'Look after your mummy,' he told the tiny tot, 'I'll miss you both but I hope to see you again very soon.'

He passed Hope over to Megan. 'Take great care of them both for me,' he said solemnly as he kissed her on the cheek.

Then he picked up his army holdall and he was gone, leaving both women in tears and little Hope crying because that was what everyone else was doing.

Nelly came to see what all the commotion was about and when she heard the news she expressed astonishment that the army could do a thing like that.

'Heartless, that's what it is,' she said shaking her head dolefully.

She whisked Hope off to the kitchen to give her a glass of milk and a biscuit, leaving Megan and Sandra alone.

Megan put an arm around Sandra to try and comfort her but Sandra was so distraught that she wasn't listening to anything Megan said.

'If I have to go by boat then it will take fourteen days to cross the Atlantic,' Sandra snuffled. 'Fourteen days with Hope fretful and no one on board that I know.'

'There will be other wives in the same position,' Megan pointed out.

'If that's supposed to make me feel any better then it doesn't,' Sandra replied with a scowl as she dried her eyes. 'Shut up on a ship for fourteen days with a gaggle of women I don't know and don't wish to know. They'll probably all have screaming kids and it will be sheer hell.'

'Yes, but remember Hank will be waiting for you at the other end,' Megan reminded her.

'Knowing how the army acts, they'll probably send him back to England the day I arrive and then I'll be in a strange country where I know no one.'

'You have the address of Hank's family so you can go direct to them,' Megan said consolingly.

'I don't know them though, do I? They're complete strangers. I might not like them! They may not like me. They may resent me taking Hank away from them. They may not like Hope.'

'Hush, for goodness' sake. You make it sound like a trip to hell,' Megan said. 'I'll go and ask Nelly to make a pot of tea and see if that will make you feel any better.'

Nelly forestalled her. She had hardly finished speaking when the door opened and Nelly came in with a tray carrying not only tea but a couple of rounds of freshly made toast.

'Here, have something to eat and drink and you'll feel better,' she told Sandra. 'Little Hope is in the kitchen eating a biscuit along with Mary. Betsy is keeping an eye on them. Hope's quite happy as can be so don't worry about her. I'll keep her with me in the kitchen until you're feeling calmer.'

'Have you brought in a cup for me, Nelly?'

'Of course I have, Miss Megan. I know you two will want to have a quiet natter about what happens next. Shame to have all your plans turned up and down like this. Have you told Dr Stott yet about the change of plans?'

'Not yet, Nelly, but we will do so as soon as we have talked things through.'

There was a moment's silence after Nelly had left and it was Sandra who spoke first. 'I'm so sorry about this, Megan, Harvey was planning to move in and now this will change everything.'

'I don't see why it has to,' Megan said quickly. 'He's moving into my room, so how will it affect things except that he'll be here for our evening meal, which of course we will all have together.'

'How's he going to feel about that?' Sandra said with a worried frown.

'I don't understand. It's not as though the two of you are strangers. You don't mind him coming to live here, do you?'

'Of course I don't. How will he feel about the new arrangement though? He was expecting to have you to himself when he's finished work at the end of the day.'

'Stop worrying, it will all work out, I know it will.'

'Even so, it's bound to make a difference,' Sandra insisted.

'The only difference you still being here will make is that I will have to reallocate some of the jobs,' Megan told her. 'I take it that you'll still want to play an active part in the running of The Haven?'

'I'd certainly like to. I can hardly sit back and twiddle my thumbs indefinitely and I have no idea when the first boatload of wives will be taken over to America. I really do think it's very bad that they have decided to fly Hank back and not let me go with him because they did promise that he could take his family with him.'

'Yes, but you thought you would be going back by ship, and I suppose it's quite another matter if they're flying him back on a military aircraft,' Megan said.

'Then why couldn't they have left him here until they were ready to transport us both back by sea?' Sandra argued.

'There is a war on, you know, and even though we are hoping that it's going to end very, very soon, we civilians don't really know what has been planned from a military point of view. They obviously have a special job waiting for Hank, one that they couldn't delay. Try and think of it as being so important that he had to return in order that you can go to America as soon as possible.'

'Yes, you're probably right. Draw up a new rota and make sure I have plenty to fill in my time, then I won't be able to think any more about what I'm missing.'

'You are quite happy about Harvey moving in here?' Megan asked anxiously.

'Of course; ignore me. Pretend I'm not here.'

'We might be able to do that as far as you're concerned, but I hardly think we can tell little Hope to ignore her favourite uncle, now, can we?'

'She's probably quite happy to stay here instead of going to America,' Sandra said ruefully.

–

It was the beginning of June before they heard from Hank and then it was only a brief note to say he was in America and working so damned hard he hadn't time to sleep let alone write letters. He hoped Sandra was well and that little Hope wasn't missing him too much. He went on to say there was so much happening but of course he couldn't comment on it and she would understand in time.

'Well, what do you make of that?' Sandra asked as she read the note aloud to Megan.

'It's what we thought, they need him for some very special job; something so important that he's unable to mention what it is he's doing.'

'That's what I took it to mean but I'm puzzled what he means when he says "I will understand in time"?'

Megan shrugged her shoulders. 'We'll just have to be patient, I suppose, and hope he is right and that you will understand what's going on all in good time. We do know that they are contemplating invading Normandy, so perhaps that's what he's talking about.'

Two days later and the news broke about D-Day.

'Do you think this is what Hank meant?' Sandra questioned.

'It seems to be a British enterprise, but perhaps the Americans are involved in some way,' Megan said. 'Let's hope that whoever is behind the invasion, it will be a success and bring an end to this terrible war.'

'They've tried before but it didn't work,' Sandra reminded her. 'You surely haven't forgotten what a disaster it was when they attempted to invade France in 1940 and ended up with the soldiers having to be evacuated from the beaches of Dunkirk in May?'

'Yes, but the Americans joined us after that so this new offensive probably does have something to do with them. Don't forget that since January this year General Eisenhower has been in command of the Allies.'

Megan was right. Eisenhower was in command and on June 5th he gave the go-ahead for Operation Overlord.

Later that day, they heard on the radio that more than 5,000 ships and landing craft carrying troops and supplies left England for the trip across the Channel to France, while more than 1,200 aircraft were mobilized to provide air cover and support for the invasion.

By dawn on June 6th, thousands of paratroopers and glider troops were already on the ground behind enemy lines, securing bridges and exit roads. The amphibious invasions began at 6:30 a.m. The British and Canadians overcame light opposition to capture beaches codenamed Gold, Juno and Sword, as did the Americans at Utah Beach. The American forces faced heavy resistance at Omaha Beach, where there were over 2,000 casualties.

However, by the end of the day, approximately 156,000 Allied troops had been successful and had stormed the Normandy beaches.

Less than a week later, on June 11th, the beaches were fully secured and over 326,000 troops, more than 50,000 vehicles and some 100,000 tons of equipment had landed at Normandy.

For their part, the Germans suffered from confusion in the ranks and the absence of their celebrated commander Rommel, who was away on leave.

Megan and Sandra took it in turns to listen to the news bulletins put out on the wireless. They were anxious not to miss any details of the Allies' progress.

They rejoiced when they heard that Hitler, believing the invasion was merely designed to distract the Germans from an attack north of the Seine River, refused to release nearby divisions to join the counterattack.

'That means they'll have to call for reinforcements from further afield and that will cause considerable delay,'

Harvey pointed out. 'I've also heard that Hitler hesitated in calling for armored divisions to help in the defence.'

The rumours were correct. Moreover, the Germans were hampered by effective Allied air support, which took out many key bridges and forced the Germans to take long detours. There was also efficient Allied naval support, which helped to protect the advancing Allied troops.

In the ensuing weeks, the Allies fought their way across the Normandy countryside in the face of determined German resistance, as well as a dense landscape of marshes and hedgerows. By the end of June, the Allies had seized the vital port of Cherbourg, landed approximately 850,000 men and 150,000 vehicles in Normandy, and were poised to continue their march across France.

Sandra worried constantly in case Hank was involved in some way although Megan kept reminding her that he had been told that he was no longer fit enough for active service.

By the end of August 1944, the Allies had reached the Seine River. Paris was liberated and the Germans had been removed from northwestern France, effectively concluding the Battle of Normandy. The Allied forces then prepared to enter Germany, where they would meet up with Soviet troops moving in from the east.

The Normandy invasion began to turn the tide against the Nazis. Not only was it a significant psychological blow but it also prevented Hitler from sending troops from France to build up his Eastern Front against the advancing Soviet troops.

'Hank was right when he said that in time we would know what he meant,' Sandra said with a smile of relief. 'The Normandy landings really have been the beginning of the end of the war in Europe.'

From then on Sandra and Megan continued to spend every minute they could listening to the news bulletins and discussing them with each other afterwards. Sandra was thrilled to hear that the Americans were dropping bombs on targets in northern France.

Sandra also scoured the daily newspaper for any mention of the American troops and although she said nothing to Megan she began to cut out any references she found and collect them all up together.

The war was on everyone's mind and references about what was going on were everywhere to the exclusion of almost everything else. Prime Minister Winston Churchill spoke to the nation on the wireless and so too did King George VI.

The American president, Franklin D. Roosevelt, told a news conference the invasion did not mean the war was over. He said, 'You don't stop until you walk into Berlin, and the sooner this country realizes that the better.'

'Yes, and the sooner President Roosevelt realizes that there are several thousand GI brides in Britain who are waiting to be transported to America the better,' Sandra added cryptically when for the second time she and Megan listened to the broadcast.

–

It wasn't until the following spring, May 8th, 1945, that the Allies formally accepted the unconditional surrender of Nazi Germany.

At the same time they heard that Hitler had committed suicide a week earlier.

'Evil man!' Sandra exclaimed. 'He's been the cause of all this trouble. It's a pity in one way that he's dead. He should have stood trial and been punished for causing so much misery in the world.'

'Never mind, it's all over now and it won't be long before you hear from the American army to tell you which ship you're going to be on,' Megan assured her.

'I'd like some proper news from Hank first,' Sandra told her. 'I still don't know if he is in America or somewhere else and I want him to be at the dockside to meet me when I do travel to America.'

'Let's hope that after waiting so long you like it when you get there and you're not homesick about leaving Liverpool,' Megan said with a smile.

Chapter Twenty-Four

Megan had looked forward so much to Harvey moving into The Haven that she found it extremely disappointing when she realized that it wasn't working out as well as she had anticipated.

She blamed Sandra. She had thought that Sandra would respect their privacy, but she didn't. When in the evening after they had finished dinner the two of them settled for a quiet chat in the sitting room, within minutes Sandra would join them and stay there, asking Harvey's opinion about the progress of the war and about things in general until it was time for bed.

Megan realized that Sandra and Harvey were very old friends and that they had known each other long before she'd come on the scene, but nevertheless she found it irksome.

She didn't say anything to Harvey because she thought it might make him feel uncomfortable, and she couldn't bring herself to mention it to Sandra, so there was nothing for it but to put up with it.

There were far bigger problems to contend with, she kept reminding herself. There had been so many girls arriving on the doorstep and asking for help that they had been exceptionally busy.

On average four babies a week had been born at The Haven in the last few months. One of the big issues was that the girls arrived not only penniless and with nothing except the clothes they stood up in, but they had no ration books either. This meant that more and more often she had to send Nelly out foraging for food. They had even sent Nelly across to the Wirral to see if there were any blackberries to be found on Bidston Hill. She had come back with enough to make jam to last them for months, although it had meant a couple of weeks with very little sugar for anything else.

Nelly knew where to go for black market butter, margarine, sugar and even meat. Buying on the black market though was expensive and even though Nelly was a first-class haggler she had to pay far more than if they had bought the goods in a conventional way.

Late on Saturday nights, shortly before Paddy's Market was closing, Nelly would go there to see what she could acquire in the way of meat, vegetables and any other produce that wouldn't keep until the market reopened the following week.

Britain's rationing system ensured that no one starved. Indeed, most of the poor were better nourished than in peacetime. But few found anything to enjoy about their fare because it was very basic and monotonous.

Housewives were using grated-up beetroots, apples, potatoes and carrots to eke out the flour and other ingredients when making cakes. Carrot and onion marmalade and rhubarb and onion chutney were some of the other combinations that people tried and relished because it was better than nothing on their bread.

People fantasized about large juicy steaks and longed for asparagus with lumps of golden butter as they chewed on omelettes made with dried egg powder. They longed to have a breakfast fry-up instead of toast with a scrape of margarine.

A further problem Megan was experiencing at The Haven was that many of the regular donations had trailed off, especially since the official end of the war with Germany. People thought that because the war was over there was no need for them to help as much.

It didn't help matters that Sandra was so very disappointed by the continued delay about her being transported to America.

As Megan kept telling her, 1 million American GIs had been stationed in Britain in the two years preceding D-Day, and in all nearly 70,000 British girls had married their GI boyfriends.

'Remember, the GIs proved to be exceptionally popular in Liverpool because of their movie star accents, smart uniforms and money, as well as being generous with items like cigarettes, nylons and sweets.'

'The GIs weren't popular with everyone,' Sandra argued. 'I remember how the local men felt threatened by the Americans with their glamour and wealth.'

'Nevertheless more than sixty thousand US servicemen married British women and they have been promised that their wives and babies will receive free passage to the US, so even though you thought you would be given special treatment, it looks as though you'll have to be patient and wait your turn.'

Although Sandra knew she had no real argument she continued to be discontented because she had to wait, but she did try to hide her resentment over Christmas, and as far as possible, they celebrated in traditional manner at The Haven.

'Here's hoping that 1946 will see us all back to normal,' Harvey said as the three of them drank a toast together on New Year's Eve.

'I'll second that,' Sandra declared gloomily. 'I haven't seen Hank now for so long that we won't know what each other looks like. Hope can't even remember her daddy.'

'She certainly recognizes his picture whenever she sees it,' Megan said quietly. 'Don't worry; you will be reunited some time in 1946.'

'Is that a prophecy or a promise?' Sandra asked mockingly.

Megan was right. In late January 1946 the first batch of war brides were transported to America.

Some 455 British war brides arrived in America on the 4th February; the same day as the first dedicated British war bride ship to leave from Liverpool for Canada arrived in Halifax.

When Sandra eventually received details and papers to enable her to go to America she suddenly became nervous and uncertain about the unknown life that now lay ahead of her.

She bombarded Harvey and Megan with questions about what would she do if she arrived in America and Hank wasn't there to meet her. What would she do if she didn't like his family, or they didn't like her? She worried about how much luggage she could take, about what the weather would be like and what they thought she ought to wear.

She was very concerned that Hope might not settle in a strange country, about the new life she would have to adjust to as well as strange people.

By the time her departure arrived both Harvey and Megan felt drained after they had finally waved her and Hope off.

'I feel like getting drunk, but I'm too tired to do so,' Harvey groaned.

'I know exactly how you feel. I think we should go home and have a quiet night. Think how wonderful it's going to be to be on our own. Let's hope that things are good for Sandra and she settles,' Megan went on. 'I've heard some terrible stories about the first brides to get there and how disappointed they were. Sometimes the husband wasn't the man he had pretended to be, other times it was his family that objected to him having married a British girl.'

'None of those things are likely to happen with Sandra,' Harvey said confidently. 'Hank's a good guy, he wouldn't have been made an officer if he had a shady past.'

'I think the American army was very much like the British army, they were so desperately in need of men they were prepared to take anyone who was willing to sign up,' Megan commented.

'Perhaps, fingers crossed, Sandra will be blissfully happy. I think we should now agree not to mention her name until we get a letter from her telling us what a wonderful place it is and how plentiful everything is and assuring us that she has done the right thing and wouldn't dream of coming back to Britain again.'

'Let's hope she tells us the truth about the place,' Megan murmured, 'because we've promised to go out and see her sometime in the future, and if we are going to take a holiday that is as expensive as that will be then I want a good time when we reach our destination.'

Chapter Twenty-Five

It took Megan some little time to adjust to not having Sandra there to talk over any problems that arose from running The Haven.

She quickly discovered, however, that in some ways Harvey was better than Sandra in this respect. He was positive, decisive and very logical. He saw right to the heart of the matter and dealt with it without quibbling.

Nelly accepted his authority without any trouble. In fact, she was always quick to say 'perhaps we ought to ask Dr Stott' whenever there was a problem, especially when it concerned one of the girls.

In next to no time the wheels were running as smoothly as ever and Megan found that there was an increasing understanding between her and Harvey.

It was a couple of months before they heard from Sandra, but when they did the news was good. She liked America and its people. In particular she was very enthusiastic about their plentiful selection of food.

'Our breakfast each day includes tomato juice, porridge or cereal, scrambled eggs, toast, marmalade and coffee,' she wrote. 'The stores here are full of food, clothes and toys of every description and the prices are even better than we knew in pre-war Britain. I'm looking forward to you paying us a visit as soon as you can so that you can see all these wonderful things for yourselves. Hank's parents are delightful; they have made me so welcome and they absolutely adore Hope. She has really taken to them and they never cease to lavish affection and goodies on her. I shall have to watch out or she will be thoroughly spoiled.'

'There, what did I tell you. Sandra is fine, better off than we are by the sound of it,' Harvey commented. 'We're still rationed for most things even though the war is over.'

The end of the war brought a good many changes even at The Haven. They still had a few pregnant girls coming to them for help because they had nowhere else to go and had been turned out by their families, but there were not nearly so many.

To start with, demobilization meant that soldiers went back to their homes; secondly, unmarried mothers were no longer the lepers they had once been. True, there were a few families who still felt that their unmarried pregnant daughter brought shame and disgrace on them, but the numbers were decreasing rapidly.

There were now so many single-parent families because the menfolk had been killed while on active service that unmarried mothers were no longer regarded as out of the ordinary. The number of girls who had been left stranded when their soldier boyfriends departed had diminished because men were no longer being sent overseas or being billeted in and around Liverpool.

As their numbers declined Megan had more time for her own life. Now that things were gradually getting back to normal she felt that it was time for her and Harvey to have their own family.

He agreed wholeheartedly but, as he sensibly pointed out, it was not feasible as long as she was running The Haven.

'It's not the sort of background I want my children to be brought up in,' he told her.

'Nor do I, but what do we do?'

'We could employ someone to manage The Haven, I suppose, and then we could buy a house somewhere else, preferably in the Wirral.'

'I don't think I can do that, not without Sandra's permission.'

'Why not? She has her own life now, I can't see her coming back to run the place.'

'No, I know that, but it is her house, remember.'

For a moment Harvey looked taken aback. 'I'd forgotten about that!' he admitted. 'Well, we'll simply have to write to her and ask her what she wants us to do about it.'

Although she agreed with him, it took Megan several weeks before she could bring herself to take his advice. It was more than simply refusing to take in any more girls and then closing down The Haven; there was Nelly to be considered.

When she did finally write to Sandra and explain all this, it sounded so cold and callous that she tore the letter up and tried again. In the end she asked Harvey to read what she had written and see what he thought.

He made one or two minor changes but he more or less agreed with everything she'd said. While they waited with trepidation for Sandra's reply Harvey insisted that they should consider taking their long-delayed holiday.

'Let's go and visit your family in North Wales,' he suggested. 'It's a long time since we saw them and your mother must be longing to see you.'

Megan agreed, and they decided that the moment the girls now at The Haven left they would go.

'Don't take any more girls in for the next couple of weeks, and remind Nelly so that she doesn't either,' Harvey instructed.

Chapter Twenty-Six

Megan took a deep breath as they reached Beddgelert. The grass seemed to be greener, the sky more blue and the mountains were like welcoming arms waiting to greet her.

Her parents were waiting to greet them and even Harvey seemed visibly to relax as he took in the mountain air and the glorious scenery.

'I can't wait to show you all the wonderful views and places there are around here,' Megan enthused.

'I thought you'd already shown me all the local sights when we came before,' Harvey said with a laugh.

'No, I really only took you to see Gelert's grave, from which Beddgelert gets its name,' she told him.

'Let's see, was that the grave of the faithful dog that belonged to Llewellyn the Great? The dog that was covered in blood and his master thought the dog had killed his little son but in fact the dog had killed a wolf that had attacked his small son. Right?'

Megan looked at him in surprise. 'Wow! You remembered it.'

'Yes, of course, and also the fact that he watered the grave with his tears, according to the poem by W. R. Spencer. "And now a gallant tomb they raise/ With costly sculpture decked/ And marbles covered with his praise/ Poor Gelert's bones protect."'

'Very impressive,' Megan said admiringly.

'Well, you were so determined that I should pay attention that I was hardly likely to forget, and when I got back home I checked it out to make sure you had the story correct,' he told her with a grin.

'Well, I'm glad you remembered, but there are other things I want to show you. There are lakes, mountain passes and wonderful views that will all stay in your mind forever. As well as climbing Moel Hebog, like we did last time, you must visit Llyn Glaslyn, the lake in a cwm on the eastern slopes of Snowdon from which our ancestors took the name for our house Yr Glaslyn.'

Megan took Harvey there the very next day. As they reached the lake the aspect opened up and was so beautiful, especially on a sunny day with the lake sparkling in the sunshine, and the distant mountain as a backdrop, that Harvey agreed it was something he would never forget.

A brisk walk up the slopes of Mynydd Sygyn gave them even better views of Llyn Glaslyn.

'Llyn Glaslyn translates to English as Blue Lake,' Megan told him.

Harvey nodded; he was gazing towards the summit of Snowdon, which loomed large to the north of where they were standing. The vista of purples and greens of the heather and bracken of summertime covered the surrounding hills.

When they reached the top of the hill close to the fingerposts that guided them on their way, Megan suggested they stop and have the picnic she had brought with them.

Feeling refreshed, they set off for Cwm Bleiddiad afterwards and very soon were descending the cwm. Here, the landscape was softer, with grassland, bracken, and rushes interspersed with rocky outcrops.

Harvey stopped to admire the view of the Glaslyn Estuary.

'What's all this?' he asked as they came across metal stanchions and the cable terminus gear.

'That's all that remains of the Cwm Bychan copper mine, where mining for ore started in the early eighteenth century,' Megan told him. 'We are walking among reminders of Wales's industrial heritage. Nearby are reminders of Wales's more recent pastoral heritage,' she added as she pointed out a number of sheepfolds that appeared to be part of the rock-strewn landscape.

They took a path that ran alongside a small stream which was forded by large stepping-stones. It made a pleasant place to stop for another break and enjoy the view of the valley below.

When they resumed their walk Megan took track leads through ancient woodlands before joining the trail that headed north through the Aberglaslyn Pass alongside the Afon Glaslyn River.

'Keep an eye open now for we are in the woodlands for Pen-y-Groes the eighteenth-century cottage that was the birthplace of Richard Owen, the Welsh bard known as Glaslyn who lived there in the nineteenth century,' Megan told him. 'Within the pass the trail is squeezed between the river and the track of the Welsh Highland Railway that runs from Caernarvon in the north to Porthmadog in the south.'

'Are you sure we're on the right road?' Harvey asked anxiously.

'I know it's not too easy to walk along here but it is worth it to see the clear waters of the Glaslyn tumbling over the boulder-strewn riverbed,' Megan explained.

On leaving the gorge Megan took a route that led across the river and entered a wide flat landscape leading them to back to Beddgelert.

'Tomorrow I want to take you to the village of Capel Curig which lies to the east of the Snowdonia,' she told Harvey.

'Hold on, I'll be on my knees if you walk me so far tomorrow,' he grumbled.

'Today is only the start; there's half a dozen other mountain walks I want to show you as well as some spectacular waterfalls, but they are at their best after rain.'

'We're only here for a week,' Harvey protested. 'What are you trying to do? Walk me off my feet!'

'I'd also like to make you walk to the top of Snowdon, although if you're very good we could go up on the train and walk down.'

'Why not take the train up and also come back by train?' he suggested with a grin.

Megan considered the idea for a moment. 'Well, maybe,' she agreed reluctantly.

When Lewis Lloyd heard of their plans, he frowned. 'If you do all that sightseeing then there'll be no time for me to show Harvey over the slate mine. I rather think it was something he said he would really like to do,' he added, looking questioningly from Megan to Harvey.

'Yes, yes, I would very much like to find time to visit the slate mine,' Harvey confirmed.

'I do understand,' Megan said, 'but there are so many places I want to show Harvey and I know we have very little time to pack it all in.'

'Then surely the answer is to stay here longer,' her father suggested.

'We'd really like to do that, but we're waiting for a letter from Sandra about The Haven.'

Her father frowned. 'Why? Is the place in trouble?'

Megan hesitated, then she said, 'Not really, but we are wondering about the future.'

'I don't understand what you mean?' Bronwyn said in a bewildered voice. 'You are still happy there, aren't you?'

'Yes, quite happy for the moment,' Megan said reassuringly.

'What do you mean by "for the moment"?' her father asked sharply.

'Well, we want to start a family, our own family and—'

'You can't do that living where you are,' her father said sternly. 'That's no place for my grandchildren to be brought up in. The war is over, you've done your bit, it's time now for you to pack up and move away from Liverpool's dockland area. Don't you agree, Harvey?'

'Yes, I do think that,' Harvey said quietly. 'I want for us to have a home on the Wirral, somewhere either near the sea or in pleasant countryside. It may not be as picturesque as Beddgelert but I can assure you there are some lovely places even in Wallasey that overlook both the Mersey and the sea and have a wonderful view of the Welsh mountains in the distance.'

'Yes, well, that certainly sounds more civilized,' Lewis Lloyd admitted. He turned to look at Megan. 'What about you then? Do you agree with what Harvey has in mind?'

'Yes, I'm in full agreement with that plan, just as soon as we can make arrangements to leave The Haven.'

'What's the problem about leaving the place? I don't suppose it's the sort of business you can sell, but you can sell the house and put whatever you get for it towards the house you want on the Wirral.'

'It's not quite as simple as that, Father,' Megan told him. 'You seem to have forgotten that it's not my house but Sandra's, and she's now living in America.'

'I see. Is that proving to be something of a problem?'

'We have written to her explaining the situation and asking what she wants to do about the premises,' Harvey explained. 'At the moment we are waiting for a reply and until we get that we can't do anything.'

'So this business of walking from one mountain to the next is more or less to take your mind off the future.'

'Yes, in a way I suppose it is,' Megan admitted.

'We know what we want to do and we will do it eventually but we must take Sandra into consideration and find out what she wants us to do about the ownership of The Haven,' Harvey added.

'I think that's pretty obvious,' Lewis Lloyd said in a businesslike voice. 'You must sell the property. She's hardly likely to want to keep it on when she's living so far away now, is she?'

'There is one problem over that,' Harvey explained. 'You see, it's also home to Nelly, who at one time was housekeeper to Sandra's family and who has helped us in running the place ever since Megan and Sandra opened it up to pregnant girls.'

'Since Nelly has been with Sandra and her family all her life we can hardly turn her out when she has nowhere to go and no family of her own,' Megan added.

'Have you considered taking her with you? When you move you will need servants of some sort,' Lewis murmured.

Megan and Harvey exchanged glances. 'We aren't really sure,' Megan said slowly. 'You see, she is in her mid-sixties and I rather think if we are going to start a family we need someone much younger than that to help around the house and to assist in bringing up our children.'

'Of course you do,' her mother said firmly. 'Make a fresh start, Megan, put all that business behind you. If you have this old woman living with you, then she'll be forever reminding you of The Haven.'

'I think I'll leave you and your mother to talk about such matters, Megan. She knows more about the domestic side of life than I do,' Lewis Lloyd stated. He turned to Harvey, 'Come on, I'll show you around the slate mine while I still have the chance.'

Chapter Twenty-Seven

Harvey found his tour of the slate mine a very interesting experience. On the way there Lewis related something of the history of the slate trade.

'Slate has been used as a building and roofing material since Roman times,' he told Harvey. 'Not long ago they found a Roman fort roofed with tiles; and they also claim that the Romans used slate for flooring as well.

'The first record of slate quarrying in this neighborhood was in 1413. Records show that in the sixteenth century the local house, Plas Aberllefenni, was roofed in slates from this very quarry,' he said proudly.

'I suppose transport problems would have meant that the slate was usually used fairly close to the quarry,' Harvey observed.

'True, but there was some transport by sea. Not so very long ago a wooden ship carrying finished slates was discovered in the Menai Straits and they thought it dated from the sixteenth century,' Lewis Lloyd told him.

'They'd transported the slate from the mine to the nearest port,' Harvey murmured.

'That's right!' Lewis Lloyd nodded. 'In the early days the slates were carried to the ports by packhorses, and later by carts. This was sometimes done by women, the only female involvement in what was otherwise an exclusively male industry,' he emphasized. 'Did you know, in 1898, a workforce of seventeen thousand men produced half a million tons of slate.'

'That sounds quite incredible!'

'I quite believe it to be true,' Lewis Lloyd told him. 'The first Monday of every month was "bargain letting day" when these agreements were made between men and management. The men had to pay for their ropes and chains, for tools and for services such as sharpening and repairing. Subs or advances were paid every week, everything being settled up on the "day of the big pay". If conditions had not been good, the men could end up owing the management money. There were other grievances too, including unfairness in setting bargains and disputes over days off.'

Lewis Lloyd paused and looked apologetically at Harvey. 'You must be fed up with listening to me, but once I get on the subject of the quarry, I could go on forever.'

'It's all been very interesting,' Harvey assured him. 'What I don't understand is why is the slate trade now in the doldrums?'

'Well, the First World War saw a great reduction in the number of men employed in the industry. Now this war has had a similar effect,' Lewis Lloyd said, shaking his head. 'It has already led to the closure of many smaller quarries, and competition from other roofing materials, particularly tiles.'

'Is that because the industry hasn't kept up with the times and made use of modern technology?' Harvey asked.

Lewis shook his head. 'No, the use of electric saws and other machinery has reduced the hard manual labour involved in extracting the slate, but unfortunately it produces much more slate dust than the old manual methods.'

'Which has resulted in more men being affected by silicosis,' Harvey said thoughtfully.

'That's right. Also the work is dangerous in other ways, with the blasting operations responsible for many deaths. The number of men employed in the slate industry in North Wales has dropped by more than half since the war started and now there are fewer than twenty quarries still open compared with forty before the war. Demand for slate is dropping as tiles are increasingly used for roofing, and imports from countries such as Portugal, France and Italy are increasing.'

'Surely there's been some increase in demand for slates to repair bombed buildings,' Harvey commented.

'True, but once they've been repaired, what then?'

'We've been told by the government that there'll also be a lot of new homes built in the near future. Won't slates be needed for those?'

'No, it's more likely they'll use tiles rather than slates,' Lewis said in a contemptuous voice.

He stopped the car at the quarry entrance. 'Here we are. I'll show you round and you can form your own opinion about the future of the business,' he said as they got out of the car and walked towards the entrance.

'I haven't mentioned anything to my wife about the state of things in the industry so we won't discuss it when we get home,' he said in an authoritative voice. 'There's no need for her to worry about it. I shall be retiring quite soon. If I can sell the mine I will, otherwise if the mine has to close it will mean all the workforce will have to be stood down.'

Chapter Twenty-Eight

Megan and Harvey arrived back at The Haven to find a letter from Sandra waiting for them. Megan read it while Harvey mixed a drink for them both. When he came back into the sitting room she took her glass from him and handed the letter to him without a word.

Megan watched his face as he placed his glass down on the table and read the letter. Taking a sip of her own drink she waited for his comment.

'Sandra doesn't seem to be very pleased at the idea of us all packing in the work we've been doing here at The Haven, does she?' Harvey said with a sigh as he put the letter to one side and picked up his drink.

'No, but we don't want to have our family here, and by the sound of it my parents aren't in favour of us doing so either.'

Harvey took a long drink and then replaced his glass on the table. 'So what are we going to do?'

Megan shook her head. 'I really don't know.'

'I suppose we could suggest to Sandra that we simply move out and leave Nelly living here to take care of the place until she comes home? Nelly wouldn't be completely on her own because Betsy Hagan and her little girl are still here and likely to remain here as they have nowhere else to go.'

'That sounds fine,' Megan agreed, 'but what about the running costs of the place? There wouldn't be any rent to pay, but there would be rates as well as heating and lighting and, of course, they would need money for food as well. Where are they going to get that from until Sandra makes other arrangements?'

'Do you think if Betsy could get a job they would be able to manage on her wages?' Harvey suggested.

'What about little Mary?' Megan asked.

'Well, Nelly could look after Betsy's little girl while Betsy was out at work.'

Megan passed a hand across her forehead pushing her hair away. 'It's a possibility, I suppose, but would Sandra agree to that?'

'I don't see why not. Anyway, Sandra will probably come home for a holiday at some time and then she could take a decision about the house and about Nelly's future depending on how well they were managing.'

'Yes, I suppose it is one solution,' Megan said thoughtfully.

'There's only one way to find out,' Harvey told her as he drained his glass, 'and that's to write to Sandra and ask her.'

It was nearly three weeks before they had an answer from Sandra. She didn't for one moment think that Betsy could earn enough to keep herself, her child and Nelly and anyway it wouldn't be fair on any of them.

'So what is the answer?' Harvey asked when Megan gave him the letter to read.

'I don't know, but we've got to do something and do it pretty promptly. Now that we've decided to give up using The Haven as a shelter for girls in trouble we also have to let the Charity Commission know that we have done so.'

'That means we can no longer accept donations!'

'Exactly! They've been a lifesaver for us but once they stop coming in then we'll have to pay all the bills ourselves.'

'Well, I suppose we can afford to do that,' Harvey assured her.

'I know, but only if we stay on here. We want to get our own home and we don't want to stay in Liverpool.'

'What did Sandra live on before this place became The Haven?' Harvey pondered. 'I've been trying to remember, but I can't.'

'Well, she told me that her mother had run this place for years as a sort of guest house for people waiting for a boat.'

'Of course! I remember now. It was a sort of high-class, halfway stopping place for people who had arrived in Liverpool from other parts of Britain and were waiting for a boat and either didn't like staying in hotels or couldn't afford them. A top-of-the-range, short-stay boarding house. Well, we can't go back to doing that again, can we!'

'It's not my idea of a future career,' Megan told him with a scathing laugh. 'Anyway, at the moment there aren't all that many people sailing away on liners for exotic holidays like there were before the war.'

'No, I agree. It might be the answer though.'

'What on earth do you mean?' Megan asked, raising her eyebrows.

'I was wondering if Nelly would be able to run it, with Betsy's help, of course. If that was possible then it would leave us free to find a house somewhere on the Wirral.'

'It is an idea,' Megan agreed, 'but I'm not at all sure that Nelly would be capable of running a place like that on her own?'

'I don't see why not,' Harvey argued. 'After all, she was living here with Sandra's mother, so she was probably involved in all that was happening here long before Sandra took over. In all probability she knew more about how to run the place than Sandra did. Anyway, there's only one way to find out and that is to ask her.'

'You mean ask Nelly?'

'That's right.'

Megan shrugged. 'Will you do it or shall I?'

'We'll do it together,' Harvey said firmly. 'We'll put the idea to Nelly, and then if she's in agreement we'll also explain to Betsy what's happening and tell her that she can either stay on here and help Nelly or else find herself somewhere else to live.'

'That's rather harsh, isn't it?' Megan protested.

'No, not at all. She has a good home here and she knows it. She also knows that her little girl thinks of Nelly as her grandmother and that she will be heartbroken if they move away. Betsy has had it easy here for several years now and it's time she worked for her keep.'

'I think she does do her fair share of the chores and is a great help to Nelly as it is.'

'In that case then it will be no hardship at all for her to help out a bit more. The two of them should be able to run a bed-and-breakfast place without too much effort.'

'I don't know,' Megan said dubiously.

'You'll be here to advise and guide them at the beginning, and they'll soon pick up the routine,' Harvey said confidently.

When they spoke to Nelly about it she stared from one to the other in silence, her hands plucking nervously at her skirt.

'I don't know what to say,' she said at last as all three of them sat there waiting for her to make a decision.

'Are you willing to give it a try?' Harvey asked impatiently.

'Well, is it what Miss Sandra wants me to do?' Nelly asked.

'She wants us to sort out some future for this place,' Harvey told her before Megan could speak. 'At the moment she doesn't want to sell it because that would leave you without a home. She would like to be able to keep a base here in England so that whenever she wants a holiday she has somewhere to stay. Now, if you say you will stay on and run this place like you used to do when she was here, before it was turned into The Haven, then we will write and tell her that and it will put her mind at rest.'

'If it's what you think she wants and it's going to keep her happy then yes, of course I'll do it,' Nelly said with a smile.

'Good! That's settled then.'

'Mind you, I'm not as young as I was back in those days,' Nelly warned them. 'I'm wondering if it's all going to be too much for me,' she added with a deep sigh.

'I am quite sure you will manage perfectly well,' Harvey assured her. 'Remember, you will have Betsy here to help you. We haven't said anything to her as yet, but if you are in agreement then that's the very next thing we'll do. We'll put it to her that she can go on living here rent-free and have all her meals and those for her little girl provided without having to pay a penny piece if she is prepared to help you to run the place. Now, how does that sound to you?'

'I'm sure she will be happy about that, except...' Nelly paused and looked worried. 'Except that her little girl keeps growing out of her clothes and shoes. I've been buying them but I've used up most of my savings.' She stopped again, her face troubled.

'Very well, we'll even agree to pay you both a small regular wage so that Betsy has money of her own to buy things for her little girl and to buy her own clothes and so on. Now does all that help you to make your mind up, Nelly?'

'It all sounds almost too good to be true. What worries me though is how do I go about getting people to come and stay here? Miss Sandra saw to all that side of things, and also to keeping the records and the books. I wonder if Betsy could be trained to do that sort of thing?' she said thoughtfully.

'I am sure she could, but don't let it worry you. At the start Megan will be here to do all that sort of thing and she will always be in the background ready with advice and guidance. All we want from you is an agreement that you will give it a trial. If, after the first three months, you really feel that it is all too much for you then we'll have to think of some other way of keeping the house and providing you with somewhere to live.'

'Yes, I suppose it is worth a try,' Nelly said rather reluctantly. 'I don't suppose it will be the same as it was in the old days, but I'll give it a go. Yes, you can tell Miss Sandra that I'll do my best. Let me know what she says.'

'Of course we will, Nelly, and I can tell you now she'll be delighted. It will be a load off her mind to know that her home here in England is in good hands and that you are doing the very thing she wanted most.'

It took an exchange of several letters to convince Sandra that this would be a suitable future for The Haven. Both Megan and Harvey wrote very detailed letters about how they would go about setting up the change of direction and assuring Sandra that they would retain a full interest in how it was organized and run even after they had managed to find a separate home of their own.

As soon as they received the go-ahead from Sandra, they arranged to have The Haven redecorated throughout from top to bottom before they placed a single advert in one of the local papers.

'I was wondering if we should ask Jennifer White to handle this side of the organization?' Megan mused when, after two weeks, they had received only a trickle of applicants.

'That's a splendid idea!' Harvey agreed. 'Remember her father is connected with the shipping lines, so she probably knows people she can contact personally at some of the shipping companies and they can recommend people to stay here.'

A month later and business was in full swing. Betsy took to it like a duck to water. She had always helped Nelly in a general sort of way but now she was the one who was taking control most of the time while Nelly looked after her little Mary.

'It's all working a treat,' Nelly reported when the trial period came to an end and once again the three of them had a meeting to decide about the future.

'Young Betsy is a real treasure. She's taken so much of the work off my hands that I've never had such an easy time.'

'Well, when she's doing the work you are looking after her little girl. Doesn't that tire you out?' Megan asked.

'Bless you, no. That child is a little angel. She's as good as gold; in fact she behaves better when she's with me than she does when she's with her mother,' Nelly added with a proud smile.

'I suppose that in next to no time Mary will be off to school,' Megan said thoughtfully when she congratulated Betsy on how well things were going.

'Nelly will miss her when that happens,' Betsy said. 'Still, it will give her more time to rest, and walking Mary to school and picking her up again in the afternoon will give Nelly any exercise she might need.'

They had a fairly small number of bookings over Christmas and Megan sounded both Nelly and Betsy out to see if they thought they could manage on their own.

'I would like to go home,' Megan explained. 'I haven't spent Christmas with my family since I've been married. It means we would be away for about a week.'

'We would like you to be here to celebrate with us,' Nelly told her, 'but we understand. Of course you and Dr Stott must do what you think best. I'm sure your parents will be delighted to have you both there with them.'

'We'll leave you a telephone number and if anything goes wrong or you are concerned about anything you have only to ring this number and you can talk to us. Understand?'

'We'll all have dinner together before we go and that includes little Mary, I'm sure she'd love to stay up late for one night.'

'I'm sure she would,' Nelly chuckled.

Their meal the night before Megan and Harvey left for Beddgelert was a real celebratory one. There were presents for Nelly and Betsy from Megan and Harvey and three for little Mary. As well as a cuddly doll, and a little pram, Megan had bought her a beautiful little winter outfit. The little red coat had its own fur-trimmed hood, and to go with it, matching red gloves and warm little red boots that were also trimmed with fur.

Mary insisted on putting them on right away and when it was time for her to go to bed she was in tears because it meant she would have to take her new little boots off.

Chapter Twenty-Nine

They reached Beddgelert mid-afternoon and the surrounding countryside had never looked lovelier. Even Harvey gave a long low whistle of appreciation as they stood outside Yr Glaslyn looking round. The tops of the mountains in the Snowdon range glistened white with snow; Moel Hebog towered over them like a benign guardian. There were a few sheep huddled together, nibbling at the sparse grass on the lower slopes, but most of the flocks had been taken inside, sheltered from the winter weather.

Yr Glaslyn stood grey and solid as a fortress as it had done for the past 200 years. There was a silence; it was almost like standing in the middle of a picture, Harvey thought.

'I'll never understand how you gave up all this to come to Liverpool,' he remarked wryly.

'I wanted to do my bit for the war effort,' Megan said softly. 'And if I hadn't come to Liverpool then we would probably have never met,' she added after a moment's silence.

'True!' He pulled her into his arms and kissed her. 'Life wouldn't be the same for either of us, would it, if we hadn't met?'

She didn't answer, merely moved closer to him and surrendered her lips to his demanding kiss.

'Come on, let's get indoors before we freeze to death,' Harvey murmured as he released her.

Lewis and Bronwyn Lloyd were expecting them and the heavy oak door was opened the moment they touched the bell pull. Inside, it was warm and welcoming with a fire glowing in the wide entrance hall and another huge log fire in the spacious sitting room.

'Come in, come in,' Lewis boomed. He held out a hand to shake hands with Harvey and enfolded Megan in a bear hug.

Bronwyn came rushing forward to kiss her daughter and to hold out her hand to Harvey, who raised it to his lips and kissed it.

A hot mulled wine was waiting for them and Lewis pressed a glass into their hands even before they could take their coats off.

Megan gave a sigh of sheer happiness as she looked round the room. A huge Christmas tree, covered in tinsel and baubles that she remembered from her childhood, stood in one corner of the room. On it hung numerous small ornamental decorations that she remembered making herself and which her mother had carefully stored away each year when the tree was dismantled.

'Now we're eager to hear all your news, but not until after we've had dinner,' her mother told them. 'Everything is ready. I'm sure you are both starving, so don't wait until you've finished your drinks, bring them into the dining room with you.'

Chicken soup was followed by lamb cutlets and roast vegetables. Megan felt almost too full to eat the delicious apple tart and cream that followed.

Dinner over, they returned to the sitting room and relaxed in front of the log fire to have their coffee. Lewis and Bronwyn sat in armchairs on either side of the fire and Megan and Harvey on the settee which had been drawn up to face the fire.

'Now, what's happening about The Haven?' Lewis Lloyd demanded as soon as the coffee was served. 'Have you decided to sell the place and get away from Liverpool?' he asked hopefully.

'Not exactly,' Megan told him. 'We did tell you that the house belongs to Sandra and we had to wait and see what she wanted us to do.'

'Surely she doesn't want to keep the place if she's living in America?' he said with a frown.

'You're forgetting there is the question of finding a home for Nelly, an old retainer who has been with the Peterson family all her life,' Harvey said.

'Ah, yes, I remember you mentioned her. So what is happening?'

Megan told him about their plan to turn it back into a short-stay boarding house which was what it had been before it became The Haven.

'I see, and does your friend Sandra agree with this?'

'She seems to quite like the idea, doesn't she?' Megan said, looking at Harvey for confirmation.

'Yes,' he agreed, 'and so does Nelly.'

'That doesn't mean you are going to stay on there though, I hope?' Bronwyn said worriedly.

'For the moment we'll go on living there, until we find a place of our own in the Wirral,' Harvey stated. 'We are training Nelly to run it, though with help from a youngish girl called Betsy and with Jennifer White to take care of the books, records and promotion of the place.'

'Jennifer White? You mean Joshua's daughter?' Lewis said in surprise.

'Yes, she's married now and living on the Wirral, but both her husband and her father have their offices in Old Hall Street, which is only a stone's throw from Chapel Gardens. She says it's no problem because she's often at their offices so she can always come and collect the books or send someone for them.'

'Well, that certainly sounds sensible, but we both want to see you away from the Scotland Road area, you know that. It's not the sort of district we want you living in, so hurry up and find that house in the Wirral,' Bronwyn urged.

'Have you any idea exactly where you want to live?' Lewis Lloyd asked. 'I believe there are some quite good properties around West Kirby, Hoylake and Heswall.'

'There are,' Harvey agreed, 'but that's rather a long way for me to travel each day to my surgery in Liverpool.'

'Perhaps you should move to another practice,' Lewis suggested.

Harvey didn't answer; he merely gave an almost imperceptible shrug.

'So where are you looking then?' Lewis persisted.

'Wallasey. My family lived in Warren Drive until their house was bombed. There are some very nice properties in that area. I've already been in touch with one or two estate agents and I have my name on their list in case anything comes up.'

Lewis Lloyd nodded but said nothing.

'I don't think I've ever been to Wallasey,' Bronwyn Lloyd murmured.

'I like it there,' Megan said quickly. 'There's a lovely promenade from New Brighton right up to Harrison Drive, and as you walk along it you can look across the

Mersey and see Liverpool on the other side and it's like a different world.'

'Well, most parts of Wallasey are certainly better than around Scotland Road,' her father stated. 'New Brighton is to be avoided. It's all right if you're young and want to spend your time on the sand, or paddling, or going on rides and roundabouts in the fairground. During the day it's so packed with trippers that you can't move. But at night, I'm told, Victoria Road and the pier are full of drunks. Most of them travel over on the ferry from Liverpool and then the police bundle them back again on the last boat. Regardless of where they come from.'

'That is certainly not the area where I am looking,' Harvey said quietly. 'As I mentioned before, I am looking for a property in the Warren Drive, Harrison Drive area. It's very quiet there and nearby is a first-class golf links.'

The subject was dropped and Mrs Lloyd began to tell them about the party they had planned for Boxing Day evening.

'We've invited all your old friends,' she told Megan. 'It will give them a chance to meet Harvey and to catch up with all your news. I'll show you the list after breakfast so that you know who'll be coming. I've also invited some cousins you haven't seen since you were quite small and they will be staying here overnight.'

The next morning it was snowing and the world outside Yr Glaslyn looked even more picturesque than it had done the night before.

'Now don't go walking anywhere and certainly don't go up any of the mountains,' Lewis Lloyd warned them. 'In fact, it might be better if you didn't venture out at all today. The snow looks inviting but it's damn slippery underfoot.'

'I promise we won't do anything risky, but I thought a Christmas Day walk as far as Beddgelert would be nice,' Megan told them. 'Harvey has never really seen the village, only passed through it when we've been coming here or when we've been setting off for a walk.'

Christmas Day passed off in a lovely haze of delicious food and happy companionship. They exchanged the small presents they'd brought with them and retired early that evening in preparation for the party the next day.

The Boxing Day evening event was well attended and a great success but by the end Megan found she had talked so much that she was quite hoarse.

When they were sitting quietly afterwards having a cup of hot chocolate before they went to bed, Harvey asked, 'Are you quite sure you want to move to Merseyside?'

'Of course I do! Whatever makes you ask that?'

'You have so many friends here that I wondered.'

'No, I have flown the nest, and although I love coming back here, and I always will, I think it was time for me to spread my wings. Anyway,' she added in a teasing voice, 'that's where you are proposing to live, so of course I want to be there.'

They planned to go back to Liverpool on New Year's Day and so they spent New Year's Eve quietly with Lewis and Bronwyn.

As midnight struck they raised their glasses in a toast to 1947 and wished each other a happy new year.

'I hope 1947 really will see you two settled in a home of your own,' Lewis said ponderously. 'It's time you settled down, Megan.'

'Yes, Father,' she answered primly. 'I don't know about settling down though; I rather think I will be embarking on a new career.'

He frowned. 'What do you mean by that?'

'Yes, my dear, what do you mean?' her mother echoed.

'I'm going to have a baby,' Megan said softly.

'You're what!'

The outburst came from Harvey. He grabbed her by the shoulders and stared at her in surprise. 'When?'

'Sometime in June, so you'd better hurry up and find that house,' she told him smiling.

He pulled her into his arms, kissing her hair, hugging her close, staring at Lewis and Bronwyn with surprise written all over his face. 'I had no idea,' he said lamely to Lewis and Bronwyn.

'Well, I never thought I would be celebrating the coming of a grandchild,' Lewis murmured, shaking his head in disbelief.

'A baby,' Bronwyn repeated. 'Oh dear, what a calamity!'

'Calamity? Whatever do you mean, Mother? Don't you want to be a grandmother?'

'Yes, of course I do, but you and Harvey aren't properly married.'

'Yes, we are; we married in a register office over two years ago.'

'That's not really being married; that's only a civil requirement to make it legal for you to live together,' her mother told her sharply. 'What about the wedding you said you would have at the church here in Beddgelert?'

'Well, we are married; we can hardly get married again, now, can we?' Megan laughed, trying to bring an end to the discussion.

'You could have a service there. I think it's called "a blessing" or something when you renew your vows to each other.'

'The important thing now is the baby,' Lewis boomed as he refilled their glasses. 'Come on, let's drink a toast to the new baby, to the new life ahead for all of us.'

'It will be so wonderful to have children running around Yr Glaslyn again,' Bronwyn sighed. 'The house sometimes seems to be dead, it's so very quiet here when we are on our own.'

'You won't be saying that when we come next Christmas,' Megan told her. 'There'll be a lusty six-month-old baby to keep you busy.'

–

'You kept that a secret,' Harvey told her later that night when they were alone. 'Why didn't you tell me?'

'I wanted to be quite sure. I thought at first I was imagining it, and that it was the result of all the stress because of all the changes we were making at The Haven.'

'Well, it's wonderful news,' he told her, 'and as you say I really will have to make sure that we have a house to move into before the baby is born. The spring is always a good time for buying a house because people are on the move. They've made their plans for the new year and so often these include a change of job or home or both. We'll find something suitable for us, don't you worry.'

'I'm not worrying; I'm leaving all that to you,' Megan told him with a broad smile.

'This will affect the future of The Haven, of course,' Harvey pointed out a few minutes later. 'You really must let Sandra know that we are definitely moving out within the next month or so, and so she must let us know if she's happy for Nelly to carry on running it. Once you have the baby you won't have much time to do anything to help her run it, and anyway I don't want you to be worried by it. Our child must come first.'

'Of course it will. Anyway, Jennifer White has already taken all the planning and responsibility for the accounts and records off my hands so I haven't really all that much involvement with the place.'

'No, except listen to Nelly's prattle every day and tell her what to do for the best when she has a problem.'

'Yes, but Betsy is taking over more and more. They'll cope, so don't you worry about it either.'

–

Before they left Yr Glaslyn, Lewis Lloyd took Harvey to one side and reminded him how urgent it was that he found a house for Megan. 'The girl needs a proper home if she is to settle down and raise a family,' he said authoritatively. 'If you have any financial problems then let me know, I'll be only too willing to help.'

'I'm sure I can manage, but thank you for the offer,' Harvey said courteously.

'When are we going to see you again? Do make it soon, and do take care of yourself, Megan,' her mother implored as they finally took their leave. 'I'm so happy for you, but I do wish you didn't have to travel so far to come and see us. And you know my health isn't as good as it once was.'

'Yes, I know, Mother, although you have seemed much better than last time we visited. Father says you're better, at least. I promise you, as soon as we are settled into a home of our own then you can come and visit us. I want you and Father to be our very first visitors,' Megan promised as she kissed her goodbye.

Chapter Thirty

When they arrived back at The Haven, Megan and Harvey found a letter waiting for them from Sandra. Megan read it through quickly and then handed it to Harvey.

'Sandra is coming back to England early in the new year for a holiday,' she said. 'Isn't that great! We'll be able to settle on what is to happen to this place before we move.'

'It certainly means I must speed things up,' Harvey agreed. 'I'd definitely like to have a house in mind even if we haven't time to settle all the details before they arrive so that she knows we are serious about moving.'

'It would certainly help to clinch matters,' Megan agreed.

'I'll contact the estate agent first thing on Monday morning and tell him how important it is to speed things up and find out what he can do,' Harvey promised.

He picked up the letter and scanned though it again. 'I see she says they are planning to be here by the beginning of February. That gives us barely a month!' he exclaimed, pursing his lips in a silent whistle.

'Not very long at all,' Megan agreed.

'I hope you're feeling fit enough to come house viewing if I manage to find somewhere,' he said, drawing Megan into his arms and kissing her.

'Try and stop me. I can't wait to have a home of my very own,' she breathed as she returned his kiss.

Exactly two weeks later they made their first inspection.

'It's a dormer bungalow in St Hilary's Drive, in Wallasey.'

'What's a dormer bungalow?' Megan frowned.

'Well, a fancy name for a bungalow, as far as I'm concerned,' Harvey said, shrugging his shoulders. 'I've seen a picture of this one and it has a very spacious area downstairs and upstairs the three bedrooms have sloping roofs and the windows are in the eaves.'

'Where did you say it was in Wallasey?'

'Almost next door to St Hilary's church,' he told her. 'It's a very nice part of the town and high up on a promontory so it has great views, right across to the Welsh mountains. You can probably see your beloved Moel Hebog from there,' he teased.

'Is it near the shops?'

'Yes; you have the choice of Wallasey Village or Liscard. Both of them are good shopping centres with plenty of choice.'

'It certainly sounds all right.'

'It's only a few minutes' walk from Harrison Drive, which has a golf course and access to the beach,' he added as he dodged the cushion she had thrown at him.

'Oh, and there's a very good school close by,' he went on as he read from the descriptive leaflet the estate agent had sent him.

'Stop, stop, I haven't had the baby yet,' Megan laughed, 'there's no need to worry about schools.'

'No, I know that, but it does mean that it's in a very good neighborhood and it's surprising how quickly time passes. It's not long before we'll have to think about schools.'

'Let's look at the house first,' Megan said. 'I might not like it.'

'I think you will.'

'We haven't seen any others yet though,' she protested.

'No, but wait until you see this and you'll know what I mean when I say it's the home for us.'

Harvey was quite right. The dormer bungalow had three bedrooms and a family bathroom upstairs, and downstairs a huge lounge with a picture window that had stunning views and an equally pleasant dining room. There was a morning room that could be used as a study as well as a downstairs cloakroom opening off the hall and a large kitchen and a utility room at the back of the house. Outside there was a manageable garden and a double garage. Even Megan had to agree that it was perfect for them.

'What about the price?' she asked.

'Leave all that side of things to me,' Harvey told her. 'Make sure you really like the house. Have another look round, check out the kitchen and make sure that it is big enough for you.'

'The house is perfect, the views are stunning and I love every inch of it. Is the garden the right size for you?'

'You mean I'm going to be the one who has to keep it in order?' he joked.

'Of course!'

'Actually, I couldn't ask for anything better. The lawn is in good shape and a decent size and the flowerbeds and shrubs have been well-planned and will be reasonably easy to keep in order. No, as you say, it's perfect. Shall I go ahead and tell the estate agent that we'll take it?'

'As long as you think we can afford it,' she agreed cautiously.

'Don't say anything to your parents until we've actually signed the deeds and completed the deal,' Harvey told her. 'I want to do this on our own. Your father has several times said he would help us out financially if necessary but I don't want to start our new life under an obligation to anyone.'

'Whatever you say, you're the boss,' Megan told him, squeezing his arm.

When they did write and tell her parents they had found a house in Wallasey that they both liked, they received an enthusiastic response. Both her parents were very relieved to know that soon she would be moving away from the Liverpool docks area.

Megan had also mentioned in her letter that Sandra was coming over to Liverpool for a holiday in February. When her mother wrote a second letter a couple of days later to say how relieved they were that they had found a suitable house, she also added, 'If your friend Sandra is going to be here in February then what about the two of you having a blessing or renewal of your vows or whatever it's called at our church here in Beddgelert? You both said that you would like to do that one day, so this would be a good opportunity to fulfill your promise.'

'Oh dear,' Harvey groaned, 'your mother never gives up, does she? To look at her she seems to be so meek and mild, yet she's like a terrier hanging on to a rabbit.'

'So you're saying I'm a rabbit now, are you?' Megan teased.

'No.' He pulled her into his arms and kissed her. 'Not a bit like a rabbit,' he said, cupping her chin with his hand

and then kissing her again so that she was unable to answer him.

'Perhaps you should write and warn Sandra what your mother expects and see how she reacts?' he told Megan as he released her.

Sandra's letter came back by return to post to say it would be lovely to do that and could Hope be their bridesmaid.

'I know she's rather young for such an onerous task but I am confident she'll do it well,' Sandra wrote.

'This is gradually growing into a full-scale do,' Harvey commented. 'What's the betting that your mother doesn't invite half the village to attend as well?'

'Of course she will, and my father will probably invite the men from his slate quarry.'

'You are joking!' Harvey frowned.

'No, not at all. My father is held in high regard because he's one of the largest employers in the area and on an occasion like this his workers as well as the villagers will all want to show their loyalty.'

'Talk about killing the fatted calf!'

'I don't think they'll do that, but they'll probably roast a couple of sheep over a spit, and the local band will play, and a choir of male voices will regale us with traditional songs.'

Harvey clamped his hands over his ears. 'I don't want to hear any more. I suppose you expect me to be there as well?'

'I most certainly do, you'll be one of the star performers,' Megan told him. She narrowed her eyes and studied him. 'You should look quite good in morning dress complete with a shiny black top hat.'

Nelly was overjoyed at the news that Sandra was coming home for a holiday.

'We've got so much to talk about,' she said and beamed. 'I never like writing letters, it's not the same as sitting down over a cup of tea and talking.'

'Sandra will probably want to sort out what you want to do about this place,' Megan said.

Nelly's face clouded. 'I know, and that bothers me. Things are going along well enough at the moment but I don't mind telling you, Miss Megan, that I'm not as young as I was and I do find it all a bit of a worry. Don't get me wrong,' she added hastily, 'Betsy works hard and manages things very well and that Jennifer, well, she's got magic in her touch the things she manages to achieve, but I still feel that I am the one responsible.'

'I know what you mean, Nelly,' Megan agreed.

'The place is doing well at the moment,' Nelly went on, 'but can we keep up the pace? That's what I ask myself every night before I go to sleep.'

'If you weren't here doing this, Nelly, then where would you like to be? What would you want to be doing?'

'That's the problem, I've nowhere to go and no family to take me in. I wish sometimes that Betsy was my daughter and that we could go and live somewhere quiet and bring up little Mary and not have to worry about anything.'

'That might suit you, Nelly, but don't you think Betsy might get restless with nothing to do all day?'

'Yes, I suppose you're right. Perhaps we ought to see if we could open a little sweet shop or tea place in some quiet village somewhere. Enough to earn us money to live on but somewhere where we could shut the door at five o'clock and not have to worry about other people. Here we are working until bedtime and every weekend as well. It's too much for an old body like me.'

'Perhaps you should tell Sandra all this and see what she thinks,' Megan said evasively.

Chapter Thirty-One

The furnishing of the house that they had found in St Hilary's Drive went smoothly and they both enjoyed the experience.

They had very few items to take with them from The Haven except a few personal belongings. The furniture at The Haven belonged to Sandra so they were able to enjoy a wonderful spending spree and furnish their new home with pieces of their own choice. The newly decorated house was a blank canvas and Megan was able to indulge her taste to the full.

They spent so much of their savings that she became alarmed. 'I think we should have made do with some orange boxes for a while until we are sure we can afford all this,' she said as she proudly surveyed the tastefully furnished sitting room.

'If you would prefer that, then we can always send this stuff back,' Harvey told her.

She shot a quick look at him and was relieved to see that he was laughing at her.

They didn't move into their new home immediately. They still felt responsible for The Haven and that, together with Harvey's work at the surgery, made it more convenient to go on living in Liverpool. They stayed either at The Haven or at the flat Harvey still owned above the surgery where he worked rather than travelling all the way across to Wallasey.

At first whenever they did go over to their new house Megan kept walking from room to room, feasting her eyes on their new possessions. She couldn't stop admiring the new carpets and curtains or touching the new furniture as if to make sure it was real and not a figment of her imagination.

The room she took a special delight in was the smallest bedroom, which they had fitted out as a nursery. There was a small cot, a large toy cupboard and nursery rhyme pictures on the wall.

In due course, a single bed or even bunk beds would replace the cot. She wanted it to be a playroom; a retreat. Somewhere their child could call its own when he or she grew older, the same as her own bedroom back at Yr Glaslyn had been.

Although she was barely four months pregnant, Harvey was insistent that she must register with a doctor, preferably in Wallasey, and book into either a clinic or hospital as soon as possible.

'I don't need to do that, I'm living with a doctor,' she reminded him.

'Yes, I know that, but it's not ethical for me to act as your doctor. Leave it with me and I'll check and find out where the nearest one is. I know there's a cottage hospital in Wallasey but it's some distance away from where we'll be living so I'll see if we can find a private clinic or maternity home that's nearer to our house.'

In the end it was Megan who found both a doctor as well as a private clinic.

'I've registered with a Dr Parker in Penkett Road,' she told Harvey. 'He's recommended a private clinic not very far from his surgery and he has said he will arrange for me to go there to have the baby.'

'Fine, if you are happy with him. What did you say his name was?'

'Dr Parker.'

'Really! I went to medical school with a Richard Parker; it could be the same man, I suppose.'

'I very much doubt it. This Dr Parker is in his sixties and grey haired.'

'Well, as long as you're confident about him. I'll check out the clinic some time. No hurry about that, as long as you are registered with a doctor. I suppose the next thing we ought to do is ask your parents to come and stay so that they can see our new house and satisfy themselves that we are as far away from Scotland Road as we can possibly be and that you are not living in a shack.'

'I think they already know that from the glowing reports I've sent them. No, I think our first visitors will have to be Sandra and Hank. They are coming over in February, remember, and that's not very far away.'

'They won't want to stay with us surely?' Harvey frowned. 'What's wrong with The Haven?'

'Well, it might be fully booked,' Megan pointed out.

'Then you'd better tell Nelly and Betsy not to accept any bookings for the next couple of weeks. I'm sure that Sandra would prefer to stay there. She'll want to go over the place and decide what to do with it and she might find it easier if the place is empty. It'll also give her a chance to have time with Nelly.'

'Yes, that might be a very good idea,' Megan agreed.

'There's far more room at The Haven than we have at the house anyway,' Harvey said as if to clinch the discussion. 'We can hardly put all three of them into the spare bedroom, and somehow I have a feeling that you won't want any of them sleeping in the nursery, not even little Hope.'

'She's probably too big to fit into a cot,' Megan said evasively.

'You wouldn't want her in there anyway, come on, admit it,' Harvey teased, laughing down at her.

'If there are no paying guests at The Haven then we can also stay there overnight if we have a late night out in Liverpool with Sandra and Hank,' he went on.

'True. You think of everything, don't you?' Megan retorted.

'Well, we haven't seen them for a long time and it may be years before we see them again, so we'll want to make the most of their company while they are here.'

January whizzed past and almost before she knew it Megan found that February had arrived and with it Sandra, Hank and Hope.

The arrival of Sandra and her family came as something of a shock because Sandra seemed to have changed so much. She'd not only altered her hairstyle but she now spoke with a definite American twang. It took Megan a little while to get used to it. Hope was now a sturdy five-year-old and already she also spoke with a strong American accent. To Nelly's dismay, she didn't remember any of them, but it only took her a matter of hours to not only know their names but also be able to find her way from Sandra's bedroom or the sitting room to Nelly's kitchen.

Nelly, of course, spoiled her with biscuits and sweets.

At first there was rivalry between Hope and Mary for attention but in next to no time they were good friends and leading each other into mischief.

Now that Hope and little Mary had become buddies, as Hope termed it, they never seemed to be apart for more than five minutes unless they were in bed and asleep. It was wonderful that they played together so well because they entertained each other.

Sandra and Hank were delighted to hear that Megan and Harvey were thinking of staying at The Haven while they were there.

'It will be just like old times,' Hank drawled with a broad smile.

'It means we'll get a lot more time together and we won't have to dash off in case we miss the last boat to Seacombe,' Harvey explained.

'Anyway, we haven't properly moved into our house over there yet,' Megan explained. 'It's now fully furnished and so on but because I'm still helping organize things at The Haven, most of the time I stay here or with Harvey at his flat over the surgery. I thought it was sensible to keep on my room here at The Haven in case I have to stay on in an emergency.'

Megan waited for Sandra to bring up the matter of the proposed church service at Beddgelert but when three or four days went by and she still hadn't mentioned it she wondered if this was because Sandra didn't want to go ahead with it.

After a phone call from her mother to find out if Sandra and her family had arrived safely, Megan decided it was time to bring the matter out into the open.

'Sure we want to go ahead with it,' Sandra said in surprise. 'Hank and I think it's the most romantic thing we've ever heard of.'

Megan and Harvey exchanged looks; Megan's was one of relief, Harvey's of resignation.

'The fourteenth is on a Saturday, and since it's St Valentine's Day, Hank and I thought that would be the perfect day to hold it. What do you think?'

'Sounds great,' Megan agreed. 'If we have it then it won't interrupt the normal church services on the Sunday.'

'Sure, then we'd really like to do that,' Sandra agreed.

'We could travel to Beddgelert on the Thursday before, and that will give us Friday to get settled in and make any last-minute changes if we don't like what has been planned by my parents. Have you brought a dress?'

'Not a full bridal ensemble,' Sandra said. 'We didn't think that was appropriate, but I have packed a cream lace dress that will serve the purpose very well.'

'That sounds terrific,' Megan enthused. 'I have a white lace one that I was going to wear with a short white fur jacket over it because it might be very cold.'

'Gosh!' Sandra frowned. 'I hadn't thought of that. My heavy topcoat will look out of place. Do you think there's anywhere in town where I can buy or hire something suitable? If I remember, there are stores in Bold Street that before the war specialized in fur coats. I wonder if they're still in business?'

'I'm sure there's somewhere here in Liverpool, but why don't you borrow something of mine? I have a cream velvet cape that's really warm and I'm sure it would look good over your dress.'

'Sounds great! Thanks, Megan. That means I only have to worry about Hope. It's so easy for the men, all they have to do is wear a smart suit and stick a flower in their buttonhole.'

'Yes indeed,' Megan agreed, and tried to hide her smile as she saw the look of relief on Harvey's face. 'I'm sure we can find a shop in town that has something suitable for

Hope. We'll take her with us and go and look tomorrow. We'll make it a girls' day out. You haven't been shopping in Liverpool for a long time but I'm sure you still know where all the best shops are. It'll also give you an opportunity to see how rejuvenated Liverpool is.'

'Sure thing, that's a great idea!' Sandra enthused. 'We'll have lunch out and that will give us a chance to talk. I must decide about the future of this place and I'm hesitant about talking about it here in case Nelly overhears.'

Chapter Thirty-Two

Their outing was a great success. They found an adorable little fur jacket and a pretty blue lace dress for Hope and she looked enchanting in them.

Their talk over lunch was very productive. Megan was able to tell Sandra what Nelly had said about being too old for the responsibility of running the place as a guest house. She also mentioned that Nelly had said how she would like to semi retire and run a little shop or some kind of a tea room with Betsy.

'I think that would be a splendid idea, but I've never liked to suggest anything like that to her,' Sandra confessed.

'I think Nelly will welcome the opportunity to do so,' Megan assured her.

'She's almost seventy, you know,' Sandra said with a fond smile, 'and she's worked all her life, so it's no wonder she feels worn out. Poor dear.'

'Betsy is very fond of Nelly, and I'm sure that if you put it to her she would be prepared to look after Nelly in her old age in return for a small house and some sort of income.'

'Yes,' Sandra replied and nodded thoughtfully. 'I wonder if they would both like to go back to Ireland?'

A couple of days later when Sandra mentioned this idea to Nelly the older woman broke down in tears. 'My darling girl, that is the stuff of my dreams, so it is, Miss Sandra. I never thought as I would ever see the old place again. To spend my last days there would indeed be heaven itself if it was possible.'

'Everything is possible, Nelly,' Sandra told her, placing her hand on Nelly's arm. 'We'll have to see what Betsy thinks of the idea.'

Betsy was equally enthusiastic. She too missed Ireland and longed to go back there but had never thought she'd be able to.

'Right, we'll see if we can sell The Haven and then set about finding something suitable in your home village or near enough to it so that you are both back where you belong,' Sandra promised. 'It may take a little time, remember,' she warned, 'and you'll have to put up with the estate agent sending people to view this place until it is actually sold.'

Both women agreed that this made no difference and they certainly didn't mind people having to be shown over The Haven because it was a means to an end and they were quite happy about it.

Sandra asked Harvey if he thought the estate agent he had used to find his and Megan's new home in Wallasey would be able to help them.

'More than likely,' Harvey said. 'He's a splendid chap and seems to have links with other estate agents throughout the country. He probably has connections in Ireland too, so he'll be able to help with that idea as well as selling this place.'

'Sounds good! Give us a few days to mull it all over and then perhaps you'd introduce us to him,' Sandra said. She looked pleased. 'Then all we have to worry about now is this church do at your home, Megan, so let's enjoy that to the full.'

Over the next few days they all celebrated in style. They had dinner out at the Adelphi or at the Stork. They even took the ferry boat across to New Brighton and had dinner at the Grand. They walked along the promenade and took Hope for rides on the swings and roundabouts in The Tower fairground.

Hank took Hope down to the Pier Head to watch the ships come and go while Harvey was at work and Sandra and Megan went shopping. When they came home she couldn't stop talking about the great gilded bird that was perched at the very top of the Liver Building.

'I think she was more impressed by that than by the ocean-going liners,' Hank laughed.

'It's so wonderful to see all the old familiar shops again,' Sandra said as they browsed in C&A, Lewis's, Marks and Spencer, Bon Marche, Woolworths and some of the exclusive shops in Bold Street.

'If only we had a fortune to spend,' Megan sighed.

'You're not broke, are you?' Sandra questioned anxiously.

'Nearly,' Megan said with a laugh. 'I've spent a fortune buying furniture and furnishing our new house in Wallasey.'

'That's where we must go next,' Sandra declared.

'I'll give you a tour tomorrow,' Megan promised. 'There is somewhere else we have to go as well; I'm a little hesitant about mentioning it again.'

Sandra looked puzzled. 'You've lost me, babe,' she said with a pronounced American drawl that made Megan smile.

When she reminded Sandra about their promise to her mother about the church wedding at Beddgelert, and that although they had decided on what they would wear they hadn't mentioned it since then, Sandra smiled apologetically.

'I know, I know, but so much else has been going on. Never mind, a promise is a promise.'

'Only if you and Hank really do want to do it?' Megan said quickly.

'We did say we would go up on the Thursday before so the answer is yes, we ought to go ahead with it,' Sandra said thoughtfully.

'Thank you,' Megan said quietly. It was such a relief that Sandra had consented without any argument that she was almost speechless.

'There's just one thing,' Sandra said. 'We can't stay up there for too long because I want to take Nelly and Betsy over to Ireland, back to the village they came from, to see if there is any property in the area that I can buy for them after I sell The Haven. There's no doubt about it that Nelly is ready to take life easier.'

'I couldn't agree with you more, and I'm so happy that you've made up your mind to sell The Haven. Will you sell it as a business?'

'Yes, if I can find anyone to buy it on that basis, or I'd be equally happy to sell it as a private home. I'll take whichever offer comes in first. Hank and I would like to complete the deal while we're here in England. We'd also like to have something in sight in Ireland for Nelly and Betsy to move into.'

'You can't possibly achieve all that before you go home,' Megan protested.

'No, but we can put it all in motion and ask the estate agent that Harvey recommended to go ahead and then leave it to you to see it through to completion. I know you'll do that for us,' she said in a positive voice.

'Of course we will,' Megan agreed, 'I think it's a perfect solution and I hope things go smoothly.'

'Perhaps we should discuss it in more detail with Betsy just in case she objects to going back there.'

'I don't think she will, especially if she is going to be with Nelly,' Megan said with a smile.

'Well, since we all agree on that, then let's pay a visit to this new house of yours and see if I approve of what you've bought,' Sandra stated.

Sandra did like the house in St Hilary's Drive. She was almost as enthusiastic as Megan. She thought the rooms spacious, she adored the views and thought the garden 'cute'.

'So you'll be happy to stay here with us when you next come on a visit to England?'

'Sure! I don't see us coming for a few years though, and long before that I shall expect a visit from you two.'

'That's right. You must come and inspect the old homestead before we pay you another visit,' Hank insisted.

Megan smiled and agreed but explained, 'It won't be for a couple of years, I'm afraid.'

'Why ever not?' Sandra demanded.

'I'm pregnant, and I wouldn't want to travel all that way with a very young baby.'

'Pregnant!' Sandra shouted the word. 'How pregnant? You don't look pregnant!'

'Well, that's probably a good thing. My mother might feel embarrassed next week if I was obviously pregnant.'

'When is it due?'

'Not until June.'

'Well, well, well,' Sandra said with an enormous grin. 'Many congratulations,'

'Thank you! Harvey is delighted.'

'June! That's only four months ahead. You should be showing by now. You're still as slim as ever.'

'Yes, I'm very lucky,' Megan agreed smugly.

'You know, I did wonder why you had furnished one of the bedrooms as a nursery but I didn't say anything because I thought it might be mere speculation or hopefulness on your part. Perhaps under the circumstances we will come back to see you in about twelve months' time in order to meet the new arrival. Don't forget to keep us posted every step of the way.'

Chapter Thirty-Three

They arrived at Yr Glaslyn late afternoon on the Thursday. Harvey and Megan took Betsy and little Mary in their car and Hank, Sandra, Hope and Nelly travelled in the other one.

Their cars drew up within minutes of each other. Nelly was stiff from sitting for such a long time but when she managed to get out of the car, she took a deep breath, looked around and exclaimed, 'Why, it's almost like being back in Ireland. All this fresh and lovely green grass is like heaven after those grey old streets of Liverpool. I'll never understand how you could bring yourself to leave a place like this, Miss Megan.'

The children had slept for most of the journey so they were now wide awake and alert. They had never seen mountains before and they could hardly believe their eyes when they saw Moel Hebog close up.

'It won't fall down on us, will it?' Mary said in a rather frightened little voice.

'No, it won't do that,' Megan assured her. 'It has been here for hundreds of years and it was here when I was a little girl. I used to say hello to it every morning when I went to school.'

'Did it say hello back to you?' Hope asked.

'No, it never said a word, but I know it liked me to speak to it. I often talked to it on my way home from school as well and I told it what I'd been doing all day.'

Hope and Mary giggled and clutched hands as they said in unison, 'Hello Mountain.'

Inside Yr Glaslyn they all gasped in amazement at how lovely the house looked. Bronwyn had taken great pains to deck the hallway out in pristine white and the glowing fire contrasted with the stark white decorations.

Bronwyn ushered them all into the sitting room and insisted on them sitting down and enjoying a cup of tea and one of their cook's famous Welsh cakes before they took their cases upstairs to unpack.

'Joshua White and Jennifer and little Joshua will be arriving late tomorrow,' Bronwyn told them. 'Mr White has an important meeting first thing tomorrow morning so he can't leave until midday. They're looking forward to seeing you all again.'

The children were very excited and also tired so Bronwyn suggested that they should be given supper early and put to bed, leaving the grown-ups time to sit down to a leisurely dinner and discuss the plans for Saturday.

'All we need now is a fine day,' Megan remarked as they sat in the sitting room after dinner enjoying a nightcap before going to bed.

'It will be fine,' her father stated. It sounded almost as if he had arranged that as well as all the ceremony that was to take place before and after they went to church.

–

Saturday was fine; sunlight dappled the road as they drove in a convoy of cars to the church in Beddgelert. As Megan had anticipated, there were men from the slate works there as well as most of their tenants and all the villagers.

The miners, each of them carrying a well-polished sheet of blue slate, lined up on either side of the path that led up to the church with the slates held high and the edges touching to form an archway for the two couples to walk under.

The church itself was packed and people were standing in the aisles as well as at the back.

Lewis and Bronwyn Lloyd had seats in their own family pew and the Whites were also in the pew with them as well as Nelly, Betsy and Mary.

Megan and Sandra stood side by side, Harvey and Hank on either side of them. Little Hope stood immediately in front of Sandra clutching a tiny posy of white violets.

The renewal of their vows did not take very long and then the church choir sang as they left the church.

Outside a male voice choir made up of men from the slate quarry and men from the village rendered love songs that brought tears to Megan's eyes.

They did not go back to Yr Glaslyn immediately. First there was a lavish spread to be enjoyed in the village hall. People crowded around the two couples to offer their best wishes for their future happiness.

They also asked Megan countless questions about where she would be living and they wanted to know all about America and if Sandra liked living there.

Nelly and Betsy spent a great deal of their time making sure that Hope, Joshua and Mary behaved themselves and didn't cause any trouble.

Mary and Hope had been firm friends and good companions up until now but Joshua being there seemed to upset this as both little girls wanted to be the one who held his hand and played with him. In order to avoid the grown-ups, they ran around the gravestones, dodging this way and that, running circles around Nelly and skipping out her way so it was left to Betsy to run after them and bring them to order.

It was late afternoon when, tired out but happy, they took their farewell from the people in the village hall and returned to Yr Glaslyn.

Bronwyn was beaming. 'Now you really are married,' she told Megan. 'I'm so pleased for you and for the baby you're expecting, I'd never thought it would ever happen.' She hesitated, then smiled and said, 'I am so much happier about things now that you're properly married.'

Megan held her close and kissed her cheek. 'Yes, Mother, I know what you mean, and you are right. Now everything is perfect.'

'You haven't told me what's happening about The Haven now that you've moved into your new house in Wallasey?' she said, looking enquiringly at Megan and then back to Sandra.

Megan left it to Sandra to tell her mother that The Haven was being put up for sale and that if all went well then in a couple of months' time she hoped that Nelly and Betsy would be moving back to Ireland, to the village they both called home.

'We're planning to buy a little shop for them, a place large enough so that they can sell souvenirs and such like, or have it as a tea shop, whatever they think best,' Sandra told her.

'That sounds as though it will be ideal,' Bronwyn Lloyd said approvingly.

'Well, Nelly is too old now for anything too strenuous but Betsy needs an interest and an income and we hope that this will provide her with both. We'll be keeping in touch with them and probably coming back for a holiday every couple of years.'

'Oh, that is good,' Bronwyn breathed. 'Megan was so worried about them. She thinks the world of Nelly. She'll keep in touch with them as well,' she said, patting Sandra's arm.

'Next year when the baby is old enough for them to take on holiday, I'm sure that's where they'll go. So that she can see Nelly and Betsy and make sure they've settled in and are happy. It means that we can go back home to America without any worries. But I'm sure we'll come over again sometime in the near future to check out for ourselves that all is well.'

'When you do, you must come and stay a few days with us again,' Bronwyn told her. 'It's been such a pleasure having you here.'

Chapter Thirty-Four

Sandra was determined that before she and her family returned to America she would take a trip over to Ireland, to the village where Nelly and Betsy had come from, to see if there was any suitable property she could buy.

'I'd like for them to know they had somewhere definite to go when The Haven is sold or Nelly will be worrying in case they find themselves homeless,' she told Megan.

'I was hoping you might come along as well,' she added, 'but I suppose it's out of the question now that you are pregnant.'

'I don't see why it should be,' Megan told her. 'I'm as fit as a fiddle. Are you planning on flying or taking a boat?'

'Whichever way you prefer. I don't suppose there's a great deal of difference time-wise. We'd have to drive out to the airport or we could simply walk down to the Pier Head. There's a boat once or twice a day still sailing to Ireland, isn't there?'

'I think I'd sooner fly,' Megan said. 'I do get seasick quite easily, especially if it's at all rough.'

'Right, we'll fly. Will Harvey come as well, do you think?'

'I very much doubt it, because they're short-staffed at his surgery.'

'OK. Now, do you think we could leave Hope with Betsy and Mary? It would be so much easier without her.

She'll be bored and tired and start grizzling. Either that or we could take Mary with us.'

'No, leave her to play with little Mary. They're such good friends they'll be no trouble at all and Nelly and Betsy will keep an eye on her.'

'Yes, I know that, and I agree that it would be for the best,' Sandra said and nodded. 'By the way,' she added, 'not a word to Nelly or Betsy about where we're going. I don't want to raise their hopes.'

'Very sensible, and I do understand,' Megan agreed.

Megan had never been to Ireland and she was quite looking forward to the trip. When she mentioned it to Harvey he confirmed that he couldn't spare the time to go with them. He was rather worried about her going.

'Do you think you should be undertaking a journey like that?' he questioned.

'You mean in my state of health?' she retorted with a cheeky smile. 'I thought you were a doctor, not a fussy old woman. Most doctors tell you to get on with things and carry on as normal. Being pregnant isn't an illness.'

'Hmm! They do, do they? You've forgotten, though, that I'm not your ordinary doctor, I'm a father-in-waiting, and I am very well aware of it. I don't want you taking any chances whatsoever. Understand!'

She reached up and pulled his head closer and kissed him. 'I won't take any chances,' she promised. 'This baby means as much to me as it does to you.'

'Hank is going over to Ireland with you?'

'Yes he is, so you can ask him to make sure I don't do anything I shouldn't. We're not taking Hope, we are leaving her to play with Mary, and Betsy will keep an eye on them. We'll only be away for one night.'

'I'd sooner you came back the same day if at all possible,' Harvey told her. 'If you do stay overnight, then you must look after yourself and take care.'

'I will, I promise.'

'If you do stay overnight then where are you staying, do you know?'

'A hotel in Dublin. We're flying to Dublin and then Hank is hiring a car there. Do stop worrying, I'll be quite all right,' she added impatiently as she reached up and kissed him.

Harvey held her close, kissing her on the brow and then on the lips. The look of concern on his face touched her and for a moment she considered pulling out of the trip. But she knew Sandra was counting on her company, so in the end she returned Harvey's kiss and said no more.

The flight from Liverpool to Dublin was uneventful. Megan had been afraid that she might feel queasy. But she felt fine, even when they descended through the mist at Dublin airport.

By the time they were through customs and had picked up their hire car the sun was shining.

The village they went to that had been home for Nelly and Betsy was not far from the airport but so very small and rural that it was like being transported back into the Middle Ages.

'They'll never make a living here from a tea shop,' Sandra said worriedly. 'It's far too remote and I shouldn't imagine they'd get more than half a dozen visitors a year.'

'We've plenty of time to look around, honey,' Hank told her. 'There must be other villages nearby that offer better prospects.'

'It's very picturesque here and similar to Wales,' Megan observed. 'I can understand why Nelly was so entranced by Beddgelert.'

'If only it was Beddgelert. Now that does attract tourists and the like,' Sandra sighed.

'We'll keep looking, honey,' Hank drawled, 'and if we haven't found anywhere by lunchtime then we'll go into the nearest hostelry and ask them to tell us the name of some of the larger villages or small towns.'

Sandra and Megan both agreed with this. Sandra spread out the map she had brought with her and suggested that they should start by circling Dublin and see if they could find something within a ten miles' radius.

'Why is it so important that you find a village so near to Dublin?' Megan asked.

'It'll make it so much easier for us when we want to visit. We can probably fly direct from America to Dublin,' Sandra pointed out when she saw that Hank was also looking rather puzzled. 'Also, it's an area that Nelly and Betsy know. Isn't that right, Hank?'

'Whatever you say, honey,' he agreed. 'So where do you want me to drive to next?'

Sandra reeled off a list of names. 'Hold it, hold it, you sound as though you're talking in another language and I can't take it all in,' Hank laughed. 'What with Bally this and Bally that and Kill something and Kin something, it's going round and round in my mind and confusing me.'

They drove round for over an hour, Sandra giving instructions of when to turn left or right. Now and again she would tell him to stop in one or another of the little towns they were passing through so that they could weigh up the possibilities of Nelly and Betsy making a living there.

Eventually they decided on three places; one was a large village, with a long main street with four shops but no tearooms, a church, two pubs and a school, and the other two were large enough to be called small towns.

'Any of these would be ideal,' Sandra confirmed as she made a note of their names in the notebook she'd brought with her. 'They're not too far from Dublin and near enough to the village where Nelly and Betsy came from for them to feel at home because they are bound to know the places all around here.'

'Do you think they would be able to make a living here though?' Megan asked dubiously.

'Yes, I do. They're quiet spots, I know, but they do get an awful lot of walkers and hikers around here and they all of them need somewhere to stop and have a cup of tea, a snack and a rest. I think any of them would be ideal.'

'So do we try and find out if there are any suitable properties available?'

Hank looked at his watch. 'You were thinking about getting home tonight, weren't you, Megan?' he chuckled.

'Well, yes, I would like to do so if it's at all possible. Harvey seemed to be worried at the thought of me staying in Dublin overnight.'

'There was no need for him to be concerned. I was planning to book us into the best hotel in town,' Hank assured her. 'But if you would prefer to fly back tonight then that's all right with me. How about you, honey?' he asked, looking at Sandra.

'I'd like to get back as well, to make sure that Hope is all right. I know Betsy will take great care of her but we've never been apart before and I'm sure she'll miss her daddy if he isn't there to read her a bedtime story.'

'Then in that case it has to be home. Do you want to have dinner here first?'

Sandra and Megan exchanged glances before saying in unison, 'No, we'd sooner get home.'

'Right then, that's what we'll do. Does this mean we'll have to come back again to see if we can find any vacant properties?'

'No,' Sandra told him, 'we have the names of the village and towns, so we'll leave it to the estate agent Harvey recommended. Let him do the searching. If he can't find a suitable property in any of the places we've given him, then I'm sure he can find something nearby.'

'He won't manage that before we go back to America,' Hank warned. 'We're booked to fly home in three days' time.'

'I know, but it doesn't matter. I'm making arrangements for Megan and Harvey to sign any papers necessary to say that we will buy the property so we don't have to worry about that.'

'Are you making the same arrangements over selling your house, honey?' Hank asked.

'I am. I'm quite settled in my own mind that everything is taken care of, so don't worry.'

Chapter Thirty-Five

Megan's baby was born in early June; a healthy boy weighing eight pounds. He had a mass of dark hair and a very lusty cry.

Harvey was delighted with his new son and immediately telephoned the Lloyds to give them the good news and to tell them that they had decided to call the baby David.

As he spoke to Lewis, he could hear Bronwyn's gasp of relief in the background as the news was relayed to her.

'When are you planning to come to Wallasey to see Megan and the baby?' Harvey asked.

There was a brief pause and then Lewis Lloyd said, 'Not at the moment. We'll let you know the date later.'

Later that day Harvey received a phone call from Lewis Lloyd to say that his wife was suffering from a summer cold and he thought it unwise for them to travel at the moment.

'You wouldn't want her around the baby either. I know at that tender age they are supposed to be immune from such germs but you never know. Perhaps we'll be able to come in a couple of weeks' time. Or, better still, perhaps you would like to come here for a break as soon as Megan feels fit enough to travel.'

Harvey didn't argue but accepted the invitation on the understanding that he would have to find out if he would be able to get the time off.

'We're a doctor down so we are rather busy at the surgery at the moment,' he explained.

'Not too busy to take care of our daughter and our new grandson, I hope,' Lewis boomed.

'No, they'll be taken great care of, I can assure you on that score,' Harvey promised.

Later that day when he went to the maternity home in Penkett Road the receptionist stopped him from going to Megan's room. 'Dr Parker is with Mrs Stott at the moment,' she explained.

'Nothing wrong, is there?' he asked.

'Oh no, a routine visit. Dr Parker always visits new patients twice a day for the first week.'

'I see. Well, I'll go up just the same,' he stated and headed for the stairs before she could stop him.

Dr Parker greeted him cordially but his attention was focused on Megan. He was grey-haired and probably in his sixties, exactly as Megan had described him. When he stood up and turned round Harvey immediately recognized him.

'Are you Richard Parker's father?' he asked.

'Yes, that's right. Do you know my son?'

'We were at medical school together. I went into practice in Liverpool afterwards and I understand Richard was planning to join the forces, so we haven't seen each other since.'

'Indeed!' Dr Parker held out a hand to Harvey. 'Richard has recently been demobbed and will be back home next week. He was abroad for most of the war, first one place and then another. Fortunately he came through unscathed. I'll tell him I've met you.'

'Yes, please do. I'd like to meet up with him again sometime.'

'I'll tell him. Your wife is doing very well indeed, Dr Stott. No worries at all, and you have a very healthy baby.'

'So he is your friend's father,' Megan said in surprise after Dr Parker had left. 'What a coincidence!'

'Yes, isn't it. It would be great to see Richard again. You'll like him. Enough about that, how are you feeling?'

They spent the rest of Harvey's visit planning the future and when she would be likely to come home. He told her about his phone call to her parents and their relief at knowing she and the baby were both doing well.

'I've said we'll go and visit them as soon as you feel strong enough to do so. There's no immediate hurry as your mother has a summer cold and is scared that either you or the baby might catch it.'

'Oh, I'm sorry to hear that. Never mind, by the time we visit them we may be able to tell them that the sale of The Haven has been finalized and that the place in Ireland is ready and waiting for Nelly and Betsy.'

'Make sure you don't go rushing around doing too much in trying to help them to pack up when they are ready to leave Liverpool,' Harley warned.

'Don't worry, I won't. For one thing Nelly wouldn't let me. She fusses even more than my mother, if that's at all possible.'

Ten days later when Harvey arrived to take Megan and the baby home he had a pleasant surprise. Richard Parker was at the clinic talking to Megan and waiting to meet him.

Richard was tall and broad with short dark hair and grey eyes. He had a wide smile and Megan thought he must have looked very handsome in his uniform. Now he was wearing grey slacks, a plain blue open-necked shirt and a Harris tweed sports jacket.

Both men seemed delighted to see each other again and before they left the clinic Richard had promised to meet Harvey in a few days' time for a night out together.

'I'm not inviting you, Megan, because I'm sure you'll be far too busy,' he said with a grin as he looked down at the baby she was holding in her arms.

'I wouldn't want to come,' she told him. 'You two will be far too busy reminiscing to even notice if I am there or not.'

'You're quite right, we have years to catch up on and to anyone else our chat will be extremely boring. We'll make it up to you at a later date,' he promised.

Harvey was so keyed up and excited when he came home a few nights' later after his evening out with Richard Parker that for one moment Megan thought he was drunk.

'Drunk with excitement,' he told her. 'You'd never guess, not in a hundred years, I couldn't believe it myself.'

'Will you calm down and tell me what I wouldn't believe! What is it that you're so excited about?'

'A partnership,' he told her, his eyes glowing. 'A partnership with Richard Parker, and it will be right here in Wallasey. Can you believe it?'

Megan stared at him wide-eyed. 'What about your present job?'

'I'll tell them that I'm leaving. There won't be any problem.'

'You'll probably have to give a month's notice!'

He shrugged as if that was of no real importance.

'I'll be working right here, right on the spot. Isn't that wonderful! No more daily commuting on the bus and ferry boat to Liverpool, no more late nights being called out in an emergency. I'll be working right here on my own doorstep.'

He pulled her into his arms and waltzed round the room. 'A partner! Not just a salaried member of a team, but as a full-blown partner.'

'Hold on, hold on,' she said, pulling away and staring at him. 'Can you afford to buy into a partnership? We spent all our savings furnishing our new home.'

'That's the beauty of it all; I don't have to pay anything. Well, just a nominal sum of a few hundred pounds, but that's nothing. Old man Parker wants to retire but the practice has grown so much that he feels it's too much for Richard to handle on his own, so he suggested to him that he should find himself a partner. Richard immediately thought of me and of course old man Parker has met me and he agreed without any argument.'

'When does all this start?' Megan asked in bewilderment.

'In August! From the first of August Richard's father will retire and Richard and I will be partners. Richard's father will stay on call for six months in case we should need his advice over any of the patients. After that, providing everything is going smoothly, we'll be on our own. Fantastic news, isn't it? Wait until I tell your parents.'

Lewis and Bronwyn were extremely pleased when they heard the news.

'Anything that means you are severing all connections with that rough area of Liverpool is wonderful news,' Bronwyn breathed with relief.

'Yes, it's a very good move and we're delighted for you, Harvey, and very relieved to know that both our daughter and our grandson are well away from the Scotland Road area. I know you've never had any trouble while you've been working and living there, but it is a very rough area so you are much better away from there.'

Harvey nodded but said nothing.

'And once you're settled into your new job and can take some time off,' said Lewis Lloyd. 'It mightn't be such a bad idea to take that proposed trip to America. I'm sure that little David is old enough now to travel and Megan fully recovered from his birth, so why not enjoy a holiday?'

He handed Harvey a cheque. 'This is a belated wedding present from us; it should cover the expense of your holiday.'

Chapter Thirty-Six

David was ten months old when Megan and Harvey took him to America to visit Sandra and her family. Megan had been wanting to make the trip to Bellingham, which was on the borders of America and Canada, for months, but first of all they'd had to pay a visit to Yr Glaslyn at Christmas and Harvey had said it was no good going to the USA before that because November was the wettest month of the year in Bellingham.

'How on earth do you know that?' Megan asked in surprise.

'I've been doing my homework. I thought you'd want to see the place when it was at its best so I made enquiries from a travel agency.'

'I see!'

'The rainy period extends from October until April. November is typically the wettest month, with numerous frontal rainstorms arriving. At the height of the really cold spell, local ponds and smaller lakes freeze solidly enough to allow skating.'

'Doesn't the place ever have any decent sunshine?'

'Oh yes, but it does have the lowest average sunshine amount of any city in America.'

'Well, at least I suppose that means we won't get sunstroke,' Megan muttered.

'Despite this, Bellingham also has mild, pleasant summers and drought is rare. Although I must warn you, wells have been known to run dry in August and September.'

'OK, I get the picture,' Megan laughed. 'You don't want us to go there in winter or in the height of summer. In that case what about March or April?'

Harvey frowned. 'That might be all right. I'll have to check with Richard Parker to find out what his plans are, and if it's OK with him then I'll see if we can book in a locum to take my place while I'm away.'

'Since you seem to be giving me a lesson about Bellingham, what other things have you found out about the place?' Megan asked.

'Well, it's in the state of Washington and is about ninety miles north of Seattle, twenty-one miles south of the Canadian border and about fifty-two miles south of Vancouver.'

'Really!'

'"It started out as four separate towns on the shores of Bellingham Bay with Mount Baker as its backdrop. Bellingham is the last major city before the Washington coastline meets the Canadian border. The city of Bellingham, which serves as the county seat of Whatcom County, is at the centre of a uniquely picturesque area offering a rich variety of recreational, cultural, educational and economic activities",' Harvey read from the pamphlet he was holding.

'Is that something the travel agent gave you?' Megan asked.

'It is. Do you want to hear any more?'

'Go on.'

'"There is an arts and cultural district downtown and a very active waterfront hosts a range of marine activities. Housing ranges from regal Victorians, waterfront bungalows and country farmhouses to downtown condominiums.

'"Prior to white settlement, the Lummi, Nooksack and other Coast Salish tribes thrived there. An English captain called George Vancouver first explored the area in 1792 and named Bellingham Bay for Sir William Bellingham, Vancouver's British navy provisioner. The city of Bellingham was incorporated in 1904 after the populations of four adjacent bayside towns voted to consolidate. Bellingham's historic character is remarkably well-preserved, with a large number of historic buildings downtown, in the Fairhaven District, and in adjacent neighborhoods".'

Megan clapped her hands over her ears. 'I feel I know the place already, so don't tell me any more,' she begged, 'or I won't want to go there.'

'I told you I'd done my homework,' Harvey said with a broad grin.

'Yes, a bit too well. You're not thinking of getting a job as a guide when you get there, are you, Dr Stott?'

'No, but I found it interesting to read about it; I like to know where I'm going,' Harvey said. 'By the way, the flight takes about thirteen hours in total, so be sure to pack whatever you think David is going to need en route into our hand luggage because you won't see the suitcase until you get to Bellingham. They may have baby food on board but it might be wise to take whatever he is most used to.'

Megan tucked her hair back behind her ears as though exhausted. 'Right, I'll remember that. This trip is beginning to look more arduous the nearer it comes. I think there's a time difference as well, London is about eight hours ahead of Washington and I suppose that could upset David's routine.'

'Not if we don't tell him,' Harvey said with a smile. 'He'll probably sleep most of the way.'

As it turned out their journey went very smoothly indeed and Hank, Sandra and Hope were waiting at Bellingham airport when their plane touched down. Almost before they knew what was happening they were at the Jacksons' spacious waterfront bungalow.

'This is quite stunning,' Megan said admiringly. 'I had no idea what sort of place Bellingham was or what your home was like. We never got round to talking about it when you came over on holiday.'

'We will have great pleasure in showing you round,' Hank assured her. 'Everything will be new for you.'

'I'm not too sure about that,' Megan said wryly. 'Harvey has discovered so many facts and details about Bellingham that he could work here as a guide.'

'Reading about it in a book or pamphlet is OK, but it can't be compared with seeing things with your own eyes and forming your own opinion of them,' Hank told her.

'If that baby of yours is awake at last then can we have a proper look at him?' Sandra asked. 'He's nine months old now, isn't he?'

'Almost ten months,' Megan corrected as she sat David up on her knee.

'Is he walking yet?'

'Almost. He's at the stage where he can pull himself up by holding on to seats and then move a few steps before he falls over again.'

'Hope has been looking forward to seeing him, haven't you, sweetie?' Sandra asked, turning to where her six-year-old daughter was staring at David, wide-eyed.

'I sure have,' Hope said and nodded. 'I've got some of my toys for him to play with. Can I get them, Mom?' she asked, looking at her mother.

'Of course you can! I'll put a rug down on the floor and then if Megan puts David down on to it you can look after him while we have a drink.'

In the days that followed Megan found that Hope was a great help. She was always ready to play with David and she was so gentle and protective that Megan had no qualms at all about leaving them together, not that she was ever more than a few yards away. The slightest cry from David, she was at his side to see what was the matter.

Sandra was keen to know what the news was about her house in Chapel Gardens and about Nelly and Betsy.

'They're both still there but the house has been sold and when we get back we'll be helping them move over to Ireland,' Harvey told them.

'Yes, we had a letter from the estate agent saying he had found a place for them and I was wondering if it was suitable.'

'Harvey has already been over to see it,' Megan assured her. 'It was a flying visit in every sense of the word, but he was there long enough to make sure that the property was sound and that it was suitable for them to run a tea shop or gift shop.'

'It's quite a big area downstairs and there's a very well-fitted kitchen which is ideal for their purpose. Upstairs there are four bedrooms so they can have a sitting room and a bedroom each if they want to do it that way. With Mary now starting school they might like to have separate living rooms so that she can do her homework in peace when the time comes. Or they can give her one of the large bedrooms and she can have it as a playroom and bedroom now, and then turn it into a combined bedroom and study later on. It will still leave them with one spare bedroom. There's a very nice bathroom and separate toilet up there as well.'

'What about the garden?'

'Well, that's on the small side and is at the back of the building. I suggested to them that if they simply had a big lawn out there Betsy would be able to cut it and they would have somewhere to sit in the summer.'

'I bet Nelly wanted to grow her own vegetables out there,' Sandra laughed.

'She did until I pointed out to her that would call for a lot of hard work and she agreed she wasn't up to it and if they were running a shop then Betsy would be busy enough.'

'What about the financial details? The estate agent hasn't finalized those yet, has he?'

'Yes, he has, and I've brought all the papers with me. The figures are extremely satisfactory. The price he managed to get for your house, Sandra, not only covers the cost of the house in Ireland but leaves a very healthy balance.'

'Enough to pay for their moving expenses?' Sandra asked hopefully.

'Oh yes, more than enough. There'll be enough left for you to fit out the shop and provide them with some stock as well as set up a standing order to pay the rates and other charges for the next five years if you want to do that.'

287

'That's wonderful,' Sandra breathed. 'Thank you both for helping us in arranging all this. Now, we'll put it all to the back of our minds and enjoy your visit. Ten days isn't long and there's so much we want to show you and so many places we want to take you to see.'

–

Their visit to Bellingham passed all too swiftly. Before they knew it they were on the plane back to London.

'It's been a great holiday and I think Bellingham is lovely, but it will be good to get back home again,' Megan admitted as the plane taxied down the runway.

'Yes, I agree,' Harvey said, taking her hand and squeezing it. 'Back to our own home and a chance to relax.'

'We still have to help Nelly and Betsy pack up and move to Ireland,' she warned him.

'That won't take up too much of our time,' he assured her.

'We also have to visit my parents at Yr Glaslyn. They'll be eager to know all about our American holiday.'

'We won't be able to do that for a while,' Harvey told her. 'I have to get back to work. Richard Parker is waiting to take his holiday, remember.'

'Yes, I know, but we don't want to leave it too long, because you don't like me travelling when I'm pregnant,' Megan cautioned.

'Pregnant!' Harvey sat bolt upright in his seat and swiveled round and stared at her. 'Are you sure?'

'Quite sure, do you think I should see a doctor?' she asked with a roguish smile.

'That's absolutely wonderful,' Harvey told her, kissing her. 'When?'

'According to my calculations it should be early September.'

'September,' he murmured, shaking his head from side to side as if he couldn't believe the news. Then he put his arm around her shoulders, drawing her closer, and kissed her again, a deep passionate kiss that told her how delighted he was and how much he loved her.

Acknowledgements

With grateful thanks to Caroline and Megan at the Caroline Sheldon Literary Agency, and to Severn House for all their support and hard work.